The Perfect Fool

BETHANY ZOHNER HERBERT

SWEETWATER
BOOKS
An Imprint of Cedar Fort, Inc.
Springville, Utah

ISBN 13: 978-1-4621-1620-1

Published by Sweetwater Books, an imprint of Cedar Fort, Inc.
2373 W. 700 S., Springville, UT 84663
Distributed by Cedar Fort, Inc., www.cedarfort.com

LIBRARY OF CONGRESS CATALOGING-IN-PUBLICATION DATA

Herbert, Bethany Zohner, 1984- author.
The perfect fool / by Bethany Zohner Herbert.
pages cm
Life is good for orphan Farrago after he becomes the new court fool, but when his friend the scullery maid is revealed to be the missing queen of a neighboring kingdom, the challenges that pour into Farrago's life may be more than he can overcome.
ISBN 978-1-4621-1620-1 (perfect : alk. paper)
[1. Fools and jesters--Fiction. 2. Kings, queens, rulers, etc.--Fiction. 3. Courts and courtiers--Fiction. 4. Orphans--Fiction.] I. Title.
PZ7.1.H49Pe 2015
[Fic]--dc23
2014033619

Cover design by Michelle May
Cover design © 2015 by Lyle Mortimer
Edited and typeset by Melissa J. Caldwell

Printed in the United States of America

10 9 8 7 6 5 4 3 2 1

Printed on acid-free paper

Chapter 1

I suppose most mothers probably don't want to hear their sons say, "Mother! Guess what! I got a job as a fool!"

Well, at least I guess they don't. It probably depends how desperate they are for their sons to get jobs. And how qualified they think their sons are for the position.

If you have a mother, that is.

Me, I think I've always been a fool at heart. And the streets would have done me in soon anyway if I hadn't—well, begun my new career. I knew that the night of the spider.

I had fallen asleep in an alleyway as usual. I'd been watching the stars for a little while, so I knew there hadn't been anything over my head. But when I sat up the next morning, a little sleepy still, I put my face right through an enormous sticky net of death. I swear the creature had been spinning its web just for me. A few more hours of working and it might have made one big enough to swallow me up.

Still, I might have recovered from that if the spider hadn't been sitting in the middle of its web and landed on my nose.

I might have even recovered from that if it hadn't bit me.

And maybe I still could have moved on with life someday if the soldier hadn't seen what happened next.

But as it was, I threw the best fit of my life. I made sounds I didn't know I could make and moved faster than someone who had just been asleep should ever have to. And somewhere in my thrashing, the spider flew off my face and ran off into the darkness of the alley and my past.

The soldier was beside himself, laughing so hard he fell over. That was actually a relief, because I knew as long as he was laughing like that he wouldn't be able to torment me. And now that we both knew how I reacted to spiders, he and the others would be able to take "torment" to a whole new level. Clutching my nose, I ran off before the thought occurred to him. Being just taller than his middle, I knew I was still too much of a child to defend myself.

I ran to the edge of the kingdom and ducked between some cottages where I plunked myself into a pile of something-or-other—rags?—so I could decide if I was going to die. But before I could, someone grabbed my arm and yanked me away.

Yes, I screamed. I'm not too proud to admit it. Anyone with my kind of morning would have screamed. Probably even with a different kind of morning.

But it was only the spinster. She lived on the edge of the kingdom and made clay pots and vases and such. She had better posture and always seemed cleaner than the average peasant woman. We who lived on the street had her figured out. She was always good for a crust of bread, but she never let us stay. We figured that it was because she couldn't keep all of us.

She sighed and pulled me into her house. While rubbing

clay on my nose, she asked me what happened, told me the soldiers would probably leave me alone if I was light on my feet and stopped referring to the king as The Great Lump, and speculated that the spider probably wasn't poisonous.

Thanks.

And then she let me take a nap. When I woke up, I was back on the streets with a roll of bread curled in my fingers. And I decided that the only thing that worried me about the spinster was the fact that her face was beginning to faintly replace the one in my head of a thin woman smiling at me.

Oh well. I ate the bread. I was hungry. I was always hungry.

The next day, there was some preacher man standing on a small box, yelling about the Good Book. I listened to him for a little while. He said that God created the world and everything in it. Now, I didn't know much about God, but I thought he was a good guy, because for some reason I had a feeling that the thin-faced woman in my memory liked him. But I couldn't believe that a nice guy could create spiders. The preacher had to be wrong. I was sure that spiders had crawled straight from the devil's palm.

But it didn't matter because that was my last night on the streets anyway. Before the night was done, I would be rescued from the spider in the alley and the soldiers, though I wouldn't consider it as being rescued at the time. At the time, I would think of it as more of a kidnapping.

It was some festival. Probably The Great Lump's birthday. Or his son's. Actually, it must have been his son's, because The Great Lump would never have thought to celebrate anything by doing something for his kingdom.

But that evening, just before the sun set, the king's fool came out to perform for all the children in the kingdom, from the street or otherwise.

He was dressed in bright yellow and had bells tied to the toes of his shoes. I bet he would've had a hard time sneaking up on someone. His hair was nearly the same color as his clothes, and he was thin and long. But the part that struck me the most was his eyes. They burned like blue fire, and there was something about his smile that I found myself coveting desperately, overcome by a strange feeling of longing.

The fool juggled nine balls at one time, and then he juggled three kittens, and then he juggled *coins*! And as he juggled, he threw them out at the crowd, yet he never seemed to run out of coins to juggle. You should have seen them. Everyone was screaming and scrambling over themselves and most of them were laughing, but a few of them were crying about not getting a coin. They shouldn't have. I stole most of the coins from those that picked them up, anyway. And the fool smiled like he had everything under control, and I wanted that smile *so* badly!

I also wanted his brightly painted juggle balls.

But when it comes to smiles and juggle balls, you can only steal one of them.

Night was falling; the minstrels and storytellers were coming out. The fool was packing up and slipping away. He had a bag with all his things in it—including the kittens, two of which had already escaped and run off. I figured he would assume his juggle balls had done the same thing. After all, he had at least nine. Would he notice three missing?

Yes. Yes, he would.

Holding the three balls I had stolen in my shirt about as

stealthily as a chipmunk with apples in his cheeks, I ducked between two shops.

The shops were deserted because everyone was out listening to the music or the stories. It was mostly dark but it wasn't pitch black yet and I had some firelight from the torches on the street.

I figured three balls was where to start when it came to juggling. Two didn't seem to count because I already had two hands, and you can't do anything with one. So I held all three balls in both hands, took a deep breath, tossed them in the air, and juggled!

It was only for maybe a second before they hit the ground, but I think it counted.

Except one of them landed on my foot and it hurt. So I cried out and then picked them up to try again. Trying to keep my toes out of the way, I threw them into the air again.

But they never came down.

Quicker than blinking, the fool was there. He caught all three balls and began juggling them in one hand faster than I could follow.

For a moment he was terrible and frightening. I tried to run. But the fool, without dropping a single ball, grabbed the side of my head before I could escape, getting mostly hair and ear.

I cried out again and tried to put on a convincing "innocent" face, not remembering that my nose was still covered in clay from the spider bite and not knowing that I was growing up to look a bit ridiculous anyway. How was I to know what my face looked like?

His eyes were still fiery and for a moment his whole face was too, but then he traded it for that smile I wanted. He had everything under control.

Well, he sure did because he had an iron grip on my *ear.* To this day I can still feel it; it's been tender ever since.

"Do you know what would happen to you if I turned you over to the soldiers for stealing?" he asked me. His voice was both sneaky and confident. This close, I could tell that his longish hair was the color of the loaves of bread that taunted me from the baker's window.

I didn't answer right away because I'd learned from experience that when someone has you by the ear and they ask you a question, sometimes they just want to yell at you and they don't want you to say anything back, so I didn't at first. But then the fool tightened his grip and I took that to mean he actually *did* want me to speak.

"I wasn't stealing! Your balls ran off. I just found them. And the punishment is a beating. Or the stocks. Both if it's me they get!"

The fool laughed and his grip loosened a little, but I still couldn't get away. "Well, you're right about not making assumptions, Little Thief. And if I hadn't seen your little maneuver, I might have had to believe you. But even if you hadn't stolen from me, I could still turn you over to them just the same."

"Please, my lord! I won't do it again! Don't give me to the soldiers!"

The fool smiled like it was really funny I called him "my lord." It probably was, but I found that it paid to be polite in tight situations. Ow! Really tight.

"Oh, but it would be fair. You cannot steal without consequences. By all rights, I should give you to them." Light from the torches bounced off his eyes. "But I don't think I'm going to."

I stopped struggling and looked at him. I would later

learn that my impression was off, but at the moment, all I could think was that his face looked sinister. My stomach got really tight and I said, "Maybe you'd better."

He laughed again, not in a sinister way, I guess, but I was still afraid. "No. I'm the court fool. I don't have to do things the way everybody else does. In fact, I get to do and say whatever I want. And I say we're going to let you choose your own punishment. You're coming with me."

Then he turned and dragged me back out of the alley, dropping all three balls into his bag with the rest of them, as well as the third kitten.

His grip tightened again, and in the darkness and flickering light, my fear got the better of me.

"Let go!" I screamed and struggled against his grasp. "Let me go!"

The fool paused and shrugged. "Very well. Have it your way. Guard!"

Of all the soldiers that might have come up the street from the crowds of people, it had to be the one who had seen me with the spider.

"No!" I squealed. Yes, squealed. I tried to press myself behind the fool who had me so tightly.

"Make up your mind, Little Thief," the fool whispered. "Me or him. I'll let you choose your own punishment."

I actually hesitated. I knew exactly what waited for me on the streets and with that soldier. My legs still held red stripes from stray whip strokes, my body held bruises from being pelted in the stocks, and my mind couldn't handle the thought or presence of the spiders that riddled the streets. I was afraid of all of those. I was afraid of the fool too, at that point, but it was only the fear of the unknown, and I quickly opted for the unknown.

"You," I whispered.

The fool smiled, a different smile than the one I wanted, but it made my fear subside a little. He released my ear and put one of his large hands on my head.

A cart driven by an ox, recently emptied of the breads and meats it had distributed to the people, began to rumble past us.

The fool met eyes with the guard. "Shall I tell them to bring down some ale or wine for you and your fellows?"

The guard's face lit up. "Both. Wine for me; ale for the rest of them."

The fool winked at the soldier and then picked me up and tossed me in the cart along with his bag of tricks and jumped up beside me.

The man driving the cart looked behind him like he was about to shout, but the fool smiled and waved, and the man immediately turned his back to us and kept driving as if we weren't there.

"If—if I really get to choose my own punishment," I stammered, "then I'd really rather choose death by pastries. That sounds fair."

The fool's laughter was so immediate that I jumped. The kitten crawled out of the bag and hid in my lap. Petting it helped me feel better.

"Little Thief," the fool managed to choke between gales of laughter, "strictly speaking, you'd already chosen it back there in the alley before I caught you."

"Really?" I sure couldn't remember choosing my own punishment because I was pretty sure I would have chosen death by pastries.

The fool nodded, calming down as he wiped tears from his eyes. "You want to learn to juggle, I'm going to teach you how to juggle. And maybe make a fool of you at the same time, which won't be difficult, *apprentice*."

I raised my eyebrows. I felt relieved and wary at the same time: relieved because learning how to juggle didn't sound so bad, at least not as bad as a beating or the stocks, but wary because he was looking all sinister again.

Chapter 2

I very quickly learned to hate the name of Fendral. Fendral was the name of the fool, and he said I could call him that. I called him other things, too, but never out loud.

At first it was strange to have an adult tell me to call him by his name instead of some title. First names sounded so . . . equal. But Fendral still had a way of making it clear that he was master when he needed to. Most of the time he seemed pretty at ease, but if I didn't do what he said, he gave me a look of fire that was usually enough to encourage my obedience—because it turned out that learning to juggle actually *was* a punishment.

I think most of it was just not being used to someone telling me what to do or paying so much attention to me. And another was practicing something that turned out to be much harder than Fendral ever made it look, especially when I was convinced that I just wasn't meant to be a juggler. A fool maybe; no one could dispute that. But juggler? Nope.

Fendral was less convinced than I was that I was never going to get it. And so he never let me quit no matter how much I whined or begged.

After about two weeks of being constantly watched, I couldn't take it anymore. I needed to get out.

As the court fool, Fendral didn't have any specific wing or place to sleep. He slept wherever he wanted. On nice nights, we slept out in the garden on benches or sometimes even in trees. If it was too cool or rainy, we slept wherever we wanted to in the castle. Fendral preferred window seats in the hallway. He felt cooped up in spare rooms or even in the servant's quarters.

So one night, I waited until I was sure Fendral was asleep. He was on a window seat and I was on the floor just beneath him. There wasn't a sound anywhere in the castle. Carefully, stealthily, like I was back on the streets already, I slipped away.

I made my way to the kitchen first and filled my pockets and an empty potato sack full of breads, rolls, and pastries that hadn't been eaten that day. Fendral had shown me that he pinched food whenever he wanted, but was careful not to take too much or take things that would be greatly missed. I ignored that as I stuffed the bag. Then I exited the castle through the scullery, into the garden, and climbed over the wall separating the garden from the rest of the kingdom.

Ah. Free again!

Running through the darkened streets I saw the moving shapes of other orphans and waifs stirring. I stopped by one. Most of the other orphans called him "Little Waif." I dropped a pastry in his hands and ran on.

"Hey! Little Thief? Is that you?"

It was Sleight, one of the older orphans. He was huddled around a garbage heap behind some houses with a bunch of other kids from the street.

"We thought the soldiers had gotten you," Sleight said,

hitting me on the arm. "What happened? What do you have?"

I smiled. "I was kidnapped by the court fool," I said. And then I opened my sack and began handing out my spoils right and left. Nobody asked me any questions after that.

With some effort, I managed to save some of my food and ran to the edge of town, where I dropped the sack and the rest of my goods on the spinster's doorstep and walked away.

Without fully meaning to, I found myself heading back to the castle. The sky was just beginning to get light, so I was pretty sure that Fendral would still be asleep and would never know that I had been out all night.

Sure enough, I crept back into the hallway and found Fendral still breathing deeply on his window seat just as I'd left him.

I was going to collapse back onto the floor and get as much sleep as I could before Fendral woke me, but then I noticed something that made me freeze in my tracks.

A pastry. All golden, flaky, and filled, was sitting on the floor where I should have been.

I was immediately suspicious. Who put it there? I never came back this way after I raided the kitchen. Did Fendral know I had gone? Was this a trap? Was it poisoned?

My stomach growled just looking at it. In my excitement, I had saved nothing for myself. Well, even if it was poisoned, death by pastries had always been my preference. I slipped over and took a deep, slow bite, feeling the crunch of the crust and then a rush of sweet cream fill my mouth. I very nearly passed out from sheer pleasure—or maybe from the fact that I hadn't slept all night. Probably a little of both.

But I finished my pastry and curled up under the window seat, feeling pretty sure that I had gotten away with everything. I didn't let myself worry about where the pastry had come from.

"How was it?"

I jumped. The voice was Fendral's, but he still looked like he was asleep. I hadn't even seen him move. Was he talking about the pastry or did he know I had gone back to the streets for the night? I put a hand to my stomach and tried to sense if there was poison in me. Finally, fearing it might make him mad if I didn't answer, I asked, "How was what?" as quietly and innocently as possible.

Fendral smiled even though his eyes were closed and his body still limp with sleep. "Seeing your street friends again."

My eyes got big, but Fendral couldn't see. How had he known? "All right, I guess," I answered warily.

"Why did you come back?"

I wasn't sure how to answer that question either. Was I not supposed to come back? Had Fendral hoped I would run off and not come back? Well, then he shouldn't have snatched me in the first place!

"I forgot to save myself some bread," I answered honestly. "There are no pastries out there." No need to pretend like I'd come back for him.

Fendral snickered in his sleep, making me jump again. One of his large hands fell from the window seat and grasped my shoulder. I tensed, waiting for some demonstration of anger through that hand.

Fendral squeezed but not too hard. "I know," he whispered. "I thought you might come back for that. Well done, apprentice." Then he released my shoulder, looking just as asleep as he had the whole time.

I couldn't move and I couldn't sleep. Fendral had known about the whole thing, even about me giving bread to my friends. Even about how I had given them all away without eating one. He must have followed me unseen. Impossible. And I couldn't understand why he didn't seem like he was angry, or why he gave me a pastry, or even why he'd touched my shoulder. The only thing that kept coming to mind was what Fendral had said when he'd first caught me. *I'm the court fool, and I don't have to do things the way everyone else does.* Maybe this was what he meant. It was all I had to go on, anyway. Settling myself with this thought, I eventually fell back asleep, and we both slept in until noon.

The last thing I heard before I nodded off was an idle thought from Fendral that slipped out quietly, "Pastries, huh?"

I suppose that I hated Fendral only for about those two weeks. Sometime after that night, I began to realize that I loved Fendral more than anything, and it became easier to do what he said.

"Don't stop. Again," Fendral ordered. I was sweating. He was sitting on the ground in the garden, twirling a fork in his fingers effortlessly without looking at it. His fingers were usually busy doing something.

"I can't get it," I insisted. What I really meant was, "I'm tired."

"You're very close to getting it," he insisted. "Just a little more. As soon as you make two complete passes, you can take a break."

I had three balls. Two passes meant completing the cascade pattern more than one measly time. I just couldn't top my one time. I couldn't control my throws enough to do it twice, and completing the pattern repeatedly was the point. It's what juggling was. In a few weeks, you'd think I'd be able to get it, but I'd never had to practice coordination before, and my arms were only just learning. And I was tired.

But I knew that Fendral wouldn't let me rest until I'd done it, but at least I knew he absolutely would if I did. So I tried again.

And again.

And again.

And I got it!

"Yes!" Fendral crowed. He leapt to his feet so fast that I hardly had time to celebrate myself. "Drop them. You're done for a while."

I let my arms and hands go slack, and I wasn't planning on using them for as long as possible, but Fendral tossed something at me suddenly and I had to catch it.

A pastry!

Fendral pulled a second pastry out from his yellow shirt and held it up like it was goblet and he was making a toast, and then he took a large bite.

I never asked questions when it came to pastries, so I did the same.

"That was a pretty small one," I commented once we were through. "Can I have another?"

Fendral grinned. "Sure can," he said, winking. "As soon as you make it look easy."

Maybe I hated him for more than those two weeks; it's hard to remember.

Fendral rewarded my scowl with that powerful smile of his that I wanted so badly, almost as if he was taunting me that he had it and I didn't. And I found myself wishing he hadn't figured out that I'd sell my soul for a pastry.

“So what did the others call you on the streets, Little Thief?” Fendral asked me one day as I tossed balls into the sky under a hot sun. “I suppose I can’t call you *apprentice* forever.”

“Just that,” I told him.

“Justhat? That’s a funny name. Not quite right for a fool, though.”

“No, I mean, what you just called me. Little Thief. Except usually they said it, ‘You Little Thief!’”

Fendral guffawed. He laughed often, as if he had a fountain of mirth in him that often overflowed and splashed on other people, making them laugh too. I wasn’t quite sure why he was laughing, but I couldn’t help at least smiling a little.

“No name?” he said. “Well then, I guess I’ll have to get creative. When I think of something, I’ll let you know.”

It didn’t take him long. He caught me the next day with a nest of items I’d stolen from the courtiers: pieces of shiny fabric, rings, jewels, broaches, a comb, and three handkerchiefs.

“I got it!” Fendral snapped his fingers in delight once he’d finished laughing. “Have you heard the word *farrago* before?”

Would you believe that I had? “Isn’t it what they feed the cows and horses?” I asked.

“It’s a mixture of all the leftover grains that they feed to the livestock,” he clarified. “It kind of means a bunch of stuff. An assortment. Your little hoard reminded me. Plus I think it sounds like a good name for a fool. I’ve always liked the way the word sounded. But you’ll be the one to be wearing it. What do you think?”

"Ffffarrago," I said, tasting the word in my mouth. "Farrago, Farrago, Farrago." I liked how it made the *ffffff* sound like at the beginning of Fendral's name. I also liked how the last part felt like it popped out of my mouth.

"I'll take it," I announced, an odd feeling of pride swelling in my chest. I liked having a name. I liked that Fendral had found it for me. I liked that it felt like mine.

"Good." Fendral slapped his leg. "But cut off the stealing. There's no need. Use your light fingers for other things. Now, see how long you can stand on your hands."

It turned out that being a fool was more than just juggling three, nine, or eleven balls. It was riddles and jokes and making funny faces. It was contortions and dancing and wit—anything to make people smile and keep the mood light. Fendral even had the court scholars teach me some letters and numbers. I had picked up numbers on the street. I had learned some letters too, but apparently there were more. With the scholars' help I was at least able to spell my name—albeit three different ways. I never could remember how many Rs or Gs.

But of all the things that Fendral taught me, that ever-elusive smile was never mine, and I found myself wanting it more and more. I wanted to be like Fendral.

Chapter 3

"All right, now who are they?" Fendral pointed to a group of women wandering in the gardens one day as we watched from the hallway balcony that opened to the outside air.

"The ladies-in-waiting," I replied readily. "Fendral? What do ladies-in-waiting do?"

"They usually attend to the queen's needs and give her companionship."

"But I thought Gridian didn't have a queen."

Fendral nodded. "Not since the prince was a toddler."

"So . . . what do the ladies-in-waiting do now?"

"Um, wait. Obviously. For a new one. Now, who are they?"

"The court minstrels." The minstrels were actually strumming things down the hall from us.

"Right. And that little minstrel is Leofrick. He's one of the few people in court about your age. Let's see, who else? Oh, there's Thea. She might be about your age. She's—"

"The scullery maid," I finished as we watched her tote water from the garden well through the back scullery door.

I cocked my head. "She's better looking than most of the other maids."

Fendral cocked his head too. "Well, she does have an evenness of face that sets her apart a bit. But let me warn you, pretty faces can be dangerous. Women are evil witches with mind powers. Don't let them get to you."

I nodded solemnly.

"Now, the woman Thea is with—"

"—is her personal slave driver. The kitchen hag."

The hag in question looked up suddenly as she carried an entire dead pig under each arm behind Thea. Fendral grabbed my head and pushed me down so the hag couldn't see me.

"That's Constance," he whispered. "I wouldn't go underestimating her if I were you. We fools can get away with calling most people most things, but even a fool should know better than to offend the master of the kitchens—and therefore master of your food."

"Right," I whispered. But, actually, I hadn't understood what he'd said. For some reason I didn't realize that he meant her *name* was Constance. So the only real name I internalized for her was the kitchen hag. And I never could seem to say it without her hearing me. Ears like a rabbit, squat flat face like a bear with its nose cut off with a body to match. The kitchen hag frightened me, and I made up for it by, well, taking foolish to a new level and always calling her what she looked like. Which was actually pretty stupid of me because—

"You kind of have a beak nose."

The little minstrel, the one Fendral said was called Leofrick, was standing next to me where I crouched next to Fendral, holding a mandolin that was far too big for him.

"Thanks," I replied. "That's what the soldiers always said."

"It's not that it's necessarily too *big*, it's just that it curves down a little. You know. Like a beak."

I nodded. I'd already agreed with him; there was no need to beat it into the ground.

He must have taken my silence as some indication that I felt wounded by his comment, because he quickly added, "But you're going to be a fool like Fendral. And it's good for fools to look funny. Me, I want to eat a lot so I have a potbelly when I grow up. So it's all right."

I looked over at Fendral, who was biting his lip and making a weird face.

"Well!" He slapped his leg and stood up. "I'm going to let you two figure it out and go do some stuff of my own." He strode away.

I looked back at Leofrick. "Potbelly, huh? Want to go down to the kitchens before the kitchen hag gets there and get started on your goal early?"

Leofrick's eyes lit up as if the thought had never occurred to him. "Yeah!"

I was becoming nearly as good as Fendral. I could juggle six balls, but not eleven yet, and I could walk on my hands, dance, and juggle three kittens. I had a *farrago* (ha-ha) of other tricks I'd picked up from my master as well.

"Our job as fools," Fendral explained to me as he was giving me a demonstration of juggling random items of different weights: a pitcher, a cannonball, and a potato, "is to keep the mood light. When we're around, we don't let others mope about. People are supposed to feel different when they're around us; they'll feel better in our presence if we keep up a light air ourselves. I find that things like juggling, contortions, dancing, and tricks are a good distraction when someone doesn't feel like laughing. And people greatly need the distraction we offer."

"Why?" I asked as I practiced juggling with sticks painted white on one end. If I could catch them by the white end every time, Fendral would let me juggle knives.

Fendral caught the objects he was tossing and set them down, stretching his arms for a moment. "Because most people never learn how to be happy, and we offer some of the only tastes they will get of laughter and pleasure. We must smile and joke and entertain no matter how heavy others feel. We," and he came closer, looking me in the eye with a strange glint, "are more important than they realize. The nobility consider us a low class, but in truth"—he couldn't help a long smile spreading over his face— "we are outside of class. And that is better even than being nobility."

Our eyes met as he spoke and I could tell that he believed what he said. I believed him too and felt lucky to be one.

One morning, the trumpeters that stood on the wall to herald important visitors or the return of the king from travels woke us all up one morning with a long low wail from their horns.

"Hmmm," Fendral muttered, squinting his eyes like he was putting all his mind to one strong thought.

"What is it?" I asked. "What do the trumpets mean?"

"The king is dead," Fendral said as he looked me straight in the eyes. "They'll bury him tomorrow. His son will take over as king."

"Really?" I wished I knew about trumpets and how the kingdom worked and such. "Who is his son?"

"Giles," Fendral replied. "I'm not even sure if he's as old as you."

"What? We're getting a new king, and he's younger than *me*?"

Fendral nodded, looking thoughtful. "The burial will be a big deal. Lots of professional mourners, because they won't be able to find any genuine ones, but still, it will be sad for the prince."

"Oh, so do we . . . stay away from that?" I asked.

Fendral gave me a curious look. "The funeral? Whatever for?"

"Well, you said that we keep the mood light. You can't keep the mood light at a . . . at a . . . when someone *dies*. When people are really sad."

"Ah." Fendral scooted closer like he was telling me a secret. "That's when we're needed the *most*," he whispered. "I'll show you."

Fendral was right about the fake mourners. Such a fuss over a great lump like the king. Everyone knew that the counselors had made all his decisions for him and he spent all his time living the high life. His son, Giles, didn't look sad as much as miserable. He didn't even cry. At least he wasn't a round blob like his father had been, but honestly, he wasn't a very inspiring person. He looked small, young, and frail, even though his dark brown hair was expertly combed under his new gold crown and his cloak helped his frame look bigger. But other than that, he looked ill. Hardly someone you wanted running a kingdom.

That night, after the actual funeral, there was a feast. All the nobles and courtiers came and the kitchen hag prepared a lot of supposedly delicious dishes to tempt the mourners into eating. Fendral and I didn't sit with them. We hid in the shadows of the room while everyone ate, snagging items off dishes as maids carried them in. The king-to-be sat sullenly at the head of the table, nobles spread to either side of him. Every now and then he put something in his mouth when someone spoke to him, but he didn't seem to enjoy it.

Finally, Fendral made his move. Snagging a basket of small golden plums, he held it on his hip as he came out of the shadows and leaned against the wall where he was still out of the way but could be seen by everyone. As soon as he made his appearance, the nobles started nudging each other and whispering. Eyes gradually turned in his direction.

Fendral ate a plum at his leisure, still holding the basket at his hip, seemingly unaware, or at least uncaring, of all the eyes on him. When he was nearly done, Fendral put the rest of the plum, including the pit, into his mouth. After a second, his eyes bugged out like he was really surprised the pit was there, and spat it into his hand, tossing it over his shoulder idly. The dining room was so quiet. Then, setting the basket down, Fendral began popping plums into his mouth. One. Two. Three. Four . . . I think five. He didn't eat them, he just held them in his cheeks, his mouth bulging with the amount. I was pretty sure I wouldn't have been able to fit more than three in my mouth if I'd tried. Fendral picked up two more and began juggling them in one hand, and three more to twirl in his other. Finally, he had all five plums juggling with both hands, and after a second—POP! He spat a plum from his mouth to join the others dancing in the air. Four more plums joined the rest with the same POP! His audience gasped and chuckled with each new addition. Ten plums. I snuck up and threw one last plum into the fray because I knew he could juggle eleven. The courtiers laughed when I did that, and Fendral winked at me. I grinned back, pretty proud of myself.

Then Fendral started eating the plums out of the air, only he didn't really. He opened his mouth like he was going to swallow one whole, but instead, he stuck out his chest and let the plum slip down his collar and into his tunic, but he exaggerated swallowing them so well that it was fairly convincing. He continued to cut down on the number of plums in the air one by one until he had seemingly "swallowed" them all, but they were really all in his shirt. Looking surprised, Fendral pooched his stomach out and turned so that everyone could see the lumps of the plums in his shirt, looking like he'd just swallowed the whole basket. The nobles laughed and applauded, even Giles. The prince's whole face lifted, and for a moment he looked like a completely different person—not just happier, but more *alive.*

Fendral bowed and all the plums ran out of his collar, making everyone laugh harder.

I laughed too, and even though I was just the apprentice and not the master, I felt proud.

Later, after most of the nobles had gone to bed, Giles called Fendral over, dismissing his attendants with a stern (and, I thought, pretty spoiled-sounding) command. While the two of them spoke in the corridor, I spied from a curtain. I couldn't hear much of what they were saying, but Giles looked worried. Suddenly, without warning, Giles grabbed Fendral around the middle, squeezing him tight and sobbing over and over, "I don't want to be king! I don't want to be my father! I don't know how to be king! What am I going to do?"

Fendral looked a bit surprised at first, but it only showed for a second before he came to himself. Fendral patted Giles's shoulder and hugged him back, which looked strange to me because I'd never been hugged before. I wondered why Prince Giles was speaking about this with his fool instead of with his counselors. Then again, I didn't. I'd seen the counselors, and I knew that I would certainly go to Fendral before them if I had a choice.

Finally Fendral pulled the prince away and knelt so he could look him in the eyes. "You were born to be a king," I heard him say. "You have nothing to be afraid of." And he smiled in such a way that I'm sure Giles must have felt silly for having had a breakdown in the first place.

"Will you help me?" Giles asked.

What? How was that supposed to work?

"Yes," Fendral answered readily. "I'll help where I can. And if I can't be there, I'll send someone else. All right?"

Giles nodded and Fendral turned him away as if he was his father. Then he came over and pulled me out of the curtains.

"Next time, make sure you prop yourself up so no one can see your feet," he counseled as if he was still teaching me a fool's trick. "We'll have to keep an eye on that one, won't we?"

I knew he meant the king, but I didn't understand why Giles had gone to Fendral, or how Fendral was supposed to help him. But I nodded. There was something about Fendral that I trusted. It didn't matter that things were strange.

It was late afternoon. Prince Giles had been King Giles for almost two months, and life was pretty boring. Fendral and I had just finished lunch and were perfecting a routine that we had planned together, tossing nine-pin pins back and forth between the two of us. I was pretty good as long as I didn't overthink things. If I ever stood back and thought about what I was doing, I always dropped one, so I had to let it become second nature to me, doing only what Fendral told me and practicing a lot.

Then, just after we'd finished an act, Fendral promptly set the pins down and beckoned me to follow him.

"We're stopping? But we only just started up again," I protested. I had picked up a rhythm that I didn't want to lose.

"Our young king is meeting with his counselors this afternoon," Fendral explained.

"So?"

"So," Fendral continued as we wound our way from courtyard through the upper extremities of the castle, "I promised him I'd be there, and that means you too, by extension."

He was talking as if things were supposed to make sense, but I felt like a tagalong simpleton. I wanted to ask him why he had promised to be there, instead of saying that the king ordered that he be there, but I didn't.

I thought we were getting close to where the king must be meeting, but instead of going through another door, Fendral slipped out of a window. It took me a moment to realize where he had gone. Fendral popped his head back in and beckoned. Fendral slipped along a narrow ledge of carved stone that led to yet another window. I followed him without too much trouble, glad that the height did not bother me; though if we'd fallen, we'd have died. Sure enough, the room Fendral and I slipped into had an important-looking sitting chair that currently held dear King Giles, and he was surrounded by a bunch of other important-looking men in long, important-looking robes. The royal counselors. Giles looked bored, and the counselors were the ones doing all the talking in loud, urgent voices as they stood in front of the grand chair. Giles's chair faced the window, and he perked up when he saw us enter. The counselors kept yelling. They spoke as if they were trying to bully him, except that Giles was acting like they weren't even there. It was a good thing Fendral didn't always wear his bells, or they would have heard him coming a mile away.

"The strike must be immediate and severe or else other provinces will start acting out as well!"

"As peasants, they have no right to make demands and we must not be subject to them! These people are simple vermin and will respond to nothing other than strict and swift punishment!"

And so on and so forth.

Fendral made a face, and the king cracked a small smile. The counselors knew that something must be wrong because they had moved on to talk of killing and carnage and yet the king grinned. This may not have been unusual behavior for Giles's great lump of a father, but it was unusual for Giles. All the counselors stopped speaking at once and turned, almost like one person, to where Fendral and I still sat perched on the large windowsill as if we'd been there the whole time.

Then, again like one person, they all started yelling at the same instant and came toward us like a flock of crows on a dead cat.

"This is an official counsel between us and the king!"

"Begone, fool!"

"We could have you thrown right back out that window!"

And so on and so forth.

Fendral pulled something out of his tunic. A pastry. He took a large bite and chewed with his mouth open. This seemed to make the counselors even angrier. I tapped his shoulder. Fendral pulled out another pastry for me. I followed in his footsteps and took a large bite too, even though

I usually preferred to eat them more slowly so as to taste them longer.

One of the robed figures stamped his foot and spun back to the king. "Your Highness! Bid them leave so that we may continue our meeting! This is our time!"

"Yes, of course, this is our time," Giles agreed. "But since he's here, we may as well get a second opinion. Since you all say the same thing, there isn't one to be found here. Fendral!"

Fendral alighted off the windowsill with a small jump, standing like the sun in storm clouds with his yellow garb in the midst of all the dark robes.

"Apparently one of the far provinces has refused to pay taxes because they say they're too high. They drove away some tax collectors with pitchforks and shovels. One of the collectors was injured. You heard what my counselors think. What do you say? Should the peasants be subdued by force and made an example of?"

"Certainly!" Fendral agreed readily. The counselors looked a bit surprised, glancing at each other and nodding as if the fool was finally speaking sense. "It will encourage all other provinces to do the same and we'll have a great war on our hands! If we're lucky, all the peasants will rebel and the counselors will have to take up arms and fight themselves!" The counselors put hands over their hearts and gasped as if Fendral had spoken blasphemy. "After all, wars are supposed to be wonderfully healthy for the state of the kingdom." Fendral took a small bite from his pastry, chewed, and swallowed. "Actually," Fendral said, draping a confused mask over his face, "maybe not if the kingdom is fighting against itself. That might be bad." He scratched his head. "I can't rightly recall. But if the counselors say it, then it must be the best course of action." Then his eyes blazed just as I had seen them that day on the streets when I first met him, like an icy fire burned behind the blueness. "But one would have to be a fool to go against the counselors, wouldn't they?" He winked.

"Well then," one of the robes asked pompously, "if you don't think the king should exercise his right and power to keep his kingdom in order, what should he do?" He said it as if he was sure Fendral would have nothing to say.

"Lower taxes," Fendral said, taking off his fool's face entirely for just a moment. "Give the peasants a nonviolent method for dealing with their government accusations. Hold a trial for the harm inflicted on the collector if you must, but if you kill any of them, the rebellions will spread like wildfire until the kingdom collapses on itself." Then he shrugged, and he was a fool again. He took another large bite of pastry. "But I still like the idea of war," he lied as he chewed. "Jolly good fun. Brilliant."

"Your Majesty, must we listen to the imbecile's opinions? Please send him away so that we may continue," one of the robes whined.

Giles nodded his head. "Indeed. We've listened to enough opinions today. Fortunately, the final decision of what's to be done lies with the king. Now be gone!"

The counselor huffed like he had just been reprimanded by an infant, which he had, but he had to obey because that infant was king. Looking to his comrades, the counselors eventually all bowed, one by one this time, and filed out.

My pastry had been finished for several minutes by this time, though I had really enjoyed the show. This was Fendral at his best, juggling balls aside.

Once the room was cleared of the jabbering counselors,

Giles raised his eyes to Fendral's. He nodded once. "Thank you," he said in a soft voice, suddenly looking much younger than he had a moment before when he'd been surrounded by his counselors.

Fendral bowed, and was suddenly serious. The bow was sincere. I did as he did because I knew I was supposed to, but I wasn't sure if mine was sincere or not.

Then it was back through the windows and into the courtyard where Fendral made me practice until sundown as if we had had no interruption.

As I tossed painted rocks and stood on my hands and made funny faces, I thought about what Fendral was doing for the king, and for me. In a way, he was master of us both. Only master wasn't the right word. Guardian? Helper? Mentor. That was it. For the first time I felt like I was more fully understanding what a fool was supposed to do, and I felt a burning desire to become everything Fendral was.

I would, too, in not many years' time. I just wish it didn't have to happen the way it did.

Chapter 5

Several years passed. At least six Christmases, I think. That's how I measured time. I could measure weeks by the church bell calling everyone to mass. I measured months every time I saw a full moon and years by Christmases, with all the feasts and merrymaking. Fendral and I were kept very busy then.

I was a few years away from being an official man, I think. I had never been sure of my age. I just knew that the king was about as old as me, and he didn't look like a man yet. He looked rather thin, as if his bones had lengthened without his stomach being able to keep up, and he often seemed worried, though he spoke commands as if he knew what he was doing. Fendral and I were present in most of the meetings Giles had with his counselors, and Fendral always came up with some different solution to the kingdom's problems than what the counselors said. Usually better, I thought. He said some things that other nobles would probably have been hanged for, and even though the counselors probably *would* have liked to hang Fendral, they couldn't. He was a fool. You don't get mad at fools;

they'll never let you forget it. Giles followed Fendral's advice without really making it *look* like he was always following Fendral's advice. Things in the kingdom got a little better. I know because every now and then I still skipped back to the streets and waved to the spinster or juggled something for my street friends. They always seemed to be doing a little better than before, and they loved my juggling.

When Fendral wasn't coaching me or performing for others, he spent his time with the brown-haired gardener lady, and when I wasn't practicing or performing for others, I liked to heckle the kitchen hag and see if I could get her to throw something good to eat at me. I know, I know. It's not smart to make enemies with the food master. It sort of happened by accident. It's not my fault she was hideous. If it wasn't for Thea, the maid, I probably would have starved. She liked to slip me things now and then even when the kitchen hag wouldn't. I made sure she never got caught.

Leofrick occasionally tried to teach me some mandolin, but he didn't have Fendral's flair for teaching—plus I was a miserable music student and preferred to listen and watch his fingers speed effortlessly across the strings. After a while, I would try to juggle to the tune and feel of his music. We eventually began performing great numbers together at all the big feasts with his music and my antics.

Then things changed for me so suddenly that it still feels like there's a knife buried in my heart. I don't think the knife will ever come out. In a strange way, I don't want it to.

I had gone to sleep in the hallway under a window with moonlight pouring through. Fendral was off . . . somewhere. I reasoned that he was either entertaining the ladies-in-waiting or snatching a thing or two from the kitchen on my behalf. The night was far spent when I felt a hand brush across my forehead. That was unusual. I stirred and opened my eyes enough to see Fendral standing over me.

Several things told me that all was not right. Fendral wasn't smiling, and he usually smiled. That in and of itself wouldn't have worried me so much, though. One couldn't be smiling all the time even if it was habit. The thing that really alerted me was that he wasn't dressed in yellow. Fendral *always* wore yellow. Always. I had never seen him in anything else. I still wore a common tan tunic and leggings, and no hat or bells over my shaggy and ever lengthening brown hair. Fendral was dressed in dark brown, with a black cloak over that. This was just not Fendral-like.

Disturbed, I sat up. "What is it?" I whispered.

Fendral bit his lip and said nothing. He looked worried, or sad, much like the king did when he had some decision to make. But I couldn't figure out what Fendral would have to be worried about unless—the thought dawned slowly—he was worried about *me*. But he wouldn't have any reason to be worried about me unless—

I gasped. Behind him, a few paces down the hall was another figure. The brown-haired gardener lady. She too was in a long dark cloak.

"You're leaving," I whispered. A horrible coldness and fear burst in my chest. It was only a feeling, but it hurt worse than anything I'd ever felt. "You can't be leaving."

Fendral hugged me. I wish he hadn't. If he had spit on me or kicked me, not that he ever had or would, I could have handled it. But he'd never hugged me before. I had never been hugged before. Kindness put me over the edge.

"I'd always thought there was nothing better than being a fool," he said softly so as not to disturb the night. "There is only one thing better, and I'm going to do that now. The court still has a fine fool. They will not miss me."

He was running away with the brown-haired woman. He was going to leave me. I clutched him so hard it must have hurt him, but I didn't care. I could see the woman still standing behind Fendral, and she was weeping. She was weeping for me. I wished she hadn't. Maybe I would have been able to hate her otherwise. But I couldn't blame her. I couldn't blame her for wanting Fendral. I couldn't even blame Fendral; in my mind he could do no wrong. Fendral had given me everything; it had just never occurred to me that it would be temporary.

"The king will miss you," I said. My voice sounded awful. I was losing my ability to speak as my terror rose.

"Which is why I must leave before he wakes up, but you will take care of him, won't you, Farrago? You'll look out for things? You'll do as I have done?"

I felt myself nodding. I was incapable of refusing Fendral anything, as much as I wanted to, but, oh, how it hurt! I had never fully felt the weight of responsibility before, but if Fendral left, I would have to bear his job alone.

Fendral pulled away and looked me in the eyes. He smiled. He was crying too, but he had far more control than I did. "Remember what I've taught you, and be your own man." He put a hand on the side of my head. "Well done." I could feel myself breaking. I'd had no sign this was coming, no time to prepare, and no idea I would react this way.

Somehow he managed to pry my hands away and stood up, turning to the gardener. Then he stopped and turned back to me where I still sat on the ground of the stone hallway bathed in moonlight. "Remember what I told you about girls?" he asked.

I nodded. "Evil witches with mind powers," I recited hoarsely. "Stay away from them."

"I was lying."

"I know."

Fendral managed a laugh, that wonderful fountain of mirth overflowing again. He knelt back down and took my head in both of his hands, turning my downcast face to his. "Well done," he said firmly. "You will be wonderful." He said it with such strength that I believed him. He pressed his lips to my forehead, stood, and ran away, catching hands with the brown-haired gardener. Their footsteps thumped lightly down the corridor until they faded, no sound of bells.

I broke down completely, sobbing as I never had before. It was frightening because I couldn't make myself stop. For at least a half hour I couldn't even move. As I wept, I felt an odd sense of familiarity. I *had* cried like this before. The face of the thin woman smiling at me came to mind. I associated this kind of pain with her, but I had forgotten. Now two faces would haunt me. All of my years on the street trying to survive told me that I couldn't cry as I was. I couldn't let anyone see or hear me. Fools never cried. Fendral never did. What if a soldier had caught me crying like this while I was on the streets? He could have done anything to me and I would have had no will to resist him.

As soon as this thought occurred to me, I felt a hand on my shoulder. I jumped with an added burst of agony.

It was Leofrick. "Hey, it's me," he whispered, holding me up from collapsing. "Fendral told me you might need me to come by tonight. I saw him leaving with the gardener girl." He took care to put a firm arm across my shoulders.

"It's all right," he said softly, not meaning that the situation was acceptable, but that I was allowed to weep.

Everything in me tried to gain control of a storm that was too big for me. Strong displays of emotion like this were dangerous; the vulnerability was deadly. I couldn't. I couldn't.

But the storm was too big and too strong.

"It's all right," Leofrick repeated.

So I trusted him.

Leofrick stayed with me all night, sitting by me even after I quieted down. When he fell asleep, I slipped away. There was no sign of me when he woke up.

I went to the only place of refuge I could think of. The spinster's. I curled up in her back garden and hid. I was glad that she lived on the edge of the kingdom. Just behind her house was a small stream where she gathered the clay she needed to make her pots. She found me in the morning but said nothing, bringing me water and bread. The spinster was old, but anyone could see that she had been beautiful when she was younger. Her hair was bright white and her brown eyes were soft, though they could turn hard when she wanted them to. Right now, though, they were soft. They were nearly always soft when they were on me, especially now. I stayed with her all day and all the next night.

The next morning I rose to my feet, feeling stronger. There was the knife in my heart, but it only hurt if my mind bent a certain way. As the day dawned, I realized to my great delight that Fendral had left me his ever-elusive smile, as well as several other faces I could use at will. I sure hoped he had spares, though it had been very kind of him to give me his smile at last.

One of the only thoughts that allowed me to face the

day was a vow I made to myself: I would lose no one else. I already had a collection of missing faces, and any remembrance of them twisted a knife buried deep in my heart. I would let no one else with that kind of power over me out of my life.

It was an impossible promise, as I was going to learn, but I made it all the same. I would bring the name of fool to a whole new level, but I didn't care. Though if Fendral hadn't confessed that he'd been lying about girls being evil, I might have been able to keep it longer than I did.

But that day, when the courtiers and servants awoke, they found me with the sun on my back, juggling pastries, taking a bite out of each in turn until they were all gone.

The kingdom of Gridian had a new fool.

Chapter 6

It wasn't any particularly fancy occasion, just the king's regular dinner. But to make sure the castle crew knew of the new order of things, I performed. I juggled, told jokes, danced, and flipped. Several of the courtiers asked me about Fendral, and I cocked my head and asked, "Who?" and danced away. I never took Fendral's smile off my face, and I hoped that after a while the nobles would stop saying his name because the sound was still a bit painful.

The women of the castle, the maids and the ladies-in-waiting and some of the duchesses, twittered quite a bit about Fendral's disappearance, and it didn't take them long to speculate about the brown-haired gardener missing too. I was glad I didn't have to explain.

After dinner, most of the nobles retired to their chambers for the evening, and the maids were busy cleaning. The sun was just on its way down. I poked my head into the dining room as the maids were clearing away dishes, hoping to snag something. To my surprise, I saw Giles. He still sat slumped in his chair at the head table, resting his chin in his hand, looking deeply thoughtful. All of a sudden I had an idea of the weight that he carried. I was drawn to his sadness like sunlight chasing rain. I had to; that's what Fendral would do.

Using Fendral's advice, I started with a distraction, tossing a half-eaten roll in a hand, and adding to it with whatever I found: a bone from a cut of veal, an apple core, a plum that had been too ripe for the nobles to consider. It had taken me a long time to manage juggling items of different weights and shapes, but with a little concentration, it was very doable.

Giles lifted his gaze as I performed. I could hear maids returning and gathering dishes behind me. After a few minutes, I abruptly caught all my items, turned, and tossed them to the nearest maid, who had a stack full of dishes. She yelped as the junk landed on top of the pile, but to her credit she didn't drop anything. I smiled at her and she went along with it, curtsying briefly before scurrying away to the kitchen.

I turned back to the king. Giles sat up and drew a deep breath.

"So he's gone?" Giles asked. "Fendral has left?"

He missed Fendral too. Maybe not quite as much as I missed him, but I knew exactly how Giles felt.

Fendral had always been respectful to Giles, so I would be too. I took the confident smile off and showed the king my real face. "Yes," I answered gently. "He left me in his place."

"Farrago," the king said as if tasting how my name would taste in place of Fendral's.

"Farrago." I nodded. Then, slipping my smile back on, I darted away.

The Perfect Fool

Fingering Fendral's yellow tunic gave me my idea for my own garb. I had found his tunic sometime after he left, hidden away where I used to hide items I'd stolen from the courtiers. Starting with that, I extracted patches from everyone I could catch who lived at the castle. I cut squares from the backsides of the dukes and duchesses and the hems of the servants. Once I had them all, I took them to Thea and pressed her to stitch them together for me.

"Maggoty meal, Farrago!" Thea cursed when I dumped my patches on her lap as she sat on her small stool in the scullery. "Shouldn't you take these to the royal tailor? Or a chambermaid? At least find someone who is better at stitching than I," she protested.

"I don't need them to be stitched beautifully, I just need them to be stitched. And I can't handle a needle." Then, just to silence her, I gave her a peck on the cheek as if that settled the matter, which was difficult because I really had to tilt my head to get my beak nose out of the way.

Thea's eyes bulged. "If Constance saw you do that, she'd come upon you like the devil!"

I shrugged again. "I'm not afraid of Constance. I just think she's ugly, and I know she doesn't particularly like *me*."

"You should be kinder to her," Thea said, and her eyebrows came together a little. I knew she was probably right. I couldn't quite admit it. I didn't feel like it. I just sat on the ground next to her, rested my chin in my hand, and sighed.

"I wanted to tell you how sorry I am about Fendral," Thea whispered. I winced. I couldn't help it. Hearing his name was painful. It had been a while since someone had offered sympathy about that. I felt Thea brush some of my hair with her hand, and the gentleness of it felt like cool water on a burn. "He left with Catherine?"

"Who?"

"The brown-haired gardener girl."

"Oh, yeah." I think I had purposely not learned her name. She was never supposed to have been important.

Thea sighed. "You know, I could be content being a scullery maid my whole life. Constance sometimes tell me I'm made for better things. But if I could choose, I think I would do what Fendral did."

I looked up at her with a question on my face.

Thea's face flushed just a little. "Oh, to run away with my true love and start a family," she confessed. "I guess I wouldn't *have* to run away, but . . . listen to me talk. I'm content being a scullery maid. I am. Not all of us girls get what we dream for, and we must learn to be content." She stroked my hair one more time and then pulled her hand away, a little stiffly. She met my eyes once when I looked at her and then wouldn't again. She began to finger my patches, placing some of them side by side to see where they would fit best.

It was suddenly awkward, and I didn't know what to say. I'm just a fool, not a confessionary. So I stood and gave her a fool's bow. "Thank you for stitching the patches, Thea," I said honestly, and ran off.

All of that happened about three years ago. I suppose I am a man now, more or less, and I suppose the king is too. Leofrick finally has his potbelly, but he plays so well that he still has girls sitting around him to hear his music. Thea has kept me alive by not letting the kitchen hag starve me.

I make a point of entertaining the servants whenever I can, her especially.

Wearing patches makes me think I am carrying people with me, and even though I don't take particular stock with all of their faces, I still feel the responsibility Fendral felt for them. Fools keep the mood light, and we're not supposed to let people feel sad for long if we can help it.

I suppose I'd always made an exception for the kitchen hag, but I found that I also made exceptions for nobles when they made my job difficult.

Chapter 7

The castle had a balcony that overlooked the rear castle gardens and grounds. It was sort of an open hallway with pillars instead of walls, open to the air, with another floor on top of that. I was strolling along that one afternoon, idly tossing painted balls in one hand when I saw Thea run into the gardens from the ground-level kitchens carrying an empty water bucket. She was only a few paces away when someone grabbed her forearm and spun her around.

I recognized him as Sir Borin, duke of Clifton. Sir Borin had the look of a bloated slug, with pasty, ever-sweaty skin to match. He might not have looked so repugnant if he wore clothes a bit larger, but as it was, he always seemed to be just barely spilling out of them. He had greasy black hair and a mustache that he must have thought made him attractive or at least covered the mole on his upper lip. He was also dripping wet, and it didn't take me long to piece together where the water in Thea's bucket had gone.

"Vile hideous mongrel!" Borin barked, his voice sounding faintly like it was bubbling out of his throat. "All the most beautiful ladies would give anything for attentions from me! And you refuse them so!" He released Thea's arm roughly, making her fall to the ground. "Well, you are not so beautiful, you dandelion head! May your hands wither in dishwater!" And he stormed angrily away.

Thea got quickly to her feet, leaving the bucket on the ground, and ran into the gardens where she ducked behind a tree and crouched low. I listened closely and could hear her faint weeping.

Saving my preparations for revenge against Sir Borin for later, I ran to Thea's tree.

Once there, I slowed my step, trying to decide what to say. Everything in me said I had to fix what had happened; my honor as Fendral's apprentice depended on it, but I didn't know what to do. I tossed two balls in my left hand idly as I thought, putting a casual face on.

"To think that all I had to do to earn Sir Borin's disfavor all this time was to dump a pail of water on him," I tried to say in an envious voice. "Why didn't I consider that before?"

"Farrago!" Thea jumped and wiped her eyes with the back of her hand. "I-I didn't hear you coming. You saw that?"

"Front row seat," I said, nodding. "Perhaps we should douse him again. It's not possible for Sir Borin to have too many baths."

Thea gave a weak chuckle through her clogged throat. "No, it—it's not that."

"Ah, so you were particularly attached to the water in the pail? You donated it to a good cause."

Thea snorted a laugh again, taking a deep breath. But she shook her head. "It's just—" She raised a hand and lightly touched her wispy hair. "I *am* a dandelion head!" she wailed. And she burst into tears again.

My left hand froze, and all the balls I'd been juggling hit the ground with heavy thumps. I bit my bottom lip and willed myself not to laugh at her. I would never understand women. Over the years I'd noticed that Thea turned many heads because she had a smoothness of feature that most of the women, nobles included, lacked. Her figure was dainty and curved; she would have charmed the fairy king if they ever crossed paths. She had grown into a woman that most other women hated for her flawless face. Her only possible blemish was her wispy light hair. Her wheat-golden hair seemed barely longer than her shoulders, but it was so light that it floated around her face like a halo. Dandelion head actually wasn't a bad nickname. She should have been *grateful* for such a redeeming flaw as her hair! Thea had only been spared worse attentions because the kitchen hag protected her fiercely and would have maimed any man who pestered her too much. I had once seen the hag throw a pan at a page boy before, and if he hadn't been the thin, quick type, he would have spent the rest of his life with an imprint of his face in iron.

"Oh, good point," I agreed with Thea as she wept. "Actually, perhaps we can make it more so." I knelt and lifted her face with my hand. She turned her tear-streaked eyes on me but stood as I positioned her with the sun on her back. "There," I said, putting on a face of awe. "When you stand just right, your hair catches the sun." And it did. Quite spectacularly, I might add. In fact, for a moment I admit she mesmerized me. For several seconds I just stared at her. Slowly, I woke up when I noticed that she was staring at me too, very intently.

Suddenly I realized to my horror that I had no idea what my face was doing. I was wearing none of my fool's masks.

When had I lost them? What if Thea saw my soul? My survival instincts kicked in, warning me to protect myself. Women *did* have evil powers! So slowly, ever so slowly so that Thea wouldn't suspect and maybe not even realize what she had seen, I slipped Fendral's *I've-got-everything-under-control* smile on. Quickly, I moved her closer to the tree and out of the direct rays of the sun. "But you really can't afford to do that too often," I covered. "The dandelions will get jealous." She smiled, her eyes squinting into crescents. "But if you'd really rather dim that power and make your hair flat and shiny like the noble ladies without a hair out of place, I know how it's done."

Thea wiped a lingering tear from her cheek, hanging on my every word. "You do?"

I nodded and beckoned her to lean in closer so I could whisper something in her ear. She did so. "Egg white," I said.

She leaned away from me. "Egg white?"

I waved my hands for her to keep her voice down. "Shhh! If the ladies found I've blabbed their secret, it will be the end of me! But it's true. They put egg white in their hair, sometimes mixed with scented oils to cover the egg smell."

Thea smiled big enough to show teeth. "Really?"

I nodded, putting on a very serious face. "But it's a dangerous practice. It changes their behavior. You see how they gather in groups and start to squabble just like a flock . . . of . . ." and just to prove my point, I bent my arms like wings and began to strut, bawking like a chicken, bobbing my head and even pretending to peck.

Thea's laugh was almost better than a pastry, so I kept up my act. I had to cover my tracks for when I had let my guard down, and hopefully if I kept this up she would forget what she had seen. I began to strut around the tree, still bobbing. When I turned back, I nearly pecked into the kitchen hag. She raised a rolling pin. I was still in chicken mode, so I leapt away just like a flightless bird might, squawking in terror as I ran with long bobbing strides, bringing my knees high. The rolling pin caught my left wing, but I escaped with nothing more than a small bruise.

Oh well. Thea was safe now, anyway. And she couldn't stop laughing for hours.

CHAPTER 8

Sir Borin!" Leofrick caught the bloated duke's attention just as the castle was gathering for dinner. "You know, I was talking to the duke of Carlson's daughter the other day, and she asked me if you inspired my 'Ballad of the Stalwart Knight.' I told her that I had collected that piece and didn't quite know the source. Tell me, do you know it?"

Sir Borin's eyes perked up and he stood up a little straighter. He and Leofrick continued in animated conversation while I busied myself behind Sir Borin. I stood and nodded to Leofrick when I was done, sheathing a pair of scissors in my belt.

"Oh, my goodness! Forgive me, sir, but I must rehearse with my fellows for the next ball. I'm sure you'll want to brush up on your dance steps as well?" Leofrick bowed and took his leave, ushering Sir Borin on his way.

A crude square that showed white undergarments sat centered on Sir Borin's rear.

"I really don't want to know how you manage that without them knowing," Leofrick commented to me as he strummed his mandolin, fingers dancing rapidly and effortlessly along the strings.

"It's just like picking a pocket," I told him. "I didn't grow up with the name You Little Thief for nothing."

"So what are you going to do with it?" Leofrick asked. "Surely you don't want to add something of Sir Borin's to your garb."

"Oh, I have every intention of adding it to my garb," I assured him. "I'm going to put it right where it came from so it will be right at home."

"How long do you think it will be before he realizes?"

I shrugged. "Judging by his number of friends, no one will ever tell him. My guess is sometime after the first lady faints."

Deciding that it wouldn't take too long for that to happen, we decided to put some distance between us and him. We headed to the balcony.

"Well, I really do have to run. The court musicians always practice together before dinner," Leofrick informed me once we were alone. "Hey, want to come along and let me teach you how to play?" He lifted his instrument and strummed it rapidly, putting on an encouraging smile.

I grinned at him. Musical instruments fascinated me. I especially liked Leofrick's prowess with them, but every now and then the movement of his fingers—oh pox, like right now—reminded me of spider legs, and I lost my nerve. But I didn't tell Leofrick that.

"No thanks," I told him. "Sounds a bit too responsible for me tonight. You go ahead."

Leofrick shrugged. "Suit yourself." And he skipped away, strumming all the while. I smiled after him. I never had to worry about what face I had on when Leofrick was around, and that was a bit of a relief. I looked out over the gardens and leaned against the railing, thinking that I had a minute or so to myself before I would be missed at dinner as well.

I guess I don't really know what I was thinking about; I was just thinking. I was also under the impression I was alone, so when I felt a faint tickle on my arm, everything in me screamed "*Spider!*" and I almost leapt off the balcony.

Leofrick roared with mirth.

"Frick! What are you doing?" I demanded as I picked myself off the ground.

"Sorry," he chortled, wiping a tear from his face. "I got distracted and came to tell you something, but you didn't hear me come back. And I thought, 'I wonder what Farrago would do in this situation?'"

"And that's what you came to? You *know* I hate your spider fingers!"

"I know. I wouldn't have done it otherwise. But, don't worry, I won't do it again, at least not for a while. Want to see something funny? You're being upstaged." And he ran off, partly so I wouldn't catch him and partly because he was genuinely interested in showing me something. I knew that if Leofrick ran despite his potbelly, then my curiosity would never be sated until I found out what was going on. I followed.

He led me down to the servant's quarters and past that to an open corridor where a small group of servants stood watching Thea. Thea had two beets and an apple, and she was juggling them. Every time the apple passed by, she took a bite. The servants chuckled at each pass as if they hadn't seen me do this and better for years.

The servants saw me and grinned, jerking their heads at Thea as if to say, "Not bad for a scullery maid, eh?"

I smiled at them and acted like I was scrutinizing Thea's performance. She must have been practicing for months in her spare time to have mastered three objects. More months still if she was able to take a bite out of one of them. Still, this was my job, and I wasn't sure if I should act pleased or miffed at being, as Leofrick said, upstaged.

Thea had to concentrate on juggling, so she didn't see me right away, but when she did she gasped and dropped the beets and the mostly-eaten apple, flushing a deep rose color and covering her mouth with a hand.

"Not bad," I commented. "Trying to steal my job?"

"No!" she squeaked. "No, I wasn't, I was just . . . practicing."

A page boy nudged me. "You can do that, right?"

"Of course he can," a chambermaid answered for me. "You've seen him do things like that and more."

"Do it!" the page boy insisted.

Thea shrugged. "I have another apple," she murmured, pulling one out of a pocket in her apron.

"Only three items? I could do that blindfolded," I insisted. Three items was nothing.

"Blindfolded!" the page boy cheered. A chambermaid pulled a scarf out of her hair and tied it around my eyes. That was convenient of them. Oh well. I might as well.

"Ready?" I heard Thea say. "Hold out your hands. Here're two beets and an apple." I had the two beets in one hand and the apple in the other. Strange, they all felt pretty round. My little audience chuckled, and just to appease them, I started to perform.

There are actually several things one can do with just

three items. I tossed my vegetables over my head and under my knees and did different patterns. I had done them so often that I truly didn't need my sight. As Fendral had once said, juggling was about great throws, not great catches. My body remembered, and I could sense where all of my items were as I threw them just so.

"Aren't you going to take a bite?" the page boy asked.

"He's forgotten which one is the apple. He's afraid to," the chambermaid said.

Ah, well, I would just have to show them. I knew exactly which one was the apple. Simplifying my juggling pattern, I brought the apple to my mouth and took a quick bite.

The bite was juicy and crunchy and—definitely not an apple. I nearly gagged. It was the strongest onion I'd ever eaten, and I don't think I'd ever eaten a straight onion before.

The servants guffawed loudly. I forced myself to finish the bite, swallowing quickly.

"Worst apple I've ever tasted!" I said. "It's not possible." I took a bite of what I thought was another beet. It was another onion. Just to be sure that I wasn't completely crazy, I took a bite of my last "beet."

Yes, it was an onion.

I caught all three vegetables and pulled the blindfold off. Everyone was weak with laughter. Thea looked like she could barely stand up.

"I'm so sorry!" she squeaked, trying unsuccessfully to lower her voice to its usual pitch. "I'm so sorry! It wasn't intentional, and *he*"—she pointed an accusing finger at Leofrick—"put me up to it."

I was busy wiping onion tears from my eyes. I could barely see. It felt like onion fumes were burning their way through my nose and brain. Perhaps that influenced my next move.

"Well, I'll take care of him in a minute," I said as I tried to focus my eyes on her. "But *you're* the one who actually did it." I pounced, catching her in a hug and pinning her arms to her sides. She was still too weak from laughter and embarrassment to fight back much, and even if she had, it wouldn't have mattered.

I swear I didn't know what I was doing. I hadn't planned on it. I was just trying to think of a fitting and playful punishment, but the only thing that came to mind was, *Well, I* do *have onion breath. What can I do with onion breath?*

That was my last sane thought. When I came to again, I was mouth-to-mouth with Thea, and I didn't know how long I'd been like that. I broke the connection.

Thea's eyes were huge, and I'm pretty sure the only face I had on was a *Maggoty-meal-what-came-over-me?* face that I'm pretty sure I hadn't used before.

There was a solid second of silence before Leofrick whooped. Then the other servants joined in. If I'd thought Thea had been blushing before, it was nothing to her complexion now. Still, I didn't let her go right away, even when she tried to pull back.

"Serves you right," I whispered, trying to cover my own shock.

"Onions," she whispered back.

"Disgusting." I nodded and released her.

"Constance is going to kill me," she said and ran off. One of the chambermaids ran after her, and the other servants, knowing that nothing else was going to top the entertainment, began to head back to their posts.

I turned to Leofrick, who was also wiping tears away.

"Hopefully Constance doesn't come after you for kissing her. I'd rather be caught between a mother bear and her cub before Constance and Thea."

That was true. "Ah. Remind me to poison your food later. We need to talk."

"It must be so much fun being you! I promise, I've only come up with these things when I've tried to think of how you would do things."

"Yes, about that. I think you need to quit."

"Well, you know what they say: 'Mimicry is the highest form of flattery,'" he said as we began to make our way back up to the balcony.

"What? Who says that?"

"The scholars. I heard one of them say that. It means that when someone tries to be like you . . . it's a compliment."

"Oh, then I'll be sure to thank you later. You'll be eating nothing but onions for months."

Leofrick punched me on the shoulder. "You don't get it, do you?" He was still grinning broadly.

I stared at him, trying to figure out why I still felt so unsettled inside. "Get what?"

"Thea. She's crazy about you. I didn't realize it went both ways until just now. You two are sunk. I can't imagine how you've been able to drag it out this long. I think you should just hang it all and get married."

"*Married*? Leo, I—you can't arrange marriages for me with girls I might like when *I* don't even have it figured out yet!"

Leofrick rolled his eyes. "All right then. I'll let it settle. Good strategy with the kiss though. I didn't see it coming. Thea's going to be floating for a week."

"I doubt it. I had onion breath, you may recall."

"True love knows no bounds."

I swatted him upside the head. Leofrick chortled. "As you like it. But you can't convince me that Thea's patch lies over your heart by accident."

I started. "No. There's a piece of Fendral's shirt showing right over my . . ." I fingered the patches over my heart. Right down the middle, there was a split. Fendral's yellow piece lay to the left, and Thea's to the right. Centered in my chest was an old patch of Leofrick's.

"I had her do the stitching for me," I remembered out loud.

"Told you so." Leofrick winked. "Well! It's been fun, but I really do have to go practice with the others." He turned to leave.

I stopped him as an idea struck me. "You're going to miss practice today. Give me your shirt."

Leofrick finally looked a little surprised. "Pardon?"

Stuffing a pillow in my gut gave me a bit of a potbelly, and I tied a dark scarf on my head about the same color as Leofrick's dark, short hairstyle. So when the musicians came out to play at dinner, I think I made a fair impression of Leofrick except for the fact that I couldn't play his mandolin at all. But I strummed and plucked and kept a serious face on the whole time as if I knew exactly what I was doing. The other musicians were fine. I had just convinced them to pretend I was as good as Leofrick, to pretend as if I *was* Leofrick.

Leofrick came out to perform later. He had squeezed himself into my shirt; his belly was a bit too big for it even if the rest of him was stringy. I had put the head of a mop on him, and we even tied a fake beak to his nose. He had seven of my juggle balls, and after tossing them into the air and catching maybe one or two, he would bow grandly or cheer in delight at his own success.

We were big hit, I might add. Even the king stayed glued to us the whole time, smiling and laughing, and it always made me feel better to distract him from his worries. I guess it wasn't too much of a punishment for Leofrick because he obviously enjoyed himself too much. I made a mental note that we would have to do this again.

The nobles enjoyed us immensely, and I admit, I loved seeing them like that. But though I stayed in character the whole night, Thea was constantly on my mind. I wanted desperately to know what was going through her head that second, and I kept wondering if what Leofrick had said was true about her . . . wanting me. I had pestered and cajoled Thea for years without giving it a second thought until recently. She had always helped me out, and I had always thought well of her. How did you know if you were in love, anyway?

The night ended when Sir Borin got to his feet and turned, unfortunately putting his rump a little too close to the face of the lady sitting next to him. She screamed and passed out. Leofrick and I dashed away in the following panic. It wouldn't take them long to trace the crime to the one covered in patches. Not that they could do anything to me. Fool's privilege. But still, Leofrick had my shirt, and while I was tempted to leave him with it, we switched back.

Finally, I dismissed Leofrick with a promise that I would find a real way to get back at him. Then I finally had some time to sit and think. I went out and climbed one of the trees in the garden so I could be alone. Night was coming softly. Part of me really wanted to find Thea and talk with her, and the other part of me felt like I would run away and hide if I saw her right then. Once I turned around and saw a figure in the kitchen doorway holding a candle, but whoever it was ducked away. I was pretty sure I knew who it was. I fell asleep in the tree.

Looking back, I wish I had called her over. I wish I had gone to speak with her instead of hiding. Because I wasn't going to speak with her again for far too long.

The town crier called midnight, and I fell out of the tree. I took my time getting my battered body to my feet and began to trot sluggishly to the castle where I determined to find a less dangerous place to sleep.

While roaming the castle, I heard voices. A page boy or two in a nightgown ran past me carrying candles. Curious, I followed them. I was awake anyway.

The pages began to slip out of a side door. I stopped one of them.

"What's going on?" I asked in a low voice.

"There's a stranger. He says he's from the kingdom of Seacrest. He wants in for the night. Says he has important business." The page beckoned me to bend down, so I did and let him whisper in my ear. "They say he's looking for the missing heir of Seacrest. Someone in this castle is royal and doesn't know it!"

I grinned. That was quite the rumor. "I bet it's you," I said, and winked. The page smiled big and ran outside. The kingdom of Seacrest? Gridian had an alliance with them, and King Giles had ordered that all official representatives be well received. I had been present in the council that had determined to make a trading agreement with Seacrest when Gridian's crops had failed one year. It had been my idea to make a peaceful arrangement instead of trying to attack Seacrest during the transition of the monarchy. That was only made possible by the recent reclaiming of Seacrest by a king who wasn't trying to take over the world with his navy. Seacrest had been a formidable enemy, and the only reason they hadn't fallen on Gridian was because Giles's father prided himself on an impressive land army, where Seacrest's army was strongest in the water.

Missing heir? I idly wondered if the real king of Seacrest had a beak nose . . .

I hid around the corner to spy on the stranger and see what he really wanted. A few moments later, the page boy returned leading an impressive soldier-looking man behind him. The man had a well-trimmed beard and big muscles, and was dressed in dark colors with a long black cape. I was sure that if the ladies-in-waiting had been there, they would have fainted at his handsome looks. His eyes looked urgent.

"I'll take you to a chamber for the night now," the page said, but the man put a heavy arm on his shoulder.

"Forgive me, but I'm far too awake to sleep and I'd rather finish my mission quickly and quietly. Seacrest is vulnerable while I'm away. So tell me, boy, I'm looking for a nursemaid. She's a big woman, looks older than me. You might not know her, but she goes by the name of . . ." He pinched the bridge of his nose as he thought. "Constance. Tell me, do you know of anyone like that?"

The page wrinkled his brow. "Um, I know a big woman, but I don't know her name. She's not a nursemaid. She's the cook. I'll take you to her."

I knew who the page boy meant. I knew who the soldier-man meant too. The page boy led the man around the corner, passing me. The man stopped when he saw me, studying me hard for a moment, and then moved on. I followed them down the hall and peered around the corner. The page was leading the stranger to the servant's quarters. Row upon row of rooms held the castle's sleeping workers. The boy knocked on one and then stepped back.

The kitchen hag appeared a moment later, draped in a huge nightgown that probably once housed a small family. She too held a candle, and she sucked in her breath when she saw the man. "Oh no," she moaned.

"I come in behalf of the rightful king of Seacrest, who has finally reclaimed his throne from the usurpers across the sea. If you are still loyal to him, bear your token." The man lifted a fist as if showing Constance something on his hand. I couldn't see what. Constance lifted her left hand and twisted a ring on her finger, showing her hand to the stranger. The man nodded. "That will do." The he turned to the page and pressed a copper piece into the page's hand. "Thank you, lad. Off with you now."

The page looked from Constance to the stranger. He looked like he wanted to stay, but Constance gave him a warning look. The boy bowed quickly and ran off, glancing at me when he rounded the corner. He winked as if to tell me to pay close attention so I could tell him what they said later.

"Where shall we speak?" Constance asked.

"I'd prefer some place where there aren't so many sleeping people who may still be able to hear us."

Constance furrowed her brow. "The scullery is the best place, I suppose. It's a small room and it's away from where any of the servants or nobles sleep."

I ran as swiftly and silently as I could to reach the scullery first. I was only barely ahead of them. The scullery *was* a small room, with two large basins for dishwashing and a pump, as well as several high shelves for holding the dishes. A pleasant window overlooked the back gardens, and I realized that Thea must have sat here and seen me practicing and performing ever since I'd first come to the castle.

But I needed to hide. Several large wooden barrels lined the far wall. I opened one. It was filled with apples. Another was half-full of onions. No way. The third was mostly empty, so I jumped in. When I say mostly empty, I mean that most of the remains of dead chickens had already been thrown out. There were plenty of downy feathers and I was pretty sure I was crouching on a couple chicken feet. The smell was horrific. I figured that as long as there were no spiders in there, I wasn't going to complain. I could see through a long gap in the boards, and I left the lid just barely ajar so I would be sure to hear. I concealed myself just as the two entered. In fact, if they hadn't been so intent on other things, they would have seen me move the lid.

I'd never seen the kitchen hag so agitated, but then again, I tried not to look at her too often.

"I am Rupert, the king's most trusted servant. It has been difficult for the king to reclaim his kingdom and track down the caretaker of his only child. He now sits on his deathbed and is desperate for an heir. If the wrong ears were to learn how vulnerable Seacrest is still, with no one to take the throne once he's gone, he'd lose his kingdom again before he died. I'm so glad I've finally found you. Tell me, who is the king's child?"

"I was starting to hope I'd been forgotten. That no one would ever come to claim her," Constance said in a low quivering voice. Her voice was always low, caught somewhere between where a woman's voice should be and a man's.

She had also said *her*. My brief, dull hope of learning that my father had been a beaked-nosed monarch cracked like a dropped egg. But in the next instant, I felt my insides freeze and tighten painfully, and it wasn't because of the smell of fowl death in my barrel. I tried to not let my mind jump to conclusions before they spoke, but in all sanity, there was only one person the kitchen hag could mean.

"Her? Ah, King Bennion will be delighted to know he has a daughter. He never got to see his child. It will be worrisome for him about getting her a husband, though. How old is she now?"

"Eighteen years. And quite a time I've had keeping the men away from her. She has her mother's beauty."

"What have you called her?"

"Thea."

There it was. My heart froze. The knife that remained lodged in my rib cage turned white-hot. I clenched my teeth to keep from groaning aloud.

"A small name for a queen," the stranger commented.

"She was such a small thing when I brought her here," Constance said in a voice that made it obvious she was fighting tears. "She's been *my* little girl!"

I saw Rupert put a hand on Constance's shoulder and pull a handkerchief out of his shirt pocket. I felt a pang of guilt. This man was as kind to Constance as if she had been beautiful. What's more, Constance was to Thea what Fendral had been to me. It made me feel that I'd somehow been disappointing my mentor every time I'd teased her.

"You will never know how grateful the king and I am

to hear that his child has been taken care of so well when he could not be there. Tell me of her. Does she know who she is?"

Constance shook her head. "She has no idea. I've had the scholars teach her to read and write in secret. She's smart as a whip. I pay off the pages with sweets to keep us posted on current affairs. I taught her to work. She's a good, hard worker. She'll make a fine queen. It's just that—"

"What?" Rupert asked gently.

Constance shook her head. "Nothing. Nothing. I just wish I had more time to prepare for this day. When will you take her?"

"I must have a few hours sleep, or I'll never be able to make the journey back, but I hope to leave before sunrise and stop at the inn on the outskirts of the kingdom by next sundown. I brought no means to transport her other than my steed, which must have some rest as well. I left him with some pages. Do you intend to accompany us?"

Constance wiped her eyes with her nightgown. "I dare not. The queen must be settled, and I'd only slow you down. She won't stand on her own two legs if I'm around. The king here is a decent sort. I'll stay and serve him. For a while at least, until Thea has found herself."

Rupert nodded. "Wise woman. Thank you for your sacrifice. We'll be in touch. May I speak with her before I rest? Surely she will need some time to prepare herself if she does not know who she is."

Constance nodded. "She and I share a room in the servants quarters. Poor thing is asleep. Go, wake her and tell her what you will. I-I'll be along in a moment. She can't see me like this. Not when she has so many other things to worry about."

Rupert nodded, patted Constance on the shoulder, and ducked out of the scullery, knocking a page who'd been listening at the door to the ground, the same page who'd shown Rupert to Constance. The page ran off.

Constance closed the door and made an awful choking sobbing sound, as if she was trying to hold back many tears. She put both hands to her mouth, and then, quite suddenly, she strode over to the barrels and I heard her knock the lids off the first two. And then mine. When she saw me, she threw the barrel on its side with incredible force, and I shot out of it as quickly as I could, hoping to get away before—

"Beastly horrid cur!" she shouted at me, bringing a fist down hard on my ear. "Years I've kept Thea away from romancing men! Then, on the eve before she is taken she can't stop talking about the court fool! Don't you think this will be hard enough for her as it is?" She kicked me in the side. I cried out once but stayed on the ground. I wouldn't have escaped anyway. I crouched low and tried to hold up my hands for protection. "Whatever made you think she was yours to kiss, onion-breath?!"

I thought she was going to hit me again, but instead she plopped down on the floor, buried her face in her hands, and bawled. It was not a pretty sound. "I'm losing her! I'm losing her! My Thea!"

My Thea. The words bounced around in my chest, jostling the knife painfully. *My* Thea. Oh, why had it taken me to the brink of losing her to realize that I loved her? How was I going to keep a queen?

I sat up on my knees once I decided that the kitchen hag—Constance—wasn't going to hit me again. I inched a little closer to her.

"Constance," I whispered. It was the first time I had ever

called her by her name. "I'm sorry. I'm sorry I've teased you so. I-I'm sorry for your pain, but," I paused, "I think we're on the same side now."

"Ah!" Constance wailed. "Nobody cares about the pain of an ugly old hag! Nobody cares for poor Constance!"

I had never really considered myself a brave person, but I put a hand on Constance's shoulder, and that, to date, took just about more courage than anything I'd ever done. "Thea does," I assured her. "And I love Thea. And I-I think I understand you now."

Constance leaned forward and cried for several more minutes. I patted her back and said nothing. After awhile, she finally quieted down.

"Well, there's nothing to be done for it now, anyway," she said as she dabbed at more tears. "We've both lost her, haven't we?"

I had been afraid to say anything, but I felt my vow swell inside me, stemming the stream of pain from the knife of loss. I had promised myself I wouldn't add to my collection of missing faces: my mother. Fendral. And now Thea . . . I simply couldn't bear it. I'd promised myself.

"Is he really taking her so soon? Tonight?"

"Before sunrise," Constance said, nodding. "Seacrest needs her."

"That's too soon."

Constance got to her feet. "It doesn't matter. This is about more than us. Don't you dare go to her. Don't try to see her. Just leave her be, Farrago."

I knew she wasn't being cruel because that was the first time she'd used my name, too.

"I've got to go speak to her. Rupert has probably frightened her to death," she said. Wiping the last of her tears away, she exited the scullery, shutting the door behind her.

I sat on the scullery floor for I don't know how long trying to think, trying to put together a plan. What if I kidnapped Thea? I doubted I could take on Rupert. Would it start a war if I succeeded? Probably. What if I convinced her to run away with me like Fendral and the gardener?

I sighed. I didn't even know what Thea wanted yet. Perhaps once the initial shock wore off, she would be absolutely thrilled to be queen. I rested my head on my knees. This just wasn't fair.

I fell asleep curled up on the scullery floor. When I woke, I jumped to my feet. What time was it? The sky was lightening. It was almost morning. Was Thea gone?

I wrestled with a want to see her and a hesitation because of Constance's warning. What if I just made things worse? Oh well. I had to know if she had left yet. I threw myself at the door. It hardly budged. Cursing, I sat on the floor and managed to open the door with my legs. Constance had propped a large barrel undoubtedly full of some heavy vegetable in the way. It took me several seconds to force the door open. Once free, I took a side door and ran around the castle, looking for signs of a leaving party.

I found them near the front gate. I ducked in the shadows so they wouldn't see me. Constance was hugging someone I could not see, though I knew who it was anyway. Rupert stood next to them while a page held the reins of a fresh horse.

"If she can ride, we could take separate steeds," I heard Rupert say.

Constance shook her head. "She can't. She's never ridden before."

Rupert made a move to put Thea on the horse, and Thea clung all the harder to Constance. Constance had to pry Thea's fingers from her gown and then shoved her to Rupert. Rupert scooped her up effortlessly in his large arms and set her sidesaddle across the horse, leaping up behind her.

"All my love, Thea," Constance said, wiping more tears away. "Godspeed."

"Courage, my lady," I heard Rupert say. "Your kingdom is in desperate need of you, and we must make haste. We don't know how much more time your father has, and he wishes to see you."

"Constance!" Thea pleaded. "Constance, will you tell him—?"

But just then Rupert dug his heels into the horse's side and the horse cantered through the barely open gates, with Thea trying to look behind her the whole time, waving, maybe reaching, as the two of them rode away.

I stepped out of the shadows, and I could have sworn I heard Thea call my name.

Constance stood staring where they had gone even after they could no longer be seen. I walked up beside her.

"Tell me what, Constance?" I asked her.

Constance didn't look at me.

"She felt badly about the onions," Constance said tersely. "She wanted me to tell you that. And she wanted to say thank you for what you did after Sir Borin. That was it."

The thought that Thea felt badly about a harmless trick pricked me, and my heart swelled in the same instant at the thought of her thanks.

I had been thinking about my vow for some time now, and I knew I would never be whole if I did not at least try to keep it.

"Constance," I said firmly. "I'm going to get her back."

"You can't," Constance said equally firmly. "If there was some way around this, don't you think I would have done it? Seacrest needs her. She was always too good for here, to live her life as a scullery maid."

The knife in my heart turned to ice. What should I do? I eventually dragged myself back into the castle, I suppose, but I couldn't shake a dull feeling of death from my shoulders.

What was the point of life if you couldn't keep people, anyway?

CHAPTER 10

I sat with my arms folded under my head on a small table in the momentarily empty kitchen. Leofrick had put a pastry in front of me, and it was still sitting there, alone, friendless, and uneaten. I couldn't bring myself to put it out of its misery.

"You're ill," Leofrick pronounced. "And you need to snap out of it. Everyone's talking. I've never seen you like this before."

"It's your fault for pointing out I was in love with Thea," I said. "And I'm open for suggestions about how to snap out of it."

"The pastry was supposed to do that."

I sighed. On any other day, under any other circumstances, that might have been funny.

Then I felt a horrible tickle on my neck and I jumped out of the chair so fast that I bumped my knees on the bottom of the table and tipped over. *Spider!*

"Ha!" a voice too deep to be a woman's bellowed. Constance stood behind me holding a chicken feather. "I knew you weren't that far gone, you great pretender."

"Constance? Maggoty meal, how did you sneak up on me like that?"

For a fleeting instant, Constance's lower lip quivered. I had just used Thea's exclamation. But the big woman quickly shrugged it off. "You're not too difficult to sneak up on, these days. And I've got work to do, so you'd better get out of my kitchen unless you want to start plucking chickens."

Willing myself to calm down, I got to my feet and trudged out, leaving the chair upset and snagging the pastry at the last minute and sticking it in my tunic for later. Surely I would be able to eat it eventually.

"I'm serious, Farrago," Leofrick continued as we made our way down castle corridors, going nowhere in particular. "You're not yourself."

"I doubt most of the courtiers have noticed. I still wear my fool's faces when I perform, and I do still perform for them."

"Yes, but you're still . . ." Leofrick struggled for the word.

"Half dead," I filled in for him.

"Yes. Yes, exactly right. And I—"

"This feels different from when Fendral left," I said, too numb to feel pain at the mention of his name. "When he left, I broke down for a few days and moved on. I don't know why this is different. I didn't break down when Thea left, but I can't seem to get over it."

"*That's* what I'm saying! You can't keep—"

A page passed us in the hall, leading a small man in a blue tunic. The page was asking the man how long it took him to ride from Seacrest . . .

I grabbed Leofrick by the shoulders. "It's a messenger from Seacrest!" I yelled in his face, my beak nose nearly touching his. "Maybe they've fired Thea and she wants to come back!" Releasing him, I followed the page and the messenger to the king's chamber.

The page knocked on the king's door, and I heard Giles bid them to enter.

Giles had a hand on his temple as he stared out his large window. He was in an irksome mood, I could tell, but I also didn't care. Maybe the messenger carried good news for me.

"Messenger from Seacrest, Your Majesty," the page announced.

The little man in the blue tunic stepped forward and handed the king a small scroll.

"The late King Bennion, Monarch of Seacrest, made final preparations to invite all who will to come and meet his daughter, Queen Theresa Mary Angeline, so that she may choose among them a fine husband who will be the new king of Seacrest."

What? They were trying to marry her off already? She'd only been gone a week and three-and-a-half days! Not that I was counting. And she couldn't marry Giles anyway! Where was *my* invitation?

"The invitation is extended first to you and then to any of the nobles of your court who you deign to give leave to attend," the messenger finished.

King Giles glanced down at the scroll as the messenger spoke. A strange smile crossed his face and he chuckled ruefully. Quickly, he rolled the scroll back up and handed it back to the messenger.

"Thank you, but relay back to your superiors that neither I nor any from my court will be vying for her hand."

The messenger bowed. "Very good, Your Highness," and he exited backward. The page glanced at me before shutting the door behind them.

I folded my arms and looked down my nose at the king. "Quite right," I agreed with him. "You'd be better sending an army down there to get your scullery maid back. Seacrest is overstepping its bounds too much."

Giles repeated his mirthless chuckle. "Well, this is a fine exchange," he said. "I've now got my fool encouraging war, and my counselors offering a peaceful solution, and I can take neither one of them."

"What have the counselors been saying?"

"Oh, they've been pressing me to pursue the new queen of Seacrest ever since Thea left."

It was strange to hear Giles call Thea by her first name. "What? Why?"

"Oh, it's wise counsel," he assured me, sitting on a large cedar chest at the foot of his bed. "It would be a smart match and a welcome union of kingdoms who have much to gain by pooling resources. It would be much stronger than the alliance you proposed earlier this year. What's more, she's only a little younger than me, and they've been quick to point out that she's quite good-looking."

"But she's your scullery maid!"

"*Exactly*, which is why *of course* I cannot marry her! I can't—I've never thought of her that way. The last thing on the counselors' minds is—is *me*. And the *first* thing on their minds is wounding you, Farrago. They just happen to be able to back their suggestions this time."

"What are you talking about?"

"Oh, please. You've been nigh inseparable since you were children. If the counselors had any doubt of your feelings for her, they've been cleared up by your pining away for her these past few days.

"The counselors would rather put you in the stocks for

the rest of your life, of course, but they figure that seeing your true love marry someone else would cause you sufficient pain to give them some satisfaction."

"That's going to happen anyway!"

"I know. I think I need to get me some new counselors."

"I say you take Seacrest with your armies! Go dethrone the fake queen and reduce her back to scullery maid! It's been done before! Her father was exiled and dethroned! Seacrest doesn't have a good enough land army to beat you!"

"Farrago! I know you're a fool, but you've always been able to back it with some sense before. I *am not* going to start a war for a scullery maid! I've been avoiding war ever since I was made king. It's ridiculous. Be grateful that I'm not doing the smart thing by going and marrying Thea myself. That's as much as I can do. Now, please, be gone." He waved his hand as if brushing me away, and massaged his temples with his other hand as if his head hurt.

"Gladly," I said and spun around back toward the door.

"Wait," Giles said suddenly.

I turned with my hand on the door.

"When I say, 'be gone,' I mean just . . . out of my sight for a while."

I put on my confused face.

Giles sighed. "I lost my last fool when he fell in love. There is no one to replace you. Don't go after her. You can't."

I felt an odd swelling of pride, the bad kind, I think, in my chest. I knew Giles at his weakest, and it didn't help that I'd grown up with him. Furthermore, we'd always had a more equal relationship than master and servant.

"Oh, can't I?" I asked in a falsely innocent voice.

Giles glared at me. "You fools think differently. I need that. I can't think on my feet when my counselors are all bawking at once. I need someone to come up with original ideas that can be backed up. Without that, I'd turn into my father." He didn't need to remind me why that would be a bad thing. "Thea is gone, Farrago. She is more removed from you than if she had died. More is the pity. No one in their right mind would ever want to be a monarch. She was better off as a maid. But now you are in different classes, and you can't cross over. God put you where you are, and He separated you. *Do not go after her.*"

My pride swelled nearly to the point of pain as it mixed with anger. Fendral had once told me that fools were outside of class, and I had believed him.

I pointed a hard finger at Giles. "I don't believe that," I said. "I'm told God is good, so I don't believe He separates people by station any more than I believe He made spiders! And let me tell you this: if you need your fools to help you with your thinking, then you're only half a king. And if you had any sense in *you,* you'd go find somebody that *you* wanted to fight for and marry *her*! Then at least she could come up with some original ideas. Haven't we fools taught you anything?"

Giles, of course, couldn't come up with any retort, so I spun around and ran out the door and down the hall, feeling better than I had since Thea had left. Most others would probably have been thrown in the dungeons for such talk, but I still had a bit of fool's privilege to say what I wanted. I might still be condemned as a traitor for actually going against the king's direct order, but the king's direct order had been pretty ridiculous. At least Giles had helped me figure out what I was going to do.

I was going after Thea. I *was* going to get her back.

"Where are you going?" Leofrick asked as he tried to keep up with me. I had a bag with some clothes from the nobility and a sack of gold coins from the chest under Sir Borin's bed in it, and I was now in the kitchens throwing food inside.

"To Seacrest," I said conversationally. "To win Thea back."

"You're crazy," Leofrick insisted.

"No," I corrected him, locking eyes with him and pointing at my face. "Fool." And I continued to stuff things in my bag.

"How are you going to pull this off?"

"I'm going in disguise."

"You're going to need more than one change of clothes."

"Nah. I like to travel light. I'll just steal more when I get there."

"You're going to pretend to be a noble? You can't even read!"

I straightened up. "I can so. Almost. Mostly. Anyway, I'll just order someone else to do my reading for me. Oh, and I need you to do something for me. Attend all the meetings the king has with his counselors, and whatever the counselors say, say opposite as long as you can back it up a little. That's the rule."

"But, Farrago! I'm not a fool. I don't have your immunity!"

"Sure you do. Just strum your mandolin really fast and put on that glazed expression you get after you eat large meal and no one will give you any trouble, and if they do, say that you've been appointed an official fool until I get back."

Leofrick pouted. "I glaze over?"

I turned to go and ran smack into someone else.

"Constance!" I nearly screamed when I looked up. "Stop that! What do you want?"

Constance put a sausage finger right between my eyes. "I'm going to let you go to Seacrest because I can't see how you're going to be able to cause any damage or hurt anybody other than yourself in the end. But if you manage to succeed, I have some terms. One: you can't do anything to harm the kingdom of Seacrest. They've been through an awful lot and they don't need any more problems. Two: don't do anything Thea doesn't approve of."

I scoffed. "Of course not. What do you think I am?"

"A fool," Constance replied immediately.

Ah, well, I guess I couldn't argue with that.

"And if you can manage to do that and bring Thea back without causing any harm to Seacrest," Constance's voice caught, "then I'll give you your weight in pastries."

My eyes got big. "Pastries!" I exclaimed, and then in sudden remembrance, I slapped my hand over my heart where I had tucked the pastry a little while ago and exploded the fruit filling in my shirt. I decided to pretend that hadn't happened. Constance and Leofrick made strange faces at me, but said nothing.

I held out my hand. Constance shook it and squeezed tight enough to nearly take my hand off, and then let go.

"Now away with you," she ordered. "You're going to have plenty of competition for her hand. Get a move on."

I clapped her and then Leofrick on the shoulder and dashed away to the stables to steal a horse.

"Farrago!" Leofrick called after me. "Don't forget to disguise your nose!"

Chapter 11

Pox! I hadn't thought about my beak nose. That would be a dead giveaway. I could shave my head and dress like woman, but I'd still be recognized instantly if I didn't do something about my nose.

I hadn't ridden before, but I'd seen it done thousands of times. I had one of the stable hands prepare a sleek brown horse for me, insisting it was for official business. (He believed me. You'd think the fact that I was a recognized fool would have tipped him off.) Then I threw my pack over the side and rode into the kingdom. I really wished I had ridden before. Even the short ride to my first destination made me sore.

It had been a month or so since I'd visited the wonderful grimy streets I'd grown up in. Actually, they looked a lot cleaner than I remembered. I made one stop before heading to Seacrest.

The spinster was standing in front of her house almost as if she had been expecting me.

"Farrago!" she said brightly. "Are you juggling horses now?"

I dismounted and tied the horse to a post that held up a small canopy over her porch.

"Not today," I said meekly. "I need a favor."

The spinster molded some of the clay she used for her pots on my face as I spouted nearly my entire life story, focusing, of course, on why I needed a new nose. I had to assume the spinster was listening while she looked very intent on what she was doing. After awhile, she peeled her creation off, still preserving the shape and stuck it in her special oven.

"It will be ready tomorrow morning," she said. "Farrago, come here."

I followed her back to her table where she cleared off some pots and bid me sit close to her.

"Farrago, if you really mean to try this, you must be prepared. You cannot just rush over there and expect your love to fall over you. In my life I've seen even fools hang for going just a little too far. Your best chance is to become a noble completely. Never let anyone know who you really are. Do you understand?"

I nodded. "I've been observing and living around nobles most of my life. I'm certain I can pretend."

"Do more than pretend," she urged. "*Be.* That means no telling jokes, no cutting patches from the backsides of anyone, and especially no juggling."

"No more juggling," I repeated.

"You will need a new name, and you may even need to prove your lineage, which means you'll need a document detailing your family line. I can help you with those as well."

I didn't bother masking my surprise. "You can? How?"

The spinster smiled sadly and sighed. "Oh, I might have

spent some time in the upper class. I was once the Lady Amalyn of Hancett Court. But that was a long time ago, you understand."

I was aghast. "*You* changed classes!" I exclaimed, probably much louder than she wanted me to. "W-why on earth would you come *down*?"

"Coming down is much easier than going up," she told me seriously. "Which is what you are attempting. I've never heard of anyone who wasn't noble managing to go up and stay up for long, and terrible things happen to them when they are caught. You will not be exempt from those things. You have to begin to think of yourself as potentially becoming the king of Seacrest if you really want to succeed."

I felt my resolve turn to butter. "I don't want to be king," I breathed, faintly remembering a time when I'd heard Giles say those exact words. I was going to try to return with Thea. I'd promised Constance. "I-I want to be a fool again after this. I *like* being a fool."

The spinster looked sympathetic. "Do you know what it means to be a spinster?" she asked.

"Um, someone who looks after the orphans on the street?" I tried.

The spinster smiled. "It means someone who never married," she said sadly. "And I suppose I should have spent the rest of my life spinning thread and weaving cloth, but my artistic talent was with clay."

"You don't really look like someone who should have never married," I said quietly.

"Oh, I could have married," she assured me. "Many times. But I had the misfortune to fall in love with the son of the cook. His name was Paul. It was a little better than falling in love with a street beggar, I suppose, but not as far as the court was concerned. He was ill-educated and plain and"—her eyes misted over—"and very kind. He used to bring me sweets from the kitchen whenever I was upset or worried and leave them for me in places where I'd be sure to find them." She smiled at the memory, and then frowned. "One of the nobles who sought my hand learned how I felt about Paul. He tried to threaten harm on Paul and expose us if I did not agree to wed him." She bit her lip. "He cornered me one night in a corridor. Paul hit him over the head with an iron pan to save me." She lowered her head. "We were going to run away, but . . . some soldiers heard the commotion and put Paul in the dungeon and before I could do anything to get him out"—her eyes shimmered—"Sir Bernard had him put to death." She sighed and straightened up. "And so I left. I didn't want anyone else."

"I'm sorry."

She shook her head. "There are worse fates than the one I've chosen. Between me and the nobles I left, I am the more blessed. I have known real love. None of them ever have, and most of them never will." She leaned forward and took my face in her hands. "Farrago, there is not a girl in the world who wouldn't want to be fought for as you are fighting for Thea. It is a hard risk, but it is worth it. Do you believe me?"

After a pause, I nodded. I couldn't quite take her story to heart because I didn't feel that either Thea or I were in danger of dying, though I did feel pity for her. The Lady Amalyn just patted my cheek and released me. "Now, get some sleep, and you'll be ready to go by morning."

When I woke, my nose itched. I reached a hand up to scratch it.

"Don't touch!" the spinster warned me sternly. "Only gently. Feel it."

Blinking several times, I sat up. I had fallen asleep on a rug in front of her fireplace. "How did you stick it on?" I asked as my fingers ran over a smooth round surface stuck where my beak used to be. It fit on the tip, top, and sides of my nose, so I could breath freely through my nostrils.

"Tree sap," she replied. "When it dries it becomes very hard. I've also painted the nose so it matches the rest of your skin. And I've packed a spare nose for you as well, simply because I don't know how well they will really wear or stick. If you lose both of them, your disguise is ruined and you must leave."

I nodded as I ran a hand over my head. "You cut my hair too? All while I was asleep?"

The lady smiled in a way that made her seem much younger and winked. "I've spent my time learning the ways of the streets as well, Little Thief."

"How do I look?"

The lady winced. "Your hair looks very nice. As for your nose, well, I'm afraid you've given up your beak for a lump."

I shrugged. "Well, if Thea had been concerned with looks in the first place, I don't think she'd ever have fallen for me."

The spinster smiled. It was her way of agreeing with me without saying anything.

"Here," she said, rolling up a scroll from the table. "This is the lineage for Sir Hubert, a duke of Poppydown."

"Aw," I groaned. "Really?" I had been hoping for a name like "Reginald" or "Cornelius" or "Richard." Hubert? Poppydown? I was trying to drop names that sounded like fools.

"He was my younger brother."

"Oh," I said, feeling my cheeks turn red. "Sounds great."

She smiled. "It's all right. Looking back on it now, it does sound ridiculous. He didn't live past infancy, but no one in Seacrest will know, even if they've heard of Hancett Court. He would have inherited the Poppydown estate." She handed the scroll to me.

"Thank you," I said sincerely. I was beginning to realize how useless my trip would have been if I hadn't gone to her first.

"Now, put your noble clothes on. Your horse should be rested, and you can leave as soon as you're ready."

I pulled on a deep blue tunic with long draping bell sleeves over my head. It was lined with gold and very comfortable. My leggings were tan and my shoes black. I'd even stolen a small hat that matched the blue of the tunic. It was small, with three corners that curled up toward the rounded center with a gold feather adorning one side. There was not a patch to be seen. In a few minutes I was again sitting on the horse I'd stolen from the royal stables, and I wished I'd brought some kind of looking glass. My hair, nose, and clothes were all different, and I was traveling by horse instead of on foot.

"You are completely unrecognizable," the spinster confirmed my thoughts. "Here." She handed me a plate of polished brass that I could use as a mirror.

I had never really studied how I'd looked before, but I could still see how different I was. If I went back to the castle right now, Leofrick and Constance would not even recognize me. Seeing how different I was sent a tremor of anxiety through me.

"Now remember," the Lady Amalyn counseled, "from now on, you are Sir Hubert. And if you want to win Thea again, it will have to be as Sir Hubert and not as Farrago. I couldn't stand it if I'd heard something had happened to you, so you must promise never to reveal who you really are. If things go badly or if you decide your cause is lost, escape without a word and you could still come back and be the court fool."

I felt strange. Afraid. Somehow I knew that things were never going to be as they had been before, and not just because Thea had gone. It helped to remember my vow. I had vowed not to let someone as important as Thea out of my life again; I had never promised that I would remain Farrago forever, as much as I wished I had.

"Thank you, my lady," I said. There was nothing else to say.

"Call me 'peasant' or 'peasant woman' from now on," she counseled me. "And now that you're all set, you must ride before someone sees you and becomes suspicious. Farewell." She gave me a smile that I didn't think I deserved; it was as if *she* was thanking *me*.

"Thank you for your directions, peasant-woman," I said in a loud important voice in case someone was listening. "Here's something for your troubles." I pulled a few gold coins out of a pouch I wore at my hip and sprinkled them on the ground. With a wink, and wearing Fendral's smile, I rode off, making a point not to look behind me.

CHAPTER 12

I knew only two things. One: the road I was on had been taken by the messengers and would hopefully take me directly to Seacrest. And two: Seacrest bordered the sea, so I figured if I got lost, I would ride until I hit lots of water.

I suppose I knew one more thing: those who do not ride horses should not ride horses, because after about an hour one becomes horribly sore. My thighs were chaffed and my rear was so sore that I spent a lot of my riding time standing up in the saddle.

But it was a small irritant weighed against the idea of seeing Thea again, so I rode on. I passed through a small forest, and then passed fields of wheat with small cottages where the farmers lived in the distance. I rode up hills and down hills. I came to a small town and passed an inn where I stayed for the night, using more coins from my bag, and stealing a bag or two more from some pompous-looking tenants who would've probably had a hard time carrying all that gold anyway. I altered Fendral's "I know exactly what I'm doing" smile to be more of a "I'm much more important that you AND I know exactly what I'm doing" face that felt like something a noble would wear.

I rode all through the next day, and just as evening was coming on, I hit a barren stretch of land. There were no houses and no crops. The ground was strewn with rocks of all sizes, and grass struggled to grow amid the choppy ground. The trail wound up and over and side to side through the expanse like a flailing snake. I rested in the saddle and let my steed pick his way along the lonely path and tried to think of what Thea might be doing instead of how very sore and stiff I was.

I had slowed my pace and the land was so still that I probably heard them coming behind me for ten miles before they finally caught up with me. They were traveling faster than I was. There were two men on horseback. They slowed their horses to a walk when they caught up to me. They both had very tan skin and tar-black hair. One was tall and stringy, little more than a skeleton, with a peasant-brown tunic, billowing leggings, and black boots with a slight point at the tips that curved upward. His hair was cut short and he had a small pointed goatee on his already long face. The second would have made all the ladies-in-waiting at Gridian Castle hang themselves for want of his favors. His black hair was cut short around the ears and flowed in thick locks on top of his head. His face was angelic, as if he could do no wrong. His eyes were large and dark, his jawline strong, and, of course, his nose was perfect and rigid and masculine. He was dressed in a dark-blue tunic, much darker than mine, with cream leggings and dark brown shoes like an English nobleman, though it was obvious that both of them were foreigners.

"Good evening to you, fellow traveler," the one who

looked like a nobleman said. "Do you know if this trail leads to the kingdom of Seacrest?" He spoke English well. His accent was faint, and I couldn't quite place it. Not that I'd ever traveled much myself.

"I hope so," I said as I tried to look like a noble and not show that I was nearly ready to fall off my horse. "That's where I'm headed."

"Would you mind if we rode with you for a short while?"

"Not at all," I agreed.

We fell into step in a line of three, with the dark nobleman in the center.

"I am Prince Kazim, and this is my servant and bodyguard, Seht. Don't bother speaking to him. He can't speak." Kazim gestured to the man on his right, who leaned forward and smiled at me. The smile made me shudder. Few if any of Seht's teeth were straight and most of them had gaps in between. They came in various shades of yellows and browns. His eyes squinted up so much that I felt certain he couldn't still see me. His cheeks were gaunt and sunken in, his features pointed. I suppose I could have forgiven his ugliness, not being prone to great beauty myself, but there was something about his expression that made me think that Seht was picturing me turning on a spit.

I forced a smile and a nod back. "I am Sir Hubert, Duke of Poppydown." I tried to make it sound much grander than it felt coming out of my mouth. "Prince of what, may I ask?"

Prince Kazim sighed and looked slightly irked. "Prince by bloodline only. My elder brother rules the land where I come from in Arabia. I seek a kingdom of my own." Kazim smiled confidently. "We have been in England many months, but we intercepted a messenger the other day who informed us of the monarchal condition at Seacrest. I am going to win the queen." He said it as if he had already succeeded.

"Oh, so you heard about that as well? That's why I'm going. Oh, I'm no threat," I added quickly, bringing my hands up as if in surrender. "I'll play the part of suitor with the others, I suppose, but I don't expect to win. It's just gossip. I'll be the center of attention with fresh news of what's going on in Seacrest, and the ladies back home will throng me."

Kazim listened to me with narrowed eyes but seemed satisfied with my explanation, especially when I insisted I wasn't a threat. What with my blob of a nose, he probably wasn't worried that I was a contender anyway.

"You travel alone without carriage or servants or even a sword at your hip. Don't most nobles keep bodyguards when they travel?"

Hmm. I suppose that did make me look suspicious. Kazim probably only stopped because he didn't suspect I was on the same errand as he.

"Oh, I do have a bodyguard," I lied quickly. "He follows behind me. He likes to travel in stealth and can rarely be detected. He's there now." I turned and gave a subtle signal to the nothing behind us.

Kazim and Seht both sat up in their saddles and turned around, trying hard to detect my nonexistent manservant, both looking wary.

Kazim looked at me and then behind us, and then at me, and then behind us. I put on Fendral's smile.

Slowly, Kazim's tense face melted and he cracked a smile. He began to laugh.

"Ha ha! Follows behind us undetected? In this stretch of flat nothing?" He laughed again. Seht said nothing, obviously, and faced forward in his saddle again, though he kept throwing looks behind us and remained alert.

Kazim wiped some tears from his eyes. "Ah!" Kazim said as he calmed down. "I cannot remember if I have ever laughed so hard. Thank you, friend Hubert."

I continued to wear my favorite smile and said nothing. Let them jump to whatever conclusions they would.

"Have you heard anything about the queen of Seacrest?" I asked him after a little while.

Kazim shook his head. "Nothing. I've gathered only that Seacrest has had her rulers overthrown several times."

"I heard that she's very ugly," I lied again. "Something about warts or boils—I can't remember."

Kazim shrugged. "Doesn't matter," he said. "If she were an old lump of a hag, it would not change my goal. I go to win my own kingdom to rule so that I may conquer more and grow stronger than my brother. If I let little things like how attractive the current queen is stop me, I would never reach my aim. You go to gather information. If you let something get in the way of that end, you will never reach it. It all depends on what one most wants."

"Oh," I said, feeling that I had lost. "Well said." He was right, of course. If only he knew what my true aim was and how far I'd already gone to get it.

We rode until the only light was what the sun chose to shoot over the horizon. I smacked my lips. I had brought bread and some meat that I had bought at the inn, but I hadn't thought to bring a flask of water.

I noticed a clay pitcher with a hinge-lid bound by a cord to Prince Kazim's saddle. It reminded me of some of the jugs that the spinster made. The lid was about the size of my palm. It had to be for water.

"Prince Kazim? Could I beg some water of you?"

"Of course," the prince replied readily.

I reached over to his horse for the clay jar. The prince stopped my hand just as my fingers touched the jug. He brought a leather water pouch from the other side of the horse and put it in my hands.

Confused, I drank first and handed the pouch back.

"Thank you," I said. "Is that wine for when you win the queen?" I asked, jerking my head toward the clay jar.

The prince's smile said that he knew something I didn't. "No indeed. Watch."

The prince picked up a small, coarsely woven horsehair sack from the back of the saddle. Reaching a hand in, he brought it back with his fingers curled around a live moth. Lifting the jar onto his lap with his other hand, the prince gave the jug a small shake and said something I didn't understand to his servant, who used some flint to light a small torch and hold it over the opening of the jar. The prince unlatched and tilted the lid back slowly. I could have sworn I heard a faint sound, like Sir Borin's slimy exhale from far away. With a quick jerk of his hand, the prince threw the moth in and snapped the lid shut again. Seht put the torch out with another "I'm going to eat you" smile.

"Camel spider," the prince said as he returned the jar to the side of the horse. "You have no idea how hard it was to catch."

I suddenly felt as if I had spiders all over me, and I drew back from the prince, fighting the urge to jump off my horse and run in the other direction. I had been sure it must have been a snake and hadn't been too worried.

"W-why . . ." I tried to keep my voice level, but it kept trying to squeak. "Why in the name of all that is sane do you keep one, man?"

The prince's smile was similar to his servant's. "I see you have no great love for spiders either. It seems to be a common fear; do not worry. I keep one because my brother hates them. We had a, uh, a disagreement, if you will. I tried to take the kingdom and he stopped me. He would have killed me by beheading, but as he himself raised his sword, he disturbed the underground nest of the spider with his foot, and it charged up his leg. Camel spiders are big, bigger than the spiders I have seen here in your England. They have two large black eyes, and two arms in addition to their eight legs that they hold out threateningly in front of them all the time. Their back part is long and sometimes very fat. They are very fast. The one I caught could only fit through the lid of my jar by curling its legs in, and it only went in because I offered it a delicacy."

He wanted me to ask what, but it was all I could do to keep from being sick over the side of my horse.

"Moths," he said. "Camel spiders hate the light, and that is why they charge you if you disturb them. They want to get into your shadow, or maybe into the folds of your clothes in order to escape the light. If I didn't hold a torch over the lid of the jar, the spider would escape and I would never be able to catch it again. Moths always go to light, and so I figured the spider had never tasted one. I feed it moths to keep it satisfied, though it would love to get out. I keep this spider because its kind saved my life. I keep one because it broke the spirit of my brother, and he will not come after me as long as I carry one. I keep one because I know I can use it against future enemies if I must." He bared his teeth in a smile. "But you do not need to worry, Sir Hubert. As you said, you are not a threat."

I felt coldness on top of my sickness. The blighter was

threatening me! I could see it in the squint of his eyes and the curve of his princely mouth that he would kill me in a second if he thought I stood in the way of his oh-so-important goal. But, at the same time, I could also see that he didn't truly think I was an obstacle, and so he must not have truly thought he was actually threatening me. In fact, my face must have read too much of my thoughts for an instant because Kazim lifted the terra-cotta jug and set it dangling on the other side of his horse, away from me. He was being courteous, but I still hated myself for revealing my weakness, whether or not Kazim was going to use it against me.

We rode for several hours without speaking. In my fatigue, I soon recovered from the nightmarish image of the spider the prince had described and could think only of how tired I was. "We are going to ride all night until we get there." The prince spoke and I jerked awake for an instant. It was dark, and Seht had lit a torch again. I saw the prince slip a rope around my horse's neck. "Let your horse fall behind," he said. "I will lead it, and you can sleep."

How could I trust the spider prince? "You will lead me while I sleep?" I asked doubtfully. Why not just go ahead and leave me behind? "Why?"

The prince looked confused. He did not have my power of face, my masks. His power was in keeping a strong default face when he needed to, but he could not show false emotion. He could not conceive that someone as ugly as I was truly a threat. I could not blame him. So far, I wasn't even sure I was a threat myself.

"We are traveling to the same place together," he said simply. "And," he confessed quietly, perhaps so that Seht would not hear, "you made me laugh."

There it was. I would have to keep Farrago in check while

I became Sir Hubert, but I believed him. He was my enemy, but he didn't know it yet, and he needn't be my enemy just now, anyway. It was strange, but I was too tired to care.

"Thank you," I said. "I would be grateful."

I leaned forward on the neck of my horse and did my best to relax while Prince Kazim and Seht led my horse to the kingdom of Seacrest.

Chapter 13

I vaguely recall my name being announced. I remember torches and a page leading my horse away and another leading me to a room. But, really, I remembered mostly nothing until I woke on a four poster bed in a room all by myself.

Well, not quite. A maid stood over my bed watching me curiously. Her cheeks and nose were covered in freckles and her brown hair hung in two braids over either shoulder. Her mouth opened slightly to one side when she spoke.

"We cleaned and pressed your clothes," she said, giving a small curtsy. "We found no others. Your nose is funny. We borrowed a nightgown for you. Would you like your breakfast brought to you or would you like to come down to the main hall to eat?"

"Um, where does the queen eat?" I asked.

The maid looked a little sheepish. "In her room mostly. But the counselors are going to make her greet her suitors this morning, I hear." She looked back and forth as if she was expecting eavesdroppers. "People are starting to think she's not very happy about having to choose the next king of Seacrest, and her husband." The maid put a hand to her mouth and her eyes bulged. "But I say too much. I'm just a simple maid and I don't know anything."

I liked my maid. It was good to know that Thea hadn't been spending lots of time with other suitors and didn't like her situation. "Thank you. That will be all. I'll be down to eat in a moment."

My maid curtsied once more and scurried out.

A long table was set with various fruits and breads in the dining hall where nobles picked at the foods or sat and talked. I saw Kazim being served a plate of fruit by Seht, and he waved me over. I saw no reason not to join him.

"So, who's the competition?" I asked as I took a seat at his side.

"Two other princes from your country, and at least seven other nobles of various ranks that I haven't learned yet. The only ones I am concerned about are one of the princes and two nobles. The others are too ugly or too stupid to win the heart of the queen or the respect of the counselors." He put a hand on my shoulder. "Forgive me, friend, but you identified yourself as not being a threat."

"No offense, no offense," I assured him. Actually, it relieved me that Prince Kazim didn't have me in his sights and was obviously going to be free with the information he learned of the others.

Seht came and offered me a plate filled with rolls and sausages and ham. It was against my better judgment because Seht troubled me, but I took it anyway.

"That one is Prince Alain," Kazim said, pointing out a handsome youth with very fair hair and skin who was surrounded by half a dozen women of the court. "He doesn't look like he has much going on behind his eyes, but that is deceptive. I am afraid the queen will admire his face too much as well. The other prince is there, Prince Meldon. He is short and clever, but he does not look the part, so the counselors will not choose him." Prince Meldon was walking down the table putting sausages on his plate as if they would make him grow taller. He had long brown hair parted down the middle, and I felt that Kazim's judgment was correct.

The other two nobles, Sir Leon and Sir Reginald, were also handsome, and Kazim seemed to think they also had enough of what the counselors were looking for to also be competition.

"Why are you worried about what the counselors will think?" I asked.

"Because the queen's power is quite limited. I heard that she spoke with her father at length before he passed, and since she had been in hiding for so long, he didn't want her to have full power until she had wed a good king. The terms are that both she and the counselors must approve, and both have power to give tests and make evaluations."

"How did you learn all this?"

"Seht has been doing some listening for me. He picked most of his information up from snatches of conversation among other servants, especially one who was listening at the door when the queen was speaking with her father."

"Any word on where the queen was in hiding before she came here?"

Kazim smiled. "No one seems to know. I suppose it was kept very secret so that the previous usurpers didn't hunt her down. Oh well. It does not matter."

"Has anyone actually *seen* the queen?"

Just as Kazim was shrugging, all the nobles got to their

feet and faced the door to the dining hall. I stood suddenly, following their gaze to the entry of the dining hall.

A grand personage surrounded by attendants came into the room.

"Egg whites," I cursed under my breath.

Fortunately, Kazim was so busy studying his prey that he did not hear me, and if he did, he didn't question my outburst.

I did not recognize her at first, but I suppose that was fair, because she did not recognize me either. Not a hair was out of place. It was woven and set just so over her already flawless face. Without the blessed flaw of her wispy hair, no one could doubt she was royal; no one could see the scullery maid that was mine.

Thea had always been small, and though her clothes seemed to bind her, they also made her seem a bit taller and more elegant, more forbidding, which was ridiculous knowing it was only Thea. Her dress was cream, and she wore a brilliant blue-green cape. It was a color I had never seen in fabric before.

Oh, but her face. It was a face of one defeated, drudgingly doing one's duty. Maybe the others couldn't see it, but Thea could not hide it from me. She was miserable. My poor Thea.

All the men in the room froze, and I heard their intake of breath. A new feeling gripped my heart and felt like it was going to crush my rib cage. Some of it was jealousy, but it was mostly a feeling of possession: Thea was mine. She loved *me*. I had grown up with her and I knew her flaws. All these others were only seeing her as an egg-haired nymph of perfection. But they didn't see Thea.

A maid standing on Thea's right, draped in simple,

elegant cream robes, stepped forward. "Announcing Queen Theresa Mary Angeline, queen of Seacrest. She will now greet her suitors one by one. Please form a queue."

All the suitors hurriedly made a line, fighting to be first. Angry, but trying to hide it, I got in line at about the middle with Kazim next to me.

One at a time, the queen faced each suitor, and a page at her side introduced each suitor in turn. Then the suitor would bow and kiss her hand, and maybe make a remark about her beauty, which only made me angrier. It was all I could do to keep on my "oh, I don't really care" face.

When Thea stopped in front of me, I worried that she would recognize me. I held my breath. "Sir Hubert, Duke of Poppydown," the page announced. Thea offered her hand. I took it and kissed it like the others. Then I was expected to say something, some idle remark about how beautiful she was or what an honor it was to meet her, like all the others.

I might have been able to control my face, more or less, but I wasn't a fool for nothing. Apparently I had no such control over my mouth.

"I don't like your hair," I said.

The entire room gasped, and it took me a moment for me to realize that what I had been thinking had actually come out of my mouth and that they would take me seriously because I wasn't the court fool. Thea's eyes became a little larger, and she actually looked at me. I mean, she had been looking at everyone, certainly, but she was suddenly really *looking* at me.

"I mean, it is too perfect," I covered quickly. "You destroy all hope of any of us one day being equal to you." I lowered my head and waited for Thea to move on.

What a true idiot I was. I go to all this trouble to

become Sir Hubert, and the first words out of my mouth are all Farrago.

Thea didn't move on right away, and after several long seconds, I looked up again. Oooh, Thea. She was looking for me. She was looking for Farrago. I gripped a casual expression on my face as hard as I could. *Oh, no you don't.* I thought. *You are not making me take my face off again.*

She might have been staring at me for hours; I had lost track of time. Finally, a blessed looked of disappointment. She hadn't found me. The look gave me both a sense of victory and pain. I had given her hope and taken it away again.

Thea moved on to Kazim. Kazim raised his eyebrows at me, but soon turned all his attention to the queen. He went on one knee as he took her hand but held it for several seconds before doing anything with it.

I knew what he was doing. By pausing, he was forcing Thea to look at *him*, to spend just a little more time with him. She did, but her eyes were dead again. I was glad. She looked at everyone the same. We might all have been invisible to her for all the attention she gave. Finally, Kazim kissed her hand. "I have traveled your country much," he said in a gentle, masculine voice, "and seen many royals. But you are the first I have seen that did not need to be announced. A blind man would know you were a queen."

Thea nodded to him. "Thank you," she said in the softest of voices.

Kazim beamed as Thea moved down the line to the next man, who assured her he loved her hair.

All in all, I had had more time with her, but Kazim had gotten the first word. She spoke to no one else. And when she had greeted all the others, she exited with her attendants, and the room exhaled.

All the men started talking, and it was either about how beautiful the queen was or about how they had all been ready to beat me when they thought I'd insulted her.

Kazim turned to me. "I know you do not intend to win her, Sir Hubert," he said with a chuckle. "But you must be careful not to make it too obvious or they'll probably kill you." He chuckled again. "Well, whoever told you she was ugly must have been playing a joke on you, I think." He laughed and patted my shoulder.

I managed a smile and a light chuckle myself even though I didn't feel like it. "They sure must have," I agreed.

Pox. Pox the whole thing.

CHAPTER 14

Thump.

I sat in my room and slowly thudded my head against one of the bedposts. It was well past dark. Tomorrow, all the suitors would meet with the counselors for a sort of group interview. There was no word on if we had to do anything for the queen yet.

Thump.

There was a faint rap at my door.

One last *thump* and I rolled off my bed and sat on the edge.

"Come in," I answered.

The door cracked and Seht slid in without any noise.

I jumped and then tried to control my gag reflex.

"Seht! What—?"

Seht swept over to me and offered a scroll, which I took reluctantly.

"From Kazim?"

Seht nodded once, looking far too merry and slimy for a servant. He was smiling, but at least he wasn't showing his teeth, and he slid out of the room again without a sound.

I shuddered and tried to resist the urge to wash myself as I opened Kazim's scroll.

Pox. I wished I could read. Well, I wished I could read better. I flopped on my belly on the bed and tried to make out the words. I caught my name at the top and figured it was Prince Kazim's name at the bottom.

Ffff —I recognized that letter from a word near the top. I liked that letter. *Fllllo. Flo. Flow-r Flower.* Flower! I knew that word! Why on earth was he talking to me about flowers?

My door opened again.

"Oh! Sorry, my lord. I was just coming to fill your basin for the morning," my maid said with an apologetic blush.

"That's fine," I assured her. "I was just . . . reading."

The maid curtsied and filled a water pitcher next to my basin on the wall.

"Tell me, um, maid, do you read?"

My maid looked over her shoulder at me as she emptied the contents of her bucket in my pitcher. "No, sir. Can't say that I do."

"Oh," I said, rather disappointed. "Heard anything interesting about the castle? About the queen or the other suitors?"

My maid's face lit up. "Oh, yes, milord," she said quickly. "Since the queen hasn't given her suitors any task, they've decided to all bring her flowers themselves tomorrow and see if they can happen upon her favorite. Have you not heard?"

"Oh! Yes, I did hear something to that effect. Just wanted to see if the news had gotten around. Thank you."

With sudden inspiration and zero dignity, I threw myself on the far side of my bed and landed with a thud, scrambling for a coin from my bag. With a flick of my thumb, I tossed it at her. She held up her bucket to protect herself and the coin clanged in.

Her eyes became big. "Thank you, milord!" she said merrily and exited backwards.

I fell backward on my bed again, staring at the ceiling. Favorite flower, eh?

All counselors looked the same to me. Same long black robes, same sneer, usually even the same voices. They all seemed like one united surly man with many bodies. The one that marched down in front of the long row of suitors was no different. We all sat behind a long table, staring up at his nose. I suppose it was unfortunate that anyone's nostrils should flare so much, so that set him apart at least.

"Running a kingdom isn't all wine and women and sending men off to war," the counselor lectured in that universal whiney counselor-voice. "A king must be able to make hard decisions and find the best solution to the hundreds of problems that may come before him."

I rolled my eyes. Dealing with counselors was another area where I didn't feel the need to wear a mask that said anything other than "I think you're ridiculous and you're wasting my time." All the counselors I'd ever met used only solutions that involved blood or carnage or caused *someone* pain and suffering.

"So today," the counselor continued as his nostrils flared embarrassingly wide, "you will each be given scrolls detailing kingdom affairs that we as a council have come across in our lives. You will each write how you would deal with the situation, and then we as a council will evaluate your responses. May I remind you," he said, smiling at us like we were babies, "the late king granted equal power between his council and the queen to choose the next king of Seacrest. So be wary of your responses." Several more robes shuffled out and set scrolls before each of us. "Begin."

Pox. I couldn't believe this. Trying to play the part, I opened my scroll like the others and spread it on the table. I blinked several times to get my eyes accustomed to the frilly writing. When so many words were put before me, I usually found it easiest to pick out maybe one or two important ones.

Sssss. All right. I knew that letter. *Pllll. Plag. Plog. Pl-ai-g. Pla-goo-ee*? Plague! There must have been some problem with a plague. Got it.

No, I didn't.

"This is a waste of time," I declared, lifting my head from my scroll. I'm fairly certain I heard a groan of, "Oh no, not him again," from the other suitors.

The flare-nose counselor strode over to me, looking down his nose very effectively as his nostrils became even bigger. I fought not to grin.

"I beg your pardon, Sir Hubert?" the counselor said icily. "If you are refusing our right to give tests and make evaluations of the suitors, there is little reason for you to remain in Seacrest."

Pox all counselors. "On the contrary. A moment ago you lectured us on the difficulty of running a kingdom. Well, I should think a king would need to use his time wisely. Surely problems could be spoken directly to me and I could respond much faster than reading and writing a response. Where I come from, the king uses scribes and only rarely writes himself except to sign his name to declarations. He can't be bothered with such menial tasks, and neither can I."

The counselor's nostrils flared in and out quickly several times. He snatched my scroll off the table so fast I jumped.

"Very well then, Sir Hubert. You will give your response verbally for all present."

Yes! Farrago did this all the time.

The counselor cleared his throat. "A plague decimates the population of your kingdom. A neighboring kingdom discovers an antidote, but it is costly. How do you negotiate exchange for the remedy, and how do you decide who receives it?"

Well, well. This one was actually a little difficult.

"First things first, a good king always listens to his counselors before making a decision. What did you or one of your comrades do in this situation? What would you *counsel*?"

My nosy friend raised his eyebrows and turned to the rows of counselors standing still as statues next to the wall while they waited for us to finish writing our responses. A small round one came forward.

"I counseled that just enough be bought to first be given to the king and those of most importance in the castle. Those next to receive antidote were those who could pay the most handsomely, thus redeeming the lost treasury. By then, the plague had taken whom it would and had left only the strongest peasants in the kingdom, thereby actually strengthening the population."

It was my turn to raise my eyebrows. "Really? Well, while I'm sure the treasury remained unharmed, no doubt you had problems with food shortages the next year due to the lack of farmers and merchants to actually produce them. And no doubt you had to quell a few uprisings from outraged peasants who had lost their families. Did you have to raise taxes later in order to support your armies to stop the uprisings, which only led to more shortages? It might be prudent to solve one problem and create as few others as possible. I can see two possible alternate solutions to this issue.

"You could have bought a small amount of antidote and given it to your chemists and scholars to analyze in the hopes that they could create more. There's no guarantee how that would work out, so you'd have to have a backup plan.

"When faced with a situation where you are completely dependent upon another kingdom for some commodity, it's best to analyze one's own resources as a potential barter. Seacrest, for example, has some of the best fishing among any of the coasts. Certain fish could be preserved and sold as delicacies. Seacrest also has master shipbuilders and could build a vessel or so for the neighboring kingdom. If your chemists figure out how to make the cure themselves, it would cut your dependence on the other kingdom. If they don't, bartering would make the other kingdom long-term dependents on your own products while you are only short-term dependent on them for as long as the plague lasts. Once the plague leaves, they still want your product and you have no need of theirs. This makes the remedy plentiful, making it possible for farmers and craftsmen to keep producing, and strengthening the overall economy with a monopoly on your own product. There would be more jobs for peasants, more money flowing into your kingdom with little flowing out, and no rebellions or shortages to deal with later. Do you follow me?" It was almost as if Fendral had entered me and spoken through me. It was exactly what he would have said; I knew it.

The short little counselor huffed like a little owl fluffing his feathers and turned to his nostril-y master.

Nose-flare was still pumping his nostrils in and out and looking like he wanted to squish me. "Interesting ideas," he commented. "No telling if they would work in a real situation, of course. We will evaluate your response with the other written ones, which will be difficult without having something to refer to."

"Yes, remembering what I said would require more brainpower," I agreed.

"You are excused, Sir Hubert," the counselor commanded.

I got readily to my feet. Prince Kazim rose at the same time from the far end of the table and walked over to the head counselor even as I left.

"My scroll," he said as he put it in the hands of Nose-flare. "I wrote my response while Sir Hubert was speaking. Some of us can handle multiple methods of exchanging information just as fast, and sometimes we must do things even when we may not like them."

Nose-flare raised his eyebrows again but not with disdain or correction. He was impressed.

"Quite right, Prince Kazim. Thank you very much. We look forward to reading your response. You are excused as well."

Kazim bowed and joined me at the door, and we exited together.

"You're just trying to get on their good side," I said as we walked down the corridor.

"Naturally," he said. "If you keep acting as you do, you will give me multiple opportunities to stand out in contrast." He smiled. "I'm glad we are after different things and are not truly in competition with each other, aren't you?"

There it was again, that hint of a grin that suggested he would kill me if I got in the way of his quest to rule his own kingdom.

"Indeed," I replied with camaraderie as false as his was. "That's a relief."

"Still, you must be careful. I would hate to lose you. Try to humor them, and be nicer to the queen."

What was he playing at? "You're right, of course. I'll try."

"Thank you. And by the way, you were right. Your answer, I mean. It was actually quite thorough. Especially your comment about not creating future problems. You think quickly."

"Oh. Um, thank you. I try."

"Now, if you'll excuse me, I must attend to the matter of what flowers to get Her Highness. You did get my scroll last night, didn't you?"

"Hmmm? Oh! Oh yes, I did. Thank you. I should get on that task as well."

"Good luck to you." He smiled and left me. I would never make sense of that man. Oh well, at least I had other tasks to occupy myself with.

Willing myself to forget how sore riding made me, I rode out into the kingdom of Seacrest. The castle itself was up a rocky incline, and the kingdom spread out on all sides, most of the cottages hugging the coastline where the fishermen lived. I rode through the town, not failing to notice how run-down the village seemed, or how the locals always kept their faces down, especially when I passed. Constance had said that Seacrest had been through a lot. They were well due for some respite.

I rode out the way I had come in, heading toward the meadows and farmland where the cottages were much more widely placed.

When the sea was a distant line, I stopped by a tree standing on the edge of the road. If I rode farther, I would pass a farmer's cottage and his land of tilled ground, but this place was undeveloped. The land was tall with weeds and grains and wildflowers. I tied the reins of my horse to a low branch where he could still graze and walked out into the meadow. I took a deep breath. Pox, it was good to be here. It was good to be away from the tightness of castle life and those beastly counselors. I hadn't realized it until just now.

I sprawled spread eagle in the field and let a mild breeze blow the stalks of plants over me. I began to fade, letting my eyes droop.

Plop!

Augh! My arms and legs jerked into the air, but the weight was on my stomach.

"Nose funny."

The weight belonged to a knee-high lump of a girl. I was no great judge of ages, but she was very small, and would most certainly have not come up to my knees. She was dressed in a clean frock, and her hair, the color of the crust of a perfectly baked loaf, was tied into two ponytails on either side of her head. She scooted forward up my chest and tapped the tip of my nose with an impossibly small finger.

"Nose funny," she repeated with that childish high-pitched baby voice and tenor that could never be mimicked by an adult.

"Hello, my lady." I sat up on my elbows. "Fancy a seat?" I scooted up further and deposited my new friend on my lap. "And it's fake, if that makes you feel any better. But even if it wasn't, you'd still say the same thing. What's your name?"

She stared at me with big blue eyes and said nothing.

I patted my chest. "Farrago," I said. "Fff-air-ah-go. What's your name?"

"Fer-go."

I beat myself on the head when I realized my mistake. "No, no! I'm Sir Hubert. Hubert. Pox!"

"Pox!" my friend repeated. "Fer-bert!"

I laughed. How refreshing she was after constantly

putting on faces for the court of Seacrest! It was really no fun being Sir Hubert.

My nameless little visitor opened her other small hand and stretched it out to me.

"Rock," she said. She had, in fact, two small pebbles. "Jug-oh."

"Are you collecting pebbles?" I guessed. "In a jug?" I looked around but saw no container.

My friend tossed the pebbles in the air and waved her hands around. The rocks hit my legs and thudded lightly on the ground.

"I have a better idea than rocks," I announced. "Can you help me find some flowers? Some yellow flowers?"

"Flowuh," she repeated. "Lello flowuh."

She got to her small, slightly bowed legs and toddled away faster than I would have given her credit for, weaving her way through plants and grains taller than she was.

She pulled at a flower when we passed one.

"Lello flowuh." She handed it to me.

"Um, actually, no. That's red," I corrected her. "I need yellow."

"Oh," she said and continued.

She led me just a little farther. I saw them before she did because I was so much taller.

"Dandelions!" I exclaimed as the field gave way to them. "Well done, little one!"

She became very excited when I began merrily picking the flowers, and happily joined me, though she often got just the tops instead of the whole flower. Every now and then I would toss her one, and she would giggle hysterically, which is another reason why I like children. It's so easy to make them laugh. We may have had a small dandelion fight, which she may or may not have won. But at least I ended up with a fine bouquet.

"Mommy," my friend said, clutching a long-stemmed dandelion in one hand.

"Yes. That's perfect for mommy," I agreed with her. "And because you were such a big help, I have something for you, all right?"

I set my bouquet of flowers down and found two palm-sized pebbles and a similarly sized hardened clump of dirt. I stood and looked in all directions. Except for the cottage in the distance with the people too small to see, we were completely alone. Hang it all, I began to juggle.

And it felt so good!

My little friend squealed so loud that at first I thought she was upset. But it turns out that squealing is how females show many emotions, including being nearly delirious with joy. She opened her mouth, clapped her hands, and jumped up and down in obvious uncontainable bliss.

"Jug-o!" she screamed. "Jug-o! Jug-o!"

Jug-o? The realization hit me suddenly. Juggle! Little snip knew the word for *juggle*!

I dropped my items suddenly.

"Ana!" A faint voice carried over the breeze. "Ana!"

Well, it sounded like I was about done anyway.

"More!" My friend, now known as Ana, begged. "More!"

But I shook my head. "Sounds like Mommy is calling you," I informed her. "You better go give her your flower."

"Flow-uh," Ana said. "Bye, jug-o man."

Pox! She couldn't go around saying that! "Wait!" I stopped her, digging into the small pouch at my side and pulling out two gold coins. "Here, this is for Mommy too." I put one gold coin in her small hand . . . and realized she couldn't hold another without letting go of her flower, so I returned it to the bag. There. Now I was "shiny-coin man."

"Oooh!" Ana made a happy baby noise.

"ANA!"

Oh dear. The peasant woman was coming this way.

"Bye, Jug-o man," Ana repeated.

"Run to Mommy!" I urged her. "And don't drop your coin!"

Ana ran into the tall weeds, and I watched just long enough to see that the rustling plants rustled in the direction of the ever-approaching woman. Then I snatched up my bouquet and ran to my horse before the woman could catch me.

I don't know why I felt so guilty. Maybe it was because I'd betrayed myself to her daughter. Oh, well. At least I had gotten what I'd come for, and I was sure of at least one of two things: I either had Thea's favorite flower or her least favorite. We would see.

"Did you get the queen a bouquet?" Kazim asked me as we entered the dining hall that night.

"Yes," I said merrily as I winked. "I did. You?"

Kazim stood up straighter. "Of course. What did you get her?"

"You first."

Kazim smiled a princely smile, all too happy to tell me.

"Roses are the queenliest flower," he said. "So naturally I got her those. But since I thought that others would think the same, I had mine painted blue and dusted with silver."

"Oooh," I commented, until I realized that made me

sound like Ana. "I mean, that's brilliant. You're sure to stand out with that."

"Her suitors have been sending bouquets all day. Her room must be full of them," Kazim said, running his eyes across his competition.

"How will we know which bouquet she liked best?" I asked.

Suddenly the double-wide doors to the dining room burst open, and Thea came running through, a lady-in-waiting running after her.

"Who sent me these?" she demanded, holding my bouquet of dandelions in front of her in a desperate rage. "Whose are they?"

The suitors all looked at one another. I clenched my teeth.

Kazim looked first at me. "You didn't—"

"I'm sorry, my lady." I put on a remorseful face as I stepped forward. "I did not mean to offend you by gracing your presence with something so . . . common . . . and homely." I chose my words deliberately.

"You?" Thea turned her whole self on me, and I tried very hard to decide if she was angry or . . . something else. "Why these? How did you know?"

"Know?" I feigned surprise. "I knew nothing."

"Then why these?"

The room was dead silent. Everyone stared at me as if they were at my execution.

"Well," I began, "as you may have guessed, your suitors decided to try and get you your favorite flowers." I paused. "And I thought that everyone would be getting you such beautiful tokens. But I got you these because, well, I guess they are my favorite flower."

"Some call them weeds," Thea said quickly.

I shrugged. "But they catch the sun so beautifully," I said purposefully. "And rather than show you something beautiful, I thought I'd show my favorite flower, or weed, as you like, how beautiful *you* were, instead." Thea's eyes began to tear. "But if they've offended you, I will personally get them out of your sight." I reached for the bouquet.

Thea immediately hugged the flowers to her as if they were a child. She stared at me very hard.

Sir Hubert, Sir Hubert, Sir Hubert, I chanted quickly to myself. *No, you don't, Thea.*

What I fool I was. Here I gripped so tightly to Sir Hubert, yet I went out of my way to taunt her as Farrago. What was wrong with me?

Finally, Thea turned on her heel and thrust my bouquet at her lady-in-waiting. Then she stopped, took out a single dandelion, and clutched it to her heart.

"Valyn, see to it that Sir Hubert sits on my right hand at dinner. I will return shortly." She marched quickly away. "And have those put in water!" we heard her voice echo down the hall.

Valyn, Thea's lady-in-waiting, gave me a confused look and then turned and ran after her charge.

Kazim looked at me. "What just happened?" he asked. "Tell me, Hubert, as a native of this country, did that make sense to you? Was she angry with you or not?"

I raised my eyebrows and tried to look like what had happened was no big deal.

"Oh, I don't know," I said casually. "I expect we'll find out at dinner."

Chapter 16

Kazim managed to sit on Thea's left hand as she sat at the head of the table. She looked surly and kept throwing me suspicious glances.

I tried to look like a pleased yet humbled noble who still wasn't sure if he had experienced good or bad luck.

"Am I in trouble?" I finally asked bluntly as Thea glared at her soup.

Thea looked like she wanted to hang me. "Why would you be?"

"Oh, I don't know. I just got a subtle hint I might be when you stormed in with my bouquet," I replied, sipping my soup casually. Thea's consternation was far too much fun.

Thea pursed her lips. "They . . . reminded me of something. That was all. It didn't occur to me that one of my suitors might bring them."

"Reminded you of something good or bad?"

Thea sipped her soup. "I don't know," she confessed.

"What other flowers were you given?" Kazim spoke up, studying the queen closely.

"Roses," Thea sighed. "So many roses. And one bouquet was stunning. Blue, glittering with silver. Perfect and painted and presentable." She lowered her eyes. "Just like me," she whispered.

I heard, but Kazim seemed too pleased that she had cited his gift to take note that she wasn't happy that she resembled the roses. "Those were mine," he said in a gentle voice.

"Were they?" Thea glanced at him and let a servant take her nearly finished bowl and serve the next course.

Kazim began to explain his reason for his choice, and I tried to listen and pay attention to Thea's mood, but a man at the far end of the table caught my eye.

Seacrest's fool.

He had a clubbed foot and walked with a bouncy swaying motion, but only partly because of his foot. He was mildly drunk, as evidenced by his bloodshot eyes and sickly smile. It took me a moment to realize that he wasn't much older than me. He was just more worn, more careless with his appearance. His brown hair was droopy and unkempt, but he might have looked decent if he ever cleaned up. He had rigid, manly features. He was dressed in two different shades of brown, light and dark, split down the middle.

I despised him as soon as I saw him.

I imagined him as the clinging influence of the evil kings that had so long ruled Seacrest and the decay that had overcome the kingdom. He approached several suitors and courtiers, men mostly, and whispered things in their ears that made them laugh. I, of course, could not hear what they were, but I knew the kind of jokes that drunken men like him were accustomed to using, and I had never used them. I would have sooner bitten Fendral than speak words like that. What's more, I noticed that when the fool whispered to the other suitors, they glanced at Thea. *My Thea.* And I didn't like to imagine what they were saying or why they chuckled or choked on their ale. The fool was making his way down the table, getting closer to us. With all my might, I stared at him and tried to put on my most fearsome expression. My "if you dare get too close to me I will bite your head off" face.

"Sir Hubert, are you all right?"

I turned abruptly to Kazim. Both he and Thea were looking at me curiously. I realized that I was seizing my knife so tightly that my hand was starting to freeze up. I pried the knife out with my other hand and flexed my fingers.

"Oh yes," I assured them. "I was just noticing your fool, Your Highness."

"Oh." Thea sneered. "The others just call him Oaf."

"Not a bad name for a fool," I commented, taking a bite of mutton and potatoes.

"You do not care for fools, Sir Hubert?" Kazim asked me.

"I detest them," I answered readily, feeling very much like Sir Hubert. "Ridiculous useless creatures, if you ask me. I don't see why they exist." Yes. That was a very Sir Hubert-ish thing to say. That should throw Thea off the scent of Farrago.

"We do not have them in Arabia," Kazim commented. "I do not fully understand their purpose. They are curious to me."

"They are supposed to entertain," I said. "They are supposed to keep the mood light, to help people smile when they need it, and to offer ideas that the counselors are too rigid to think of. They are supposed to do many things, but when they do not, they are despicable." I jerked my head down the table. "Like *Oaf* over there. That is *not* how I was—" *Watch it!* Farrago screamed inside me. "Um . . . accustomed to having fools in Poppydown," I finished with difficulty. I shoved more potatoes in my mouth. That had been too close.

"My lady!" Oaf was suddenly there, bowing to Thea, who was shooting daggers at him. I was quite certain that in his current state, he had no ability to judge what the queen, or me, for that matter, thought of him, or how much we wanted him to suddenly drop dead.

"Forgive me," the fool said quickly, reaching behind Thea's ear. She tried to object, but he brought his hand back deftly with a beautiful white handkerchief embroidered with white roses.

Thea jumped and put a hand to her chest, where I assumed the kerchief had once hidden. I clenched my teeth. So he wasn't just a man of crude jokes, ale, and limping. He specialized in sleight-of-hand.

"That's—!" Thea started.

"Belonged to the old queen, your mother," Oaf finished for her. "Be still, my lady. I didn't think behind your ear was the best place for it."

His voice reminded me of Sir Borin but perhaps a little deeper. He had that same slimy rasp in his throat.

"Wait! I think I've found something else!" Oaf insisted, bring the kerchief quickly across his hand. A dandelion rested in his palm. Thea gasped. Oaf pulled the kerchief across again, and the dandelion was joined by one of Kazim's blue roses. I heard Kazim's short intake of breath. He had our full attention; he was more powerful than I had given him credit for.

"So," Oaf mused, setting the three items down in front of us, the kerchief in front of the queen, with the dandelion to the right and the rose to the left. "The three of you made it to dinner together, did you? A curious trio. And the queen must choose one. Well," Oaf leaned closer to me so that he was between Thea and me, "dandelions are common, surely, but once they take root, they're hard to get rid of." Then he leaned over between Kazim and the queen. "But they do not compare to the beauty and majesty of the rose. No. One can almost forget they had ever seen anything ugly in the presence of such a cleverly crafted token," Oaf turned the rose in his hand so that the silver dust glinted. "One can almost wish to leave the dandelion behind."

Thea's eyes widened. She snatched up her handkerchief, shoved her chair back, knocking Oaf to the ground as she did so, and stood and ran out of the dining room. Valyn, her attendant, came out of nowhere to follow her.

Oaf, still on the ground, gave us a smile I didn't like as he got to his feet, leaning to one side because of his foot. It was partially a drunken grin, and partially something very alert and sinister. He bowed slightly before he hobbled away to whisper in the ears of everyone down the other side of the table.

"Curious man," Kazim murmured, eyeing Oaf warily. "I suppose he must not know that you are not after the queen."

You're not after the queen, I thought harshly. *You're after the crown and kingdom*. I'm *after the queen*.

"He must not," I agreed with a light, dismissive grin. "He must not."

Chapter 17

"Well, Sir Hubert! You have good taste. I have a tunic just like that with me," Prince Alain commented as we made our way to dinner the next night.

"Do you? We should match one of these nights," I joked with him. Not that that would be possible. It was his tunic. Red. Very fetching. I was pleased that it fit me so well.

"Indeed!" Alain said with a smile as he took the seat to the right of where Thea would be sitting. Sir Leon, another suitor Kazim thought was competition, was already sitting to her left. Pox. Of course I wouldn't be able to sit with her every night. And I also felt pretty certain that if Thea hadn't insisted, I never would have won a place at her side. These two must be favored by the counselors. I made my way a little down the table and sat between two nobles native to Seacrest's court as Thea entered and took her place at the head of the table.

I so badly wanted to interact with her more. I wanted to speak with her, to feel her out; I had not seen her all day.

"She has been speaking of you."

I jumped, throwing my fork in the air. Oaf stood

behind my chair, speaking in my ear. I quickly picked up my knife and tossed it, catching it easily by the blade, ready for throwing. My action had been quick and only mildly betrayed me as Farrago. No one would think anything of it.

"Be gone, fool," I said in my most dangerous voice. "I want none of your tricks."

"Tricks? I am a harmless entertainer, as you well know. And surely you are bursting with the question: favorable or unfavorable?"

He was baiting me. He wanted me to show my interest. "Unfavorable, of course," I said, spoiling it for him. "What else could it possibly be?"

"It is strange for a suitor to not care about the opinion of the one he pursues," Oaf commented. "Unfavorable it may be, but she has not been speaking of any other suitor unless she is directly asked, and even then, she has nothing to say. I thought you would appreciate the information."

I held the knife lightly between my middle and forefinger. "I would appreciate the sight of you dangling from the gallows," I said venomously. "Now *that* would be entertaining."

"You speak harshly to a poor, harmless, crippled fool," Oaf said with false sorrow. "But I do not think you are as uncaring about our lady's opinion as you seem. Why would you have come here?"

I flipped the knife to hold it by the handle and turned so that the sharp edge of the blade sat gently over where Oaf's no doubt equally crippled heart rested.

"If you know what is good for you, you will not trouble me again," I said firmly, narrowing my eyes and tucking the knife away in my sleeve. If anyone had been observing us, the most they could have discerned was that we were having an animated conversation, and perhaps that I liked playing with knives, but I didn't care about that.

"As you wish, my lord, as you wish," Oaf said hurriedly. "But I have just one more piece of information you might actually find interesting."

"I doubt it."

Oaf continued anyway. "We have a few new faces come to join our coven of counselors," he said in a slimy voice. "They bring new news from the kingdom of Gridian. Apparently their court fool is missing. And there's even darker rumors that say he has ties to our queen and might cause trouble."

I gasped before I could catch myself. "Oaf," I hissed, "I *will* cut your tongue out if you meddle with me."

Oaf held up his hands as if in surrender. "Oh trust me, my lord, if the fool is caught, it will not be because of my tongue. I would just hate to be him if he *were* ever discovered. They've done terrible things to enemies here, and the queen is not in full power yet, and she won't be until she is married. Good night, brother," he said quickly as I opened my mouth to say something more. Then Oaf extended his hand by my plate, palm down. He flipped his hand palm up, and the fork I had tossed was there. When I didn't take it, he tossed it on my plate and ran away on his hands.

I felt sick. Oaf knew. Did that mean the counselors knew? Was I already caught? Was I done for? Should I flee?

No. I had done nothing to worry anyone about my intentions. If anyone *knew,* then I would surely be dead already. But no one thought I was taking this suitor-business seriously. If there were whispers, they were running on suspicion only. Oaf had pieced things together, but I could still attribute that to the fact that he was still, after all, a fool, and possessed the queer abilities of such. He still thought differently.

I could not eat. I glanced at Thea striving to respond to the questions and banter of the two suitors at her sides and excused myself.

I made my way down corridors, tipping my head to maids as I passed, forgetting that I was supposed to ignore them. I climbed several floors higher than my room. I knew the routine. Out one window, move along the narrow edge of stone to the next window, and back in.

Except I didn't go in. This was the queen's chamber. I sat outside. Fortunately for me, this castle had gargoyles carved along some of the windows, certainly around the queen's window for protection. I sat on the neck of one of them and waited for Thea to return.

I fell asleep. Heights did not worry me, so it seemed like the next second that I heard female voices entering the room.

"Valyn!" I recognized Thea's wail. "Every night I tell myself that I'll put on a good face and be happy about everything, and every night I am reminded why I hate my life."

"You were better tonight," Valyn encouraged her. "Better since that fit over the dandelions. But—"

"But you would do so much better than me if you were in my shoes," Thea finished.

I heard something snap. I chanced a peek into the window to see that Valyn had snapped a hairpin in two.

"Yes!" Valyn said through gritted teeth. "I would give anything to be where you are! Almost. Granted, I'm not sure who among your suitors I would pick, but to be in your position! You have no idea what a relief it was when my father and I learned there was an heir to the throne. We had already worked so hard to rid the kingdom of the usurpers. But we couldn't make anything work for long without a blood heir. And then when the king became so ill, it looked like everything would go back." Her voice cracked. "Back to the way it was."

Apparently that had been bad.

I looked again to see Valyn rubbing her temples and Thea with her head in her hands sitting in front of a looking glass.

"This isn't about you," Valyn whispered, putting a hand on Thea's shoulder.

Thea's eyes were wet. "I know. I've learned what this kingdom has gone through. I've learned who I am supposed to be. I think I could do it. I really think I could. The fear isn't quite as bad anymore. It's just that I'm not—I'm not a *queen*. I'm not better off than I was before! I've been reduced to an object. I would rather be a scullery maid with love than a queen without. If I thought that any of the suitors saw me as anything other than a ticket to power, I would have him. I could go through with it. But I'm just a pretty thing, and I can't be convinced that any of them see me as anything other than that. None of them see me as something with a soul. If any of them knew what I had been before—"

"Careful! You're father wanted you never to speak of what you were in the past, even to me. I know what you were, and it doesn't matter. And you must give them time. All we need is someone who will make a good king. The counselors are charged with evaluating that quality. You *have* been given the freedom to put forth your own tasks for them. They came up with the flowers themselves. Why not have them write you poems? Or maybe dance with them? Spend a little time with each of them to get to know them better."

Thea banged a fist on the table before the mirror. "No! It's all farce! They're all putting on faces and airs anyway. How can I ever expect to see who they really are if it's so easy for them to act pleasant for a little while? I don't trust them! I know why they're here, and it isn't for me! Why don't the counselors just assign one to me and stop giving me the illusion of choice?"

"Your father was genuinely trying to give you a choice. The counselors would gladly assign you, and you would regret it. You do have some power."

"Bah. All I can do is refuse or accept who the counselors choose. They do everything else for the kingdom. I don't have any power and I won't have any power until I wed, and even then, my husband will have final say in everything."

"Before you marry, you have the power to give final commands to the army in the event we are attacked," Valyn said helpfully.

"And that had better not happen," Thea insisted. "I can't send men off to die. I can't do this."

"I think you should just hang it all and marry Sir Hubert."

Thea's eyes blazed. She stood and kicked her chair over. I had never seen her so angry. "I do not want to marry Sir Hubert! I hate him! I hate him!"

"Then why have you been speaking of him every night? Why does everything he does affect you so?"

"Because!" Thea yelled, stamping her foot and calming a little. "Because I believe him to be a demon sent to torment me. I-I keep seeing things I *want* to see that aren't there. He—"

"He reminds you of someone you fell in love with before," Valyn said gently as she led Thea to the edge of her bed and bade her sit. "And I gather that he was common, someone you can't have. I would have thought that if Sir Hubert was so similar, you could accept him."

Thea shook her head. "I don't want a fake. I'd rather have someone completely different. Sir Hubert is not my love. He likes to torment me. Sometimes I think he knows what he's doing, but that's just wishful thinking again. If Farra—" Thea's voice froze entirely. She'd come so close to saying my name. I shuddered with pleasure at the thought of her saying my name, but she stopped as if her slip caused her pain. It reminded me of how I'd felt when people still mentioned Fendral's name after he left. It stung. "If my love were here pretending to be a courtier when he was really common, what would happen to him if he were found out?" Thea whispered.

Valyn was silent for a moment as she considered. "The counselors would swiftly have him put to death," she said softly. "You must let go of that hope for your own sake. He cannot come after you. You must let him go and move on."

Thea nodded. "I was never really sure if he loved me back anyway. Never sure. Some things happened just before I left . . . maybe if I had stayed a little longer . . ."

"Assume he did not," Valyn encouraged. "Whatever was true, tell yourself that he did not return your affection. That will help."

Thea nodded. "I so love the idea of him coming after me that I keep seeing him in Sir Hubert. I would give *anything* to believe that he was coming after me, that he wanted me. That he loved me too." Thea's voice became softer and softer, and it seemed as if all her hope was fading with her voice. I realized I was trembling. I had to hold myself back from throwing myself through the window and spoiling everything. Valyn had said they would kill me if I was found out. So what was I going to do? Remain Farrago and try to run away with her? What would become of Seacrest? What of those poor people I passed in the street? Of Ana? Should I remain Sir Hubert and try harder to become king like the spinster said? The thought made me ill. Or should I remain Farrago and run away as if I'd never been here? Thea need never know I had come for her . . . but I so wanted her to know. It was so important to her. Why didn't I have a better plan? Why didn't I know what I wanted beyond Thea? Was I going to please Constance? Or the spinster? Or no one in order to stay alive? *Why?* I brought my fist down on the stone gargoyle in frustration.

"What was that?" Valyn asked. I heard her coming toward the window.

Pox!

Valyn pushed the latched glass open further. It opened outward. Without thinking, I flipped myself over the gargoyle and dangled, holding on to its stone head for all I was worth.

"Hmmm. Perhaps it was just a gull," I heard Valyn say as she pulled the window closed all the way. Her voice was much more muffled as she continued. "Now, let's put all that behind us. The counselors have already sent messages to the suitors about their next evaluation, and you're involved, and you're not going to like it, but I think you should go through with it."

I really wanted to stay and listen to whatever Thea wouldn't like. I hadn't gotten word of our next evaluation yet, but after so nearly getting caught, I made my way back along the narrow stone ledge and back through the window I had come in. I ran back to my room. Part of me sang. She loved me! Well, she loved Farrago, but she hated Sir Hubert. I could hardly blame her for that. I felt the same way. If only I knew how I was going to make this work.

Chapter 18

Wham! Wham! Wham!

A maid, not my usual chambermaid, made the mistake of leaving her broom in the corridor while she emptied chamber pots.

Wham! Wham! Wham!

She rushed in just as I was finishing.

"Sir Hubert!" she howled. "What are you doing?"

I was standing on a chair, beating the top corner of my room with the broom as hard as I could.

"Um . . ." These things were always hard to explain. "There was a—a web."

"A spiderweb? Well, I'm sure you killed the spider. And, please, next time just call a maid. We're always around." She seemed worried about the state of her broom and looked like she wanted to scold me further but knew she couldn't do that to a noble and a guest.

"Yes, miss," I said, far more politely than I was supposed to as I handed the broom back to her with my head downcast. She took it, gave me a "you should know better" look, and left. Actually, I hadn't seen a spider; I wouldn't have had the courage to beat the web if I had. But it made me feel better to know that the spider's home was dead at least. That much I could do.

Plus, the physical exertion was good for my brain. Normally juggling helped me think, or else wiped my mind of thought. But I wasn't allowed to juggle. Pox. Maybe I should go find Ana again.

There was a faint rap at my door. I jumped to attention and made a mental note to learn the names of my maids. *Casual*, I told my face. *Bored.*

"Come in," I called, sitting at the edge of my bed with my chin in my hand.

But instead of my maid, Kazim put his dark, flawless face through the door and stepped quietly in.

"So, you are awake," he commented. "Did you hear that banging sound?"

"Banging sound? Oh. I think one of the maids saw a mouse."

"Ah." Kazim readily accepted my answer.

"Can I help you?"

"I wanted to ask you if you'd heard what's next."

"Next? What do you mean?" It was probably the thing that Valyn had said Thea wouldn't like. In my distraction, I had nearly forgotten, but I was dying to know.

Kazim looked to his left and picked up a small scroll on a table that I had not noticed.

"You should really read these when they come through."

"I didn't notice it. It can't have been there that long."

"It came by this afternoon," Kazim said.

"I assume it's important."

Kazim replaced the scroll on the table. "Day after tomorrow, there will be a Tournament of Princes."

"A *Tournament of Princes*?" I repeated. "Sounds . . . important."

Kazim gave me a curious look and chuckled. "Incredible. I come here about what I think to be a serious matter and I can't seem to stay serious very long around you. Yes, it's important. It's really just an opportunity for the suitors to show off, but I feel it may determine who actually becomes king. Each will choose their preferred weapon and battle up through the ranks to a victor. Victors fight other victors until there is an ultimate champion. That champion will be first to dance with the queen at a ball that night. And he is promised a kiss."

All my masks fell off with a clatter. "What? A kiss?" No one could kiss my Thea except me! No wonder she wouldn't like it! I scrambled to put my Hubert face back on. "Gross."

I had never seen an Arabian laugh so loudly before. "I don't know why I bother!" he said, once he'd calmed down. "You make me lose my thoughts. Oh, yes. I've been investigating what weapons the other suitors favor. Two prefer jousting, but most prefer swords. One an axe or other weapons that can be used in close range. I came to ask what weapon you favor."

I let my wariness show on my face. "Did you just go up to all the other suitors and ask them and they told you?"

"No. I used subterfuge or paid off their servants for information."

I just looked at him.

Kazim exhaled. "You are wise to be cautious," he said, sitting on the cedar chest at the foot of my bed. "After all, we should be enemies. And the other suitors have much to fear from me but—" He paused, considering. "There is something different about you. I cannot name it. You are the only man I've ever met that I have trusted so quickly. Forgive me if I seem bold. I only asked so that I could help."

"Help . . ."

"So the other suitors don't assume you are easy picking and kill you off."

"I thought you said it was just an opportunity for the suitors to show off!"

"It is, and it is not supposed to be to the death, but some of the others might go too far. I do not intend to kill anyone, because I do not think it will be necessary, but some of them see this as their only chance to impress the queen and they may overdo it. So, please, what weapon do you prefer?"

Oh, *why* was he pressing me for answers? I didn't know! "The sword, I suppose. If that's what everyone else is doing."

"What kind? Do you have a strategy? A specialty? How do you fight?"

"The sharp kind. And I plan on flailing a lot."

Kazim put a hand to his forehead as if in exasperation, but he was smiling.

"What's *your* weapon?" I countered.

Kazim glanced up at me with a chilling smile. He put a hand to his hip where a sheath dangled.

"Persian scimitar," he said, drawing a wicked blade out with a metallic hum. The blade was narrow with a dangerous curve and an even more dangerous edge. The hilt was long.

"Well, that's certainly . . . fearsome," I said. At least I hadn't said "evil."

Kazim turned the blade a few times. "Better for slashing than for stabbing, and the curve keeps it from getting your horse's ears when riding." He resheathed it. "The day after tomorrow. I will be practicing near the stables most of the day until then. You are welcome to join me." He bowed. I inclined my head in return, and he exited.

I didn't like this game. Throwing myself back on my bed, I thought until I fell asleep with Alain's red tunic still on.

I was performing for Gridian Court. Leofrick stood next to me playing an impossibly beautiful and happy piece on his mandolin. Giles and Constance and many other familiar faces from the court looked on with applause. I heard a squeal of delight and looked down to see Ana clapping her small hands. Suddenly I found myself tossing the balls forward instead of up, but they all returned to me. Thea stood before me, her hair in blessed dandelion form. We tossed the balls and juggled between each other. I was shocked. I'd had no idea Thea was this good! When we met eyes, we both stopped juggling, but the balls continued to float around us. We stepped closer, and Thea took a large bite from an onion. I laughed and moved to embrace her . . .

But the sudden shout of a man and scream of a horse woke me. I was on my four-poster bed where I still lay as Sir Hubert. No! I pulled pillows over my head and tried to force myself back into my dream. I bet if I'd stayed, Fendral would have shown up.

It was no good. I couldn't get back. Curse whatever

woke me. But I recognized the sounds: the stomp of horse's hooves on soft dirt, the clang of metal against wooden uprights. Someone was jousting, or at least practicing. Of course. The blasted tournament was tomorrow. My soul filled with dread at the prospect of my reality verses my wonderful dream.

And all the dream left me with was knowing that I wasn't going to just run away and leave Thea hanging. Which meant that I had work to do today.

All the other suitors seemed to have woken early to begin preparing and training. After returning Alain's red tunic, I put on just a simple white tunic one of the maids had left in a drawer and decided to skip breakfast and make my way to the armory. No one was about except for maids, to whom I tipped my head respectfully, startling them. Rounding a corner, I very nearly tripped over a drunken figure, but I caught myself at the last minute.

Oaf was dead asleep under a window, his crippled leg sticking out into the hallway while the rest of him slouched against the wall. Drool was making a trail out of the corner of his mouth and down his neck. He breathed like a horse. Clutched in one slack hand was a mostly empty bottle of ale. I was no great judge of liquor, but I could tell that it was an expensive brand, far too dear to be in the possession of the court fool, one would think.

I couldn't resist.

I ran back down the hall and bumped into my maid.

"Sorry, miss!" I helped her to her feet. "What's your name?"

My greeting was unusual, and it took my maid a moment to decide how she should answer.

"Um, Alyss, my lord."

"Alyss, I need a bucket of mop water. Preferably used."

It was a trick pouring the water from the bucket into the narrow mouth of Oaf's bottle without spilling everywhere, but considering the other liquids I could have chosen to fill the bottle with, I considered myself quite kind. Oaf didn't stir through the whole process, and while Alyss looked a little guilty, I suspected it was more because she didn't want to stop me.

"Thank you, my lady!" I said brightly as I handed the bucket back to her. Alyss looked anxiously from bucket to Oaf's bottle a few times before deciding she had better get away with the evidence and darted out of sight.

Unable to wear anything but a smile, I ran the rest of the way to the armory, passing suitors sparring and trying on armor and riding horses and jousting and all sorts of things. The armory was at the far side of the rear courtyard, and I pushed the wooden door open to let myself in.

"Can I help you?" a burly man wearing a thick leather apron asked testily. His skin was suntanned, he sported a short beard, and his head looked just a tad too small for the rest of his blubbery bulk.

Farrago wanted to shrink back, but Sir Hubert wouldn't have done that, so I held my ground.

"I need a sword. Or a weapon or something."

He gave me a suspicious look. "Don't you bring your favorite weapon around with you?"

"I don't have a favorite weapon. And I like to travel light."

"Hmmm," he grunted. "Well, come and see."

Once the initial greeting was over, the burly man, Tom, wasn't as bad as he came across at first, rather like a bear in porcupine clothing who always spoke gruffly but thought of more than just tearing your head off all the time. Since I couldn't give him any specifics on what I wanted other than "probably a sword," and "sharp," he fitted me with a light broadsword. I swished it a few times.

"Haven't you ever used a sword before?" he asked.

Nope.

I glanced at him self-consciously. "There was never really a need," I said. "I specialized in . . . other things."

Tom grunted again and then started right into a lesson as if I'd asked for it. I hadn't, but I appreciated it. He coached me on stance, thrusting, swinging, and footwork. I was good at the footwork, bad at thrusting, and maybe passable at swinging. In a few hours he determined that I had potential but there was no way I should plan on winning anything the next day.

"You could always forfeit and just watch," he suggested. "Better than getting pummeled."

No, no, no. That was the way other people thought. I had to come up with something.

"These fights aren't to the death," I said. *I hope*, I added to myself. "What's going to be the main objective?"

Tom stroked his short grizzly beard. "Disarm and force to yield," he said. "That means you must rid your man of his weapon and hold your own to his throat so he must surrender."

Disarm. Disarm. I'd seen swordsmen disarm their foes, but it required a skill and precision I just didn't have yet. At least not with the sword. I needed something else.

I looked up and down the rows of weapons. There were battle-axes and spears, lances, and dozens of different swords. My eyes rested on a flail for a moment. It was a short stick with a small chain and a ball with evil spikes all over it. I'd seen them used before. One could pick up terrific speed by spinning the ball and then letting it fly. I couldn't seem to take my eyes off the ball; it reminded me of juggling, and perhaps the chain . . .

"Tom," I asked curiously, "do you have a flail with a long chain I could practice with?"

A moment later, I had Tom positioned in front of me holding a sword while I spun the flail at my hip. Tom had fitted a longer chain and a smaller spiked ball to the end while I spun from the chain, with the rest coiled in my other hand.

"Now just hold still this first time," I told him as if I'd done this hundreds of times before.

"If you strike me, I will personally bring this hilt crashing down on your noble forehead," Tom promised grimly.

I chuckled even though I knew Tom wasn't joking, and that I would probably die if he bashed me. But I had a theory that I felt certain would work. My mind went back to learning how to juggle with Fendral.

"Farrago, you're too worried about catching the balls again," he had instructed me one day as I stood sweating with the effort of mastering the balls.

"I thought that was the point,*" I panted.*

"No." He gave me a wink that infuriated me. "That only looks like the point. Juggling is the art of great throws, not great catches. Once you teach your arms to control your throws, catching will become second nature and you won't need to think about it."

I knew I had mastered throws. I was as good at juggling as Fendral had ever been. Surely the ball on the flail would respond to a good throw.

So I tried it, tossing the spiked ball over the blade as close to the hilt as I could. Once the links came in contact with the metal blade, the ball spun around the sword several times and I yanked it out of Tom's hand.

Tom cringed, but once he realized the sword was missing and that he hadn't been touched, he lightened up.

"You did it!" he shouted happily. Then in the next second he caught himself and looked surly again. "But I bet you can't do it again."

"Let's try it," I said, giving him that same wink Fendral had given me.

The rest of the day was spent sparring and throwing chains. We practiced and practiced and practiced. More than once I had to run for my life from Tom across the courtyard because I'd missed, but by the time the sun was setting I felt certain I could consistently use my chain to disarm my opponent even during battle. And Tom hadn't killed me off.

"You might just be all right," Tom said as he drew a big arm across his forehead. "Bless me, but I don't know why I spent all day coaching a noble. But there's something different about you, Sir Hubert. I've never met a noble humble enough to let a peasant teach them in the first place, but you didn't seem to care."

Pox. I had to be careful of that. Sir Hubert surely wouldn't have interacted with a peasant so readily. But I had needed him, and Farrago hadn't cared.

"Yes, well," I cleared my throat, "peasants are refreshing after some of the nobles I have to be around all day."

Tom thought that was a fair statement and clapped me on the back, nearly-but-not-quite knocking me over.

"I hope you win, Sir Hubert," he said. "It's high time we had a decent king on the throne."

There it was again. That reminder that if I got what I

wanted, that might mean being forced to become king. I smiled back at Tom, fitting my masks back firmly into place. I wanted to win, but I didn't want to be king. I would have to figure that out soon.

Chapter 20

All the suitors were talking about the tournament at dinner that night. Sir Reginald and Prince Meldon sat on either side of Thea tonight, speaking animatedly to each other about what they had done all day. Thea made humming sounds as if she was paying attention, but she wasn't.

"I didn't see you today, Sir Hubert. Are you ready?" Kazim asked as he took a seat next to me.

"I think so," I said casually.

"Did you find a sword that agreed with you?"

"More or less. At least I got to work on my flailing a lot." Ha! I hadn't even realized how clever that would be! Flail, flailing. Ha!

The meal was good, and I chatted casually with the courtiers and suitors. Prince Alain sat directly across from me and we talked about tailors, which meant I had to do a lot of lying about who made my clothes. The courses came by until servants put pastries before us for dessert.

"Don't eat your pastry," a maid whispered in my ear as she set it before me.

What? I *wanted* my pastry! But then I caught sight of

Oaf at the far side of the dining room. He was entertaining some scullery maids with some sleight-of-hand, but he glanced in my direction and I was quite certain that he knew perfectly well who had corrupted the last of his ale. His revenge no doubt sat before me.

So I forced myself to ignore what surely only *looked* like the warm buttery flakiness of bread hugging some undoubtedly toxic yet usually wonderful filling.

But I was afraid that I would forget the servant's warning, so I decided to get rid of my pastry before it killed me.

"Hey, Alain," I said casually, "how much do you want to bet I can't hit Oaf with my pastry from over here?"

Oaf was too far away to hear me and was deeply engrossed with a small audience of a few maids and pages.

Alain checked the distance. "Hmmm. Five gold coins," he said. "Pastries are harder to throw than you think, and fools are harder to hit."

"Done." I stood and picked up the pastry, curled my wrist, and flung it easily at Oaf.

I had known I was going to hit him. I just hadn't fully taken into account that Oaf must have had experience with people throwing things at him.

Oaf caught the pastry with one hand without looking. His audience gasped. In one motion, he broke the pastry in two, checked the insides, and flung one half back at me.

I was still standing; I could catch it easily. It looked like it was filled with nothing but custard. But as it spun, something black broke away from the cream filling and continued to fly at me.

In an instant of sudden horror I tried to throw myself backwards away from it as it spread its legs toward me trying to steady itself. Maggoty meal, it was still *alive.*

The large black spider landed squarely on my chest, and I went mad. With an awful cry, I fell backward onto my chair, knocking it over as I desperately swatted and swiped at my front with my hands. I hit the spider off, and it landed on the floor where it began to run. Ladies took up screams as the custard-covered monster tried to escape. I knew the spider was no longer on me, but I continued to beat at my chest as if there was still some clinging spider-influence that I couldn't get rid of.

Kazim flew off his chair and stomped the spider with a single powerful step. The screaming stopped almost instantly. But I was still swatting and I couldn't breathe. I didn't understand why my hands were covered with custard until I realized that the pastry must have hit me as well. I hadn't noticed it.

Kazim turned and pulled me to my feet. I was not in control of myself and shrank away, repelled by the thought of the spider still smeared on his foot. Kazim gripped both of my wrists, forcing me to stop beating myself.

"He's fine," I heard Kazim say, and I realized he was speaking for the benefit of everyone else who must have been watching me. "It just caught him by surprise. He just needs to get cleaned up and compose himself."

Kazim, by holding me still, probably made me look less crazy than I felt.

"Calm down," he whispered.

He was right. I knew I needed to calm down. There was something about realizing my situation that helped pull me out of my terror at least a little; I was suddenly able to think of something other than the fact that the spider had been on me.

"I-I'm all right," I said, relaxing my arms, though I could

still feel myself trembling just a little. "I'll be right back," I lied. There was no way I was going to show my face for the rest of the evening.

"Do you want me to come with you?" Kazim asked.

He was being kind. Really? I didn't trust him, and a small nagging feeling in my head told me I was right not to trust him, but in this instant, I felt sure Kazim was being genuinely kind. Still, I shook my head.

"As you wish," Kazim said and released me.

I looked to where Oaf had been, and he was of course gone. Unable quite yet to put a mask on, I walked briskly out of the dining room without turning around.

Pox. That whole incident must have made Kazim look good and me look ridiculous. I was used to looking ridiculous, but I couldn't afford that here. Not in this way.

I entered my room and washed my hands in the basin, pulling my tunic over my head, touching the place where the spider had landed on my bare chest. The skin was faintly red where I had beaten myself, but other than that, nothing. Nothing was there. It hadn't hurt me, so why could I still feel the tickle of tiny legs?

"I bet you didn't want people to see that."

I spun around, all the muscles in my arms and chest tightening with instant rage. Oaf sat cross-legged on my bed, looking happy and evil.

"Oaf, I could kill you for that," I hissed, still trembling, though this time with anger I wasn't sure I could control. I had always fought so hard to not advertise my greatest fear. All the survival instincts in me told me I was setting myself up for torture if I declared my weakness, and just now Oaf had betrayed it for me.

"If it makes you feel any better, ale is rather my

weakness," Oaf confessed merrily. "But only the absence of it, not the presence of it."

"Then I will see to it that you dry up and wither away without it when I am king," I said through clenched teeth. Not that I suddenly wanted to be king, but I had to make it a good threat.

But Oaf knew it was fake. He threw back his head and laughed a sickening laugh. "You'll never be king!" he cackled. "You'll be *dead*! There's only enough room for one fool in this kingdom, *dear Farrago*!"

He jumped off my bed and scurried to the window much faster than someone with a clubbed foot should have been able to. Hearing Oaf say my name brought on a whole different kind of fear.

"You have nothing but suspicions, Oaf! You cannot kill me with that!"

"All in good time." Oaf grinned and vanished out the window. I wanted to believe he had fallen, but I could not.

I went to my bed, swung both fists in the air and brought them down as hard as I could on the mattress. I beat my bed over and over until I exhausted myself. Then I slumped on the floor and gripped my hair with both hands, closing my eyes. Fear and anger ebbed a little to make way for the most horrible feeling of loneliness I had ever felt. I had been weakened, threatened. I was afraid. I wanted to tell Leofrick, or Fendral. But they were gone. I had left them. I felt surrounded by enemies. Perhaps I could go find Tom or Ana. But my insides clenched at the thought. They both thought I was Sir Hubert. Everyone but Oaf thought I was Sir Hubert, and I didn't want that. I wanted someone to know who I was and still be my ally.

Crumbling on the floor, I lay there in agony and didn't move until I escaped into sleep.

Chapter 21

Sunlight managed to find its way to me even though I was on the floor on the far side of my bed. There was a pillow under my head and the blanket from my bed had been draped over me. How had that happened?

I heard the click of my door, and it was pushed just barely open. Whoever was on the other side pushed the door open all the way when she saw I was awake.

"Are you all right, my lord?" Alyss asked in a worried voice.

I put a hand to my head. I had a slight headache, but I was all right. My intense feelings had dulled and I was more myself.

"Yes," I said as I tried to shake sleep from my head. It was tournament day. "Did you do this?" I gestured to the blanket.

Alyss nodded. "Oh, my lord! I'm so sorry. I should have stopped you playing that prank on Oaf! He can be a beastly horrid sort, he can! He seems harmless and fun one moment but so frightening and dangerous the next! Everyone knows he's in league with—"

"Peace, Alyss, you have nothing to be—wait. What? What about Oaf?"

"He's awful!"

"No, not that part. The last thing you were going to say."

Alyss was silent for a second, trying in the midst of obvious concern to retrace her train of thought back to what she had been going to say. "You mean about how he works with the counselors?"

"He's in league with the counselors," I said. Of course he was. How else could he get such fine ale? That explained how he knew some of the things he knew, especially if one of Gridian's counselors had come to Seacrest. What on earth were they waiting for? Any of Gridian's counselors would not hesitate a second to kill me. Then perhaps I was right. Perhaps they just weren't entirely sure about me yet, or else they were waiting for the right moment, for me to really betray myself.

"Sir Hubert, you . . . he didn't tell you . . . did he?"

"Who, Oaf? Tell me what?"

Alyss looked down, began to wind her apron in her fingers, and wouldn't meet eyes with me. "Nothing," she said softly.

I got up and crossed the distance between us, kneeling in front of her so I could meet her downcast eyes, and unwound her hand from her apron, holding both her hands in mine. I made her uncomfortable, probably because she thought I was a noble and because I still didn't have my shirt on, but I needed to know whatever she did. "You don't have to be afraid of him, you know," I consoled her. "I'm distracting him far too much for him to do anything to you," I said with a smile. "He hasn't done anything to you, has he?"

Alyss shook her head. "It's not me you should be worried about, my lord. It's you! It's him! Oaf loves to blackmail. The counselors pay him good ale to find things out about people. Sometimes he tells them and sometimes he uses what he learns for other things. He'll hurt you. He finds out your secrets and he'll hurt you or use you."

"What hold does he have on you, Alyss?" I asked gently. Maybe it didn't matter as far as it concerned me, but I wanted to know as much about my enemy as I could, and maybe see if I couldn't free her somehow. Besides, the Farrago in me didn't like to see anyone in such distress if there was something I could do about it.

"Please, sir, it—it was just once. It was nothing. There was no queen for such a long time. No one was using them. Some of the other maids and I—we just tried on some of the dresses when no one was looking. Except Oaf caught me. He knows. He said it could get me in trouble, but he wouldn't tell if I did what he said. So last night he came at me and I—" She looked miserable. She didn't want to tell me, but she was going to. "I told him about the mop water in his bottle, and that's why he put the spider in your food." She began to cry. "I'm so sorry, my lord! You've been very kind to me, and I repay you with that!"

Personally I was relieved. I had worried it was something much worse. In fact, just to prove it, I laughed. "Oh, Alyss! I never wondered how he found out it was me. I expected him to know. If he had to go frightening you to learn about that prank, then he's not as clever as we thought. And just for the record, you can't get in trouble for the dresses. Even if Oaf strode right up and told the queen, she wouldn't care one jot. In fact, she'd probably let you try them on all you wanted. Don't let him get his way anymore, all right?"

Alyss's face lightened considerably. "Really?" she asked. "Y-yes. Yes, my lord!" She went into a low curtsy.

I released her hands and stepped back. "Now, off with you. I've got a tournament today."

"Yes, my lord!" Alyss said again, wiping her eyes and scurrying to the door. She paused before she exited. "I hope you win, my lord!" and she ducked away. She was a nice girl. And pretty. I imagined her sitting in front of Leofrick as he played, and I made up my mind to introduce them . . . someday.

But pox. There it was again. Blast it all, I didn't want it, this king business. Somehow, someday, I wanted to be me again. With Thea. I very much doubted I would be able to be me again without her anyway.

Oh well. First things first. I had to go steal some clothes.

Sir Reginald had some very fine clothes that fit me well. Green and a deep brown. They felt suitable for a tournament day. Now, breakfast.

Suitors were still trickling in to the dining hall, and I was pleased I wasn't late. After my talk with Alyss, I was feeling much better, so I didn't even mind greeting Kazim at the table.

"How are you today, my friend?"

It took me a moment to realize he was talking about the spider from yesterday. The memory made me shudder, but I shook it off quickly. "Quite well," I said truthfully. "Um, thank you. For killing it. It did . . . catch me by surprise."

Kazim gave me a knowing look. He already knew that spiders terrified me, but he didn't press the point or rub it in. I listened again for the nagging feeling that told me not to trust him. It was still there, and I knew it was right because that same nag had told me to be nicer to Constance even though I hadn't been.

"I notice I haven't seen Seht with you for the past few

days," I mentioned as we ate fruit and bread. This morning I avoided the pastries.

Kazim smiled. "He has been away doing some digging for me on some of the other suitors, just the ones I am concerned about. He got back late last night. He is sleeping now, but he will be at the tournament."

"Oh." I took a bite from an apple. I hadn't missed him. I was only glad that Kazim obviously was not wasting time digging dirt on me. "Where is the tournament, exactly?"

"The tournament grounds out past the town. I visited it yesterday. The peasants are probably gathering there now."

"What? You mean the whole kingdom gets to watch us?"

Kazim shrugged. "Naturally. They are the ones to be ruled, after all."

"Oh, yes. Naturally." I snagged a large sausage. I hoped the day would only be marginally humiliating.

Very quickly it seemed we were riding down to the stadium followed by small crowds of raggedy-looking children. Most of the kingdom was already there surrounding the arena and filling long benches. The greater part of the arena held a long jousting divider, and closest to the canopy where the royalty sat was a large circle marked off for hand-to-hand combat. That's where I would be fighting. That's where I would see if one day of flail practice and nearly a lifetime of juggling would save me.

On a raised platform with a beautifully decorated canopy sat all the counselors, several nobles, and, of course, Thea. Thea looked too beautiful for being seen as a mere trinket to win one a kingdom. In part it was her own fault. She never should have put egg white in her hair. She should have left it in all its dandelion glory. That would have been a better way to weed out the unworthy than this ridiculous tournament.

Then I saw Seht leaning against the dais and momentarily forgot about Thea because he was smiling at me the way a vulture would smile at a dead dog, if vultures could smile. Oh, how I'd missed him. Missed him the way I missed a stomachache.

Since we had met eyes, I smiled back and looked into the crowd of faces, giving a small signal to no one in particular. Seht's face immediately became serious as he tried to follow my gaze to see who I'd signaled to. He ran into the crowd, no doubt in hopes of putting a face to my nonexistent manservant. I felt a lot better.

"Hubert." Kazim's voice pulled me out of my thoughts. "Hubert, did you know? I didn't think you jousted."

I gave him my full attention. "What are you talking about?"

"The schedule for the first combatants. You're first, and you're not in hand-to-hand combat. You're up to joust with Lord Percival."

Pox that Oaf. And the counselors. They had to be setting me up for failure.

"I'll get them to change it," Kazim insisted.

"No." I shook my head. There was no point. "No. I'm sure they can't change it. I'll just—I'll just figure it out. Don't worry about me."

Kazim nodded, but he looked sorry. Why? *Why did he look sorry?* The man was starting to convince me he was more of a fool than I was. There was no possible reason for him to want me to succeed in any of this. I didn't understand.

Oh, well. I had other things to worry about. Two squires ran up to me and took the reins of my horse.

"This way, my lord," they said. "Jousters are outfitted in that tent." They pointed to a blue tent just outside the arena and pulled my horse along. I didn't look back at Kazim. Once at the tent, I dismounted, let the squires take my horse, and entered the tent to get outfitted for my probable demise.

"Tom!"

Tom was bent over a grinding wheel sharpening an ax. He stopped and held the blade up to his eye. "I didn't think you jousted, Sir Hubert," he said, setting the ax down.

"I don't! The counselors have it in for me. I haven't even seen what other events I'm signed up for."

"You're in the ring with whatever weapon you choose for your other events. But first you have to get past Lord Percival."

"Tom, I've never jousted a day in my life."

He nodded. "I figured. I don't think you have much hope, but I'll tell you all I can. Come on then."

Tom fitted me with some chain mail and then some heavy armor, all the while talking about how one jousts.

"It takes months of practice to hold a lance," he said, picking one off a rack in the tent and handing it to me so I could feel its weight. "The rules are different for actual tournaments, but here, you'll only joust until one of you knocks the other off the horse. See that?" Tom touched the tip of the lance and I shifted my hold so I could see it too. The tip was a metal spread with three small stubby points. "That's called a coronal. It's designed to not pierce good armor, just to force you off your horse."

"All I have to do is stay on my horse . . . ," I wondered aloud. "Tom, perhaps I should tell you: I'm not really against cheating at all."

Tom paused as he took the lance from me to put back on its rack. "Me neither." And he smiled in a way that made me like him a lot more.

Chapter 22

I could only see through a small slit in my helmet, and my breath hit me back in the face each time I exhaled. I suddenly felt very strange. Unpleasantly strange. Fear. Had I been afraid before? Yes. When Fendral left, and when I'd put a hand on Constance's shoulder to comfort her after Thea left. This was different. This was like running from soldiers on the street as a child, except here I was supposed to run *toward* him. And he would certainly be running at me.

I heard a crier announce something I couldn't hear fully, and then my horse jolted as someone hit his rump. My steed shot out into the field straight toward Lord Percival.

I believe it took me about a second to decide I absolutely detested jousting. It was impossible. Bouncing with the horse, I could barely see through the slit in the helmet much less hold my stupid lance straight. But Tom had told me that without having ever practiced, I shouldn't expect to do any better. My only goal was to stay on the horse, and the rope under my breast shield and knotted around the horn of my saddle should help with that.

To my credit, when Lord Percival and I finally came within lance range, my lance scraped his side. True, it didn't hit straight on, but at least I didn't look like a *complete* beginner.

Lord Percival's lance, as expected, hit me square in the chest.

The fastness and sheer weight of it took me by surprise. I'd had no time or means to prepare for what it would actually be like. The rope around my middle went taut against the saddle, which pulled at the saddle straps and, of course, at the horse.

The horse must have been surprised as well; he couldn't have been expecting to feel himself thrust backward as well. So my steed, mid gallop, was forced to rear back. Tom had told me to lean back as far as I could once I was hit so that the horse could keep running, but the rope had risen to above my belly button as I'd ridden, and I couldn't fall back as I should have.

In the frozen seconds after I was hit, I realized what would happen. The horse would have to fall, and my legs would be crushed if the horse didn't end up on his back, in which case all of me would be crushed.

Without thinking, I brought my left wrist up to the rope even as I was falling. Tom had concealed a small knife there to cut the rope afterwards. Quickly, with a single slice, the already taut rope snapped. I hit the ground first, tipping and landing on my back, and then it was head over heels away from the horse, who hit the ground just missing me.

So I was unhorsed. I'd lost. Oh well. That was to be expected. If I won my other two matches then I would still be able to compete to the next rounds. The knife had even jabbed into the dirt instead of into me somewhere. I was pretty rattled and felt, well, *bent* would be the best word, I guess. I stayed still for a few moments before deciding it was safe to move. My horse, still flailing his legs, hurriedly got to his hooves and bucked away, snorting angrily as attendants came to catch him. I began to shed my armor. The whole event had been pretty bad, but it could have been worse. I suppose I just should have forgotten the rope in the first place. Pox whomever had signed me up for this.

Oh, wait. I knew. The counselors. My dear friends. Pox them forever.

A few squires helped me to my feet as Lord Percival took a victory lap. I was surprised that with the armor on I had felt only pressure, not pain from the blow. I raised my arm to show the crowd I was not dead, and there was a round of polite applause. Feeling a tad fragile, I made my way back to Tom's tent.

"Well, *that* didn't work," I announced as I sat on the ground.

"You're not hurt?" Tom asked, putting a hand on my shoulder.

I shook my head. "A bit shaken is all."

"Sir Hubert," Tom said in a way that commanded my attention. I looked up at him. "I'm truly sorry it didn't work."

It was strange to hear an apology coming from such a burly, rough-looking man. But he was sincere. "I do not blame you, Tom," I assured him.

"You'll win your next two bouts," he said, "and then you can still work your way to the top. You must try to win."

All right, I had to ask. "Why?"

"Because I'd rather have you on the throne than some stuffed-shirt pompous prince, that's why. Seacrest has had enough of them."

I supposed that was a compliment. "Thank you," I said with a shake of my head. He wouldn't get what he wanted, but he was being nice all the same. "Who's my next match?"

"You're in the ring with a Sir Leon."

"Grand. I'll get my flail."

By this time I had decided that I liked the name of my weapon about as much as the weapon itself. The name had about as much grace as I felt like I did in a fighting situation.

I had to wait for one more joust and two more battles before it was my turn again. Kazim won his own bout so quickly that I became more convinced he wasn't to be trusted. A few quick strokes with his light scimitar and his opponent was unarmed and on his knees with Kazim's sword at his throat. Alain was plenty good with a sword as well, though it took him longer to best his own opponent.

Then it was my turn again. In the ring, we wore chain mail over our heads and a mail shirt with a breastplate and some strategically placed armor on our arms and legs. I didn't like the weight, but all I really needed was the use of my arms to throw my flail and the ability to sidestep blows.

Sir Leon, when he wasn't dressed for battle, always seemed to have his eyebrows raised as if he was either surveying everything around him or else hadn't quite made up his mind about everything around him. I had heard him laugh once at dinner, and it was annoying. Donkey brays were more pleasant. He must have been aware of how hideous his laugh was because that was the only time I'd heard him. His hair was golden brown and tightly curled. More than once I'd had to resist the urge to stretch out one of the small curls and let it go. Other than that, he had high cheekbones and a strong jawline that women-folk found attractive. Well, Kazim was concerned about him because of his looks anyway.

We stood in opposite ends of the circle surrounded by peasant-folk cheering and shouting. A crier stood ready to hit a gong.

"Ready!" the crier yelled. Sir Leon drew his sword, and I held the long chain of my flail in my left hand as I began to twirl the small spiked ball in the other. The stick was still at my hip. I heard a murmur from the crowd. Some of it was laughter but most of it was curiosity. Flails weren't normally used like this. The chains were shorter, the balls bigger, and the wielder held on to his weapon by the stick, never by the chain. Well, they were about to be surprised.

"Fight!" I heard the crier shout. Sir Leon, holding his sword with both hands, came at me at a run, bringing his sword down heavily over his shoulder. I sidestepped him easily and flung the ball at the back of his head, making him fall to his knees. The crowd laughed. Leon got quickly to his feet to come at me again. He didn't charge, but he took calculated steps forward as he swung his sword, forcing me to step backwards. With each swing, I sent the ball of my flail to hit the blade aside. I just needed a good angle. Finally, Leon brought both arms to one side for a particularly hard swing that would certainly knock me down if it made contact. But in his preparation, he also made himself completely vulnerable. I saw my opportunity and threw the flail.

The spiked ball brought the chain around the sword at least three times, and with a hard yank to one side, Leon suddenly had no sword.

Leon swung only his hands, throwing himself off balance, and before he could get up again I picked up his own sword and held it to the neck of the weaponless Leon, still trying to figure out what had happened.

"Do you yield?" I demanded, pressing the sword just under his chin where the chain mail didn't cover.

Leon still looked a little surprised. Looking up at me, he chuckled, which fortunately wasn't as bad as his all-out laugh. "Sure," he said with a shrug. "I guess so."

The crowd roared. And I was only getting started.

Next I fought Duke Ellington, an average-sized man at least ten years older than me with an unfortunate turn up to his nose, making him look a tad piglike. Before he had swung his first blow, his sword was out of his hands and the tip was at his throat. It didn't make him look good, but he was never really in the running anyway. He was ugly, short, old, and not particularly bright. Like Kazim had thought, no worries there.

I raised both fists in the air and let my head fall back. I had won two of my three initial battles. I was still in the fight! Huzzah!

Even after Lord Walter, Sir Marcus, Prince Meldon, Sir Miles, and even Sir Reginald, I still hadn't lost a bout. Since so few of the suitors preferred jousting, it was all hand-to-hand combat now, and none of them quite knew how to defend against a flail with a sword. I even had a rematch with Lord Percival.

Lord Percival was a great bearded fearsome lump whose obvious strength was, well, strength. He couldn't quite manage to swat the ball aside with his sword, and his blade made contact with the chain early. To his credit, it actually slipped off twice. He had been watching me and wasn't about to let his sword go for the world.

After my second failed attempt to get his sword from

him, he was feeling pretty good about himself, and I was a little worried. I really did not want to lose to this guy again. So when Lord Percival swung both arms to one side for what he undoubtedly expected to be my final blow, I threw my flail around his ankles and tripped him up.

He hit hard.

Quickly pulling my flail back, I stood on his wrists so that he couldn't lift his sword, spinning my weapon to land a blow on his head if I needed to.

"Do you yield?" I threatened, spinning the spiked ball in a blur.

Percival made a sour face and grumbled something.

"Sorry?" I said, almost hoping I'd be able to hit him again.

Percival glared at me. "Fine," he said. "I yield."

Ha!

Of course, all of my fights happened between all the other suitor's matches. Kazim and Alain had yet to lose. Both of them wielded swords that could be used with one hand.

For most of his matches, Kazim merely quickly disarmed his foe and held his sword at a vital point. None of his matches had lasted more than a few minutes. Kazim's armor was very light. He wore a small breastplate as his only form of protection.

Then Kazim battled Sir Reginald. By that point, Sir Leon had already been disqualified for losing too many bouts. Sir Reginald fought fiercely and kept Kazim in the ring longer than any opponent so far. Even with both hands, Reginald was fast enough to block most of Kazim's fast slices. Then Reginald, during a brief pause while they both caught their breaths, backed up for a running blow and took off at Kazim.

Usually, such moves were easy to sidestep, though they did put terrific force behind the blows. Kazim wasn't weakened enough for the move to threaten him, but as he stepped to one side for the two of them to trade sides in the ring, he brought the sharp curve of his blade across the unprotected back of Reginald's ankle.

It had been such a small and quick slash that most of the audience hadn't caught it.

Reginald stumbled, falling to one knee. He jumped up again, turning, but as soon as he tried to take another step, he fell.

Reginald couldn't use the foot that Kazim had slashed. He was finished.

There was something deliberate in Kazim's move that troubled me, and I couldn't shake the feeling that Kazim had saved that cut for his last few opponents. And it hadn't escaped my notice that before this tournament was over, I'd have to face him.

I was so troubled by Kazim's disabling blow to Reginald that perhaps that was why I didn't fare so well against Alain.

Alain favored a long sword, but it was either light enough or else he was strong enough to wield it with one hand. His extended reach and swiftness of movement had been distinct advantages that had served him well. Also, it was to my disadvantage that he'd already had opportunity to observe me in the ring and knew how I fought. Alain was swift enough to block the spiked ball when I threw it. Then he deliberately let the chain catch his blade, brought his blade to the ground, and stepped on the chain as he pulled his sword free. Holding the blade to my neck, he forced me to yield.

If I lost against Kazim, then I had lost the tournament. But first, the battle was between Alain and Kazim.

It was Alain's stick-straight long sword against Kazim's curved Persian scimitar. They each held their sword in one hand, and had won all their matches mostly due to their speed. The crowd was eerily silent.

"Fight!" the crier yelled.

Kazim and Alain reacted in the same instant, meeting swords midway. Blows and blocks continued to clang out faster than any sword match through the entire tournament. Neither was getting any points off the other.

I'll admit, I was worried. It wasn't the same fear I felt when I'd been about to joust with Percival. It was just a powerful uneasiness. Kazim was going to do something awful to Alain before the fight was over. Part of me wanted to look away and not watch it, but I couldn't quite bring myself to do it. After all, I'd be fighting Kazim next.

The fight went strong without slowing for several minutes. They'd have to wear each other down until one of them made a mistake big enough for the other to take advantage of. I kept waiting for Kazim to try to slash Alain's foot.

Then Alain took a risk and stopped his blows long enough to take a powerful thrust at Kazim, undoubtedly hoping the greater length of his sword would give him the advantage he needed.

Kazim was barely able to sidestep it; the sword caught his tunic to the side of his small breastplate and tore a hole through. Without missing a beat, Kazim brought his sword down across Alain's unprotected and vulnerable face.

The crowd gasped. For an instant, Alain stood there with his eyes wide, trying to get his mind around what had just happened. Slowly, a red streak began to glow on his face from his left temple down to the right side of his chin, jumping his eye, missing his nose, and slicing his lips. With a cry, Alain dropped his sword and fell to his knees, covering his face. Blood seeped through his fingers. Kazim pointed his sword at the fallen prince but didn't ask if he yielded. He merely stood watching with his sword at the ready. But something was wrong. Alain cried out again, but it wasn't because of pain, and it wasn't because he'd lost the tournament. I felt sick inside. There had been something deliberate in that particular blow, something sinister. Finally, the crier named Kazim as the victor, and attendants came to lead Alain away to get his face looked at.

Then it was my turn to fight Kazim in the ring.

CHAPTER 23

I was deep in thought as I adjusted my chain mail. I shed some of the armor on my arms and legs. Anything to make me faster. Besides, I doubted Kazim would slash those. After thinking it over, I strapped my arm coverings to the back of my heels, protecting the place that Kazim had slashed on Reginald. As for my face, well, I guess there wasn't too much to do about that. If Kazim decided to carve my face, I'd never been particularly handsome to begin with.

Kazim was tired; that was at least something to my advantage. We made eye contact from across the ring. At first, Kazim looked only tired and maybe even sad. But then his face composed itself into a peaceful mask of docility. He looked calm. Regal even. It was like he had shaken off the last fight as if it had never happened. There was something about his look that calmed me as well, as if he was telling me not to worry. Well, no such luck. I was still uneasy. Maybe after this whole tournament was over I would feel better. If I wasn't dead, I was sure Kazim would tell me why he had done what he'd done to his last two opponents.

Then the crier shouted, "Ready!" and then "Fight!" and I stopped wondering about what had just happened and put all my concentration into that second.

Kazim did not spring right away as he'd done with Alain. With sword drawn, we circled each other, my flail humming at my side as I spun it, trying to decide what best to do. Just as a test, I threw my flail out a few times. Kazim knocked the ball back easily each time. Then Kazim attacked, coming at me swiftly. I stopped spinning the flail and used just the chain to block his sword, stretching a section between my hands and forcing the blade just past its mark every time. Kazim stepped back and smiled in an encouraging way.

I tried to ignore his face, and instead spun my flail again and sent it toward his ankles, hoping to trip him up. Kazim jumped and dodged my throws easily. Pox. I'd known that none of my previous moves would work. How else could I use my flail?

Kazim came at me again, and we had another round of my blocking his blade with my chain. He was very fast, but I still sensed he was going easy on me. He had pummeled Alain relentlessly until he'd found an in to throw a blow. He paused between attacks now. Perhaps it was because he was tired, but I didn't think so. In any case, I was certainly feeling myself wearing down. Kazim's sword was difficult to block with only a chain.

Trying to think of something Kazim wouldn't, I threw my flail again, this time wrapping around his wrist, binding him to his sword. If only he'd been holding it with both hands, I might have been able to do something. Yanking, I jerked Kazim off balance. His collected face cracked with surprise and annoyance. As he fell, he brought his other hand around and shoved the chain off his wrist and onto the blade. Before he could pull his sword free, I pulled down on the chain, forcing the blade into the dirt. I smiled.

I shouldn't have.

I don't think Kazim planned it; I think he just reacted, because there's no way he could have known. I'd almost even forgotten myself.

With his blade down, Kazim brought the hilt of his sword up and rammed me directly in the middle of my face.

I heard a cracking sound. My eyes filled with tears as pain filled my face. I lifted a hand to cover my nose and pull away.

My false nose had shattered.

Well, not entirely; it had cracked. Some shards had flown off, but I could feel most of my false nose still on my face. I could also feel blood, warm and flowing. If I hadn't had something to hide, I would have continued fighting, but this kind of blow would reveal me. I had lost.

Putting both hands to my face, I dropped my flail.

"Jug-oh!"

It was a little cry of fear, and I knew exactly who it belonged to. I tried to lift my head just a little, but my eyes were still tearing too much to see properly.

"Jug-oh man!"

I think I was more worried that she was concerned about me than that someone might actually be able to understand what she was saying. She shouldn't be watching this. I just needed to get off the field.

"Yield," I whispered. It was difficult to speak normally, my voice sounded clogged with my nose cracked, so I tried to use as few words as possible.

Kazim righted himself and held the tip of the sword in my face until the crier announced him as victor. In the next instant, Kazim was at my side before the attendants got there.

"Are you all right?" he asked earnestly. "What—what happened?"

You rammed me in the face! That's *what happened*, I wanted to say but of course couldn't. At least his statement confirmed that he hadn't known about my nose; he just didn't understand about the sound or the few shards raining down, or why I had quit at such a minor wound.

Not that I was going to confess anything to Kazim. I pulled away from him and let the attendants escort me to a nursing tent inhabited by physicians.

"A bandage. All I need is a bandage," I begged of them, trying to swat their hands away.

One of the physicians knelt in front of me. It was a girl. A nurse. She wore a white wimple that framed a round and very young face. I finally let her bring my hands down and slipped the largest pieces of the false nose into one of my boots. The whole thing had broken off into two main pieces with probably hundreds of dust-like shards.

"Oh, that's—" She put some fingers on the bridge of my nose and pressed. It didn't hurt. It would have hurt if Kazim had struck my real nose. "—unusual," my nurse finished. She probably didn't see many nose wounds that changed the victim's nose from round to beak-like. The spinster had given me a spare nose, but it was back at the castle in my small bag with my fool's clothes. I would have to keep *this* nose covered until I got back and could put it on.

Still, it wasn't until the fake nose came off that I realized how uncomfortable and irritating it had really been. And surely, it must have made me look so ugly. So many of the suitors had such flawless faces. How could I really expect Thea to fall in love with Sir Hubert?

My nurse took a wet rag and dabbed the blood away and cleaned my face. She gave me a wad of a rag to stem the continued bleeding, but that was all I needed. Had it not been protected, my nose would have been broken.

I could hold the rag there enough to cover my true nose until I was able to replace it, but I decided to take a long strip of rag and tie the lump in place over my nose so that no one would ask to see on my way back. Everyone knows there's nothing more attractive than tying a great bloody lump of cloth to your face.

Pox.

When I came out of the tent, all of the suitors, some of them bandaged and sitting but most of them still in good order, had all lined up in front of the canopied dais where Thea and the counselors sat. All except Alain.

Kazim stood in front of the line, directly in front of Thea. Thea looked worried. Her lips were pressed tightly together as she rose to her feet.

"Prince Kazim!" the announcer was shouting. "You have bested all of your opponents in combat and are hereby declared the victor of this Tournament of Princes!"

The audience applauded and shouted appropriately, but I couldn't quite decide if they were pleased about the outcome or merely fulfilling their role as onlookers.

"And as winner, you shall be bestowed the crest of Seacrest!"

A page handed Thea a small pillow. Thea took a round golden medallion on a wide blue ribbon from the pillow and held it up. Kazim stepped forward and Thea placed the crest over his head.

"And a kiss from our beautiful queen!"

I gasped. Now? Just like that? The crowd murmured in excitement. Thea went pale and looked with large eyes at the announcer like she was deciding if she had been left the power to hang those who displeased her.

Kazim stayed calm and quickly snatched Thea's hand, pressing his lips lightly against it before releasing slowly. I saw Thea exhale. The crowd groaned in disappointment.

"Oh, fine," the announcer corrected. "To be *properly* given, I'm sure, after their exclusive dance at the suitor's ball tonight. Look well, you who dwell in the great kingdom of Seacrest. He could be your new king!"

More polite applause. I wondered if the kingdom now really favored Kazim, or if they were just playing their part. The crowd began to disperse, heading back to their run-down dwellings and sagging kingdom.

I wondered if it was pointless for me to remain in Seacrest.

Once back at the castle, I pulled my small bag out from under my bed and hunted around for the spare nose the spinster had put in, snugly tucked and wrapped in my patched fool's clothes. I ran my fingers over some of the patches and felt a horrible sadness. There was the yellow of Fendral's shirt, and the cream of Thea's sharing the space over my heart. There was Leofrick's after that, and over my belly a dark square from Constance.

"Farrago," I whispered, tapping my own chest and drinking in the sound of my own name. "Farrago." I closed my eyes and imagined myself performing in Gridian Court again, eleven balls dancing in the air. I felt my fingers twitch hungrily with the memory of juggling. Then I looked back at Thea's patch. The one she herself had stitched so close to my heart.

"I'm so sorry I didn't catch on sooner," I whispered to the patch, to Thea as if she could hear. "I guess that's the risk you take if you fall in love with a fool. It's not entirely my fault, you know. I didn't—I just didn't *know*. I just didn't *think*." If only I had caught on sooner. Maybe Thea and I would have been married before anyone ever came to make her a queen. What would they have done then? Would they have made me king? Would someone have killed me off to make room for a real one? Would they have had me compete in this same ridiculous competition to prove myself? I guess I'd never know. I had been too thick to figure things out sooner.

"I think I probably had your first kiss," I mused to Thea's patch. "I'm sorry I didn't win your second, but I will have your last."

There. A new promise I wasn't sure I could keep. Bring them on.

A quick trip to the kitchen and I had stuck my new nose on with some honey and the bleeding had ebbed.

I was my blob-nosed Sir Hubert all cleaned up again. My tunic was a light grayish-silver that I hoped made me stand out. Alain hadn't been in his room, so I'd borrowed another one of his tunics because they fit so well. He had good taste in clothes.

I entered the ballroom. Of all the rooms that looked like they had had a beating in the hands of the throne usurpers, this room looked as if it had been protected. The extravagant, checkered-tiled expanse of a room was currently well lit with torches and candles and a roaring fire at the far end. Tables lined one end of the room filled with trays to be picked from for dinner that night, and chairs lined the walls. Some couples were already dancing as a small band of minstrels played in the corner. They were very good, but all of them very old. Once they were gone, Seacrest would undoubtedly be hard-put to find new ones.

I saw Thea sitting in a chair at the opposite end from the huge fireplace with Valyn next to her. I had never seen her so well adorned. Her golden dress matched the small crown on her head, the hair folded up flawlessly under it. The glow bounced of her skin and made her look radiant. If only she didn't look so put out. The two of them were speaking rapidly to each other, and while I had the impression that Valyn was trying to calm her queen down, I couldn't hear them exactly.

Then I made the mistake of looking around again. Kazim was right next to me. I jumped.

"Sorry," Kazim said immediately. "I didn't realize you hadn't heard me approach. I see the bleeding has stopped."

I composed myself, putting on a casual face. "Think nothing of it. And, yes, my nose is feeling much better."

"You wear a false one. Why?"

I kept my face on, but I felt my anxiety rise. "Have you told anyone else it is false? Do you think they already know?"

Kazim shook his head. "I do not believe so. They did not feel the crack when my hilt hit your face, nor did they notice or examine the small shards that fell. And I see you have a new one, so they will not suspect. Do not worry. I have told no one. Why do you wear it?"

Kazim was not about to get a word of truth out of me about that. "I find my real one rather unbecoming."

"You might have done with a better replacement," Kazim pointed out.

"I'll tell you what," I said, hiding my irritation with him, "once this suitor business is ended, I'll explain in more detail. Agreed?"

Kazim nodded. "I know I have no right to ask you about your secrets. You can hide what you wish. I only hope that—" he broke off, looking troubled.

"Hope that?" I prodded.

"Hope that it is not anything that would come between me and my end. For your sake, Sir Hubert. I like you."

"Is that why you spared me in the ring? You surely could have done worse."

"You were better in the tournament than I thought you'd be; better than you let on. You were difficult because I had never fought with such a weapon before, but I had been able to study you. If I had fought you first, you might have beaten me."

"Really?"

Kazim shook his head. "No. Not really. I was never going to lose."

"What did you do to Reginald and Alain?"

Kazim sighed and his eyes squinted a little more with thought. "I only crippled Reginald so that he could not dance with the queen tonight. He will heal in time."

"And Alain?"

Kazim's face became hard. He took a moment before replying. "I broke him," he said in a deep and even voice.

"Broke . . . what do you mean?" I was feeling sick again.

Kazim looked at me. There was both determination and remorse on his face. It was an odd combination. "Prince Alain was continually proving himself my most threatening competitor in all areas. While eavesdropping on the conversations of the counselors, I learned that he was additionally favored because he was a native of this country. Otherwise, we might have been equal. And that was not good enough. On his travels, Seht visited Alain's land. He learned only one thing that I thought I could use: Alain is very vain."

I opened my mouth to speak, but nothing came out. Kazim caught my feeling.

"I did not enjoy it. I regret that it was necessary. Finding how to break someone is one thing, carrying it out is . . . distasteful. And delicate."

"Where is Alain now?"

"I heard that he was preparing to leave. I have not seen him since—"

"Since you cut his face off," I snapped quickly before I could catch myself. And I also wasn't sure Alain was preparing to leave, because I had just raided his closet and it didn't look like anything had been packed.

Kazim bristled. "I attacked an undesirable weakness. I could have just killed him."

"He probably prefers that you had."

"Probably." Kazim rubbed his temples with a hand and took a deep breath. "Do not think less of me, my friend. I could have done worse."

"Would you have done worse to me?"

"I had hoped to merely threaten you quickly enough that you had to surrender. I had no plans for wounding you. I had to be quick when fighting against your flail became—frustrating."

I felt a sudden, powerful loathing for Kazim that took me a moment to smother. I could not have him as an enemy yet. If he knew how I was truly connected to Thea, my life would have several reasons to be over quickly; I was beginning to feel how fragile my life could be if I made a wrong move.

"Oh, I don't think less of you," I lied with a smile. "I do not want the same thing you want." Truth. "I was merely enquiring about your techniques and how much you had thought them through." Half-truth. "You're very . . ."—think, think, think—"formidable in your goals." Truth. Very much a truth. There. Had I balanced them all out?

"Thank you." Kazim put on his usual face, the one that came across as both beautiful and harmless. He patted my shoulder. "Let's enjoy the ball."

"Yes, let's." I squinched my face into a tight fake smile once he turned his back.

But as for "enjoying the ball," no such luck.

It started out pleasant enough. I was starving and quickly filled my gullet with various delicacies from the tables: small roast quails, rolls, potatoes, deviled eggs, fruits, ham, fish, and little hard things I couldn't figure out how to eat. A page showed me that they were clams and you had to break them open. Apparently they were a "live by the sea" kind of thing. They also tasted like gristle, which as far as I was concerned was an "I'm so hungry I'll eat anything" thing, which I was, so I did. A pig with an apple in its mouth was sitting on a bed of greens with onions surrounding it. I slipped an onion in my tunic for later.

I was just washing out the taste of the clams with some wine when I chanced a glance over to the far wall lined with chairs. Sitting out of the way on a chair near the door was Oaf. Seht stood next to him. I wasn't sure if they were having a conversation or not, because I'd never heard Seht speak a word of English. But he was looking at Oaf with a grin as Oaf spoke. All I saw was Oaf take a finger, trace down his face, and laugh. Seht smiled wider and nodded.

I felt my muscles tighten again. It was obvious who

they were speaking about. I had hoped to avoid Oaf, and I would have even then—

If he didn't have Alyss on his knee.

Alyss sat very still with her head lowered, hands clasped in her lap, looking as if she was pretending not to be there. Oaf had an arm lightly around her waist. She glanced up and met eyes with me. Afraid, she gave the barest shake of her head.

Don't do anything, she seemed to be saying. *He wants a scene.*

Of course he wanted a scene.

Noticing Alyss's movement, Oaf turned away from Seht and saw me. His smile was delighted and inviting. He was practically begging me to react. He lifted a hand and ran his fingers down one of Alyss's braids. I looked away quickly, certain that if I gave him too much attention he'd probably kiss her, and I knew that if he did, he would get the scene he wanted.

I set my cup down and looked around the room. Thea and Valyn were no longer sitting where they'd been. I had to find them. I began running through the ballroom dodging groups of people in conversation.

There they were. Talking to Sir Reginald who was sitting with a bandaged foot and one crutch, obviously telling the queen and her lady-in-waiting about the fight and trying to downplay his injury.

"Valyn!" I ran up to her. Valyn turned from the conversation to look at me, raising her eyebrows with a look that I usually only got when I was Farrago. I tried not to look at Thea. "Um . . . I . . . my maid made up my room with too many pillows the other night, and I was thinking that they should maybe be moved to Sir Reginald's room, considering his injury. During the ball would probably be the best time. Like right now. You're in charge of the maids, right? I think my maid's name is Alyss. She's over there, looking terribly idle for a chambermaid, don't you think?"

"But I don't—" Sir Reginald started, but I kicked him—in his good leg—and he started again. "Ah, well that's very considerate of you, Sir Hubert. I'm sure I would be glad of . . . an extra pillow."

". . . Yes," Valyn said suspiciously. "Well, that's a fine gesture. I'll go tell her of your request."

"Actually," I stopped her, speaking softly, "if you must, tell them it was Sir Reginald's idea and leave my name out of it. Please?"

Valyn was giving me the strangest look. "V-very well, Sir Hubert. I'll be right back." She walked off. I forced myself to not watch and tried not to look too triumphant. Well, I may have given a casual glance just enough to see Valyn bark a quick order and Alyss jump off Oaf's lap and run away. Victory. And no scene made.

Plus, I was with Thea.

"Oh! Good evening, Your Majesty," I said as if I'd just noticed her. "What did you think of the tournament?"

Thea's eyes narrowed. She didn't like me, but I didn't mind because I knew the only reason she didn't like me was because I reminded her of me.

And that made me smile.

"It was, um . . ." She struggled for a word. ". . . diverting." She hadn't appreciated it. Men beating on each other to show off probably wasn't her idea of romantic. "How's your nose?" With a curious look, she raised a hand to touch it.

I leaned back. She'd surely be able to tell it was fake if

she touched it, plus it wasn't stuck on as well as the last one. "It's still very tender," I half-lied. "It could have been a lot worse. The bleeding has stopped, anyway."

"Well, good," she said idly, lowering her hand.

"Are you looking forward to your dance with Prince Kazim? I was confused about the kiss. Did the hand count?"

Thea's eyebrows came together with worry, but she seemed to catch that her face was telling too much of her mind. She tried to smother it with no doubt what Valyn had told her was a more arrogant and queenly look. The actual result forced me to bite my lip to keep from laughing.

"I don't know," she tried to say casually. "I haven't had a chance to speak to him about it yet."

"Ah." I reached into my tunic and pulled out the onion, taking a large bite as if it had been an apple.

"Maggoty meal, Hubert! What are you doing?"

"Hmm?" *Ow.* My eyes began to water as the onion burned my mouth and throat. "Oh, sometimes my head feels a little stuffy." I shrugged. "Onions clear me right up. Want some?" I was sure Kazim would love it if she reeked of onion. Let him try to kiss that. I held the onion out to her. Thea jerked away from my outstretched hand, looking at me like I was the devil himself; not because I had offered her a bite of my onion, but because Farrago was the only person she'd seen eat such a foul raw root like that.

"Ladies and gentlemen!" the announcer from the tournament interrupted us. He parted the crowd with his voice so that the center of the ballroom was clear. "It's time for our victor to start things off for us. Prince Kazim!" The room applauded loudly. Kazim stepped out of the crowd near the announcer and walked purposefully to Thea, who I thought was going to faint, and not for romantic reasons. I tried to figure out what it was she was so concerned about. Kazim cut quite a figure striding across in his princely best. His tunic was a dull bronze color and his leggings and shoes black. The bronze set off his dark skin impressively, and he matched Thea's gown well. Once to Thea, he bowed and offered his arm. Thea hesitated, and I could almost see her throat throb with her heartbeat. Was she nervous about the ball in the first place? Probably. As a scullery maid, participating in a ball like this would be completely new. Had Kazim's success in the tournament bothered her? Likely. Or maybe she was just like any other girl and was intimidated by his looks.

Pox. That was probably it.

A moment before her pause would have become awkward, Thea took his arm and followed him to the floor. A nod from the announcer and the minstrels took up an elegant tune. My enemy and my love began to dance together.

Once she was gone, I suppressed a gag and dropped my onion into the wine cup of Lord Percival as he passed by. Absolutely foul. I wondered what it said about me that I was so willing to torture myself in order to torment Thea. Wiping my mouth on my sleeve, I gathered myself a bit and watched her dance.

Little by little, I was overcome with a sort of restlessness as she twirled and stepped so close to Kazim. I wasn't exactly worried, because I didn't think she liked him, but they made a handsome couple together. Pox! I couldn't stand still. I wanted to do something. Helplessness began to find its way into my restlessness.

I nearly ran into Valyn with my anxious strides. She'd returned quickly after giving Alyss the order that had allowed her to escape from Oaf.

"Oh, sorry, lady." I bowed slightly and stood next to her, trying to hold still. Finally I leaned over to her. "Does she like him?"

"I don't know," Valyn answered readily, staring at them with such intensity that they must have felt it. "She *should*. They make a striking couple, don't you think?"

"Oh, I don't know," I answered a little too swiftly. "The queen comes across as so delicate; I've always thought he looked a bit stiff for her."

"Hmmm," Valyn murmured, taking me completely seriously. She sniffed the air and looked at me with a wrinkled nose. "You reek of onion," she said.

"Thanks," I said back, not taking my eyes off Thea.

I waited several more seconds. "Valyn?" I whispered.

"Yes?" she whispered back.

"Dance with me."

She was aghast. "Why?"

"Because people are supposed to start to dance once the first couple gets it going. That's how we do it in—" wait. Where was I from again? "Poppydown," I finished confidently. "And I'm going crazy standing still." I pulled her onto the floor before she could protest, twisting my head to keep Thea and Kazim in sight.

We passed the happy couple, both of them looking surprised to see someone else dancing, or maybe just surprised to see me. We spun around each other, and I kept trying to meet eyes with Thea. I found that I had to be careful to not dance as Farrago. Most nobles did not spin their partners so much or bend their knees up to their shoulders or arch their backs quite so far. I had to think elegant. And I did, except for one thing.

For part of the dance, I held Valyn by one hand, and

Kazim did the same with Thea. Prancing in opposite directions, we passed each other, and just as I passed Thea, I bobbed my head.

Hopefully not too much, but it was a bob similar to how a chicken moves its head when pecking. I tried to do it when I thought Thea was looking, but it was hard to tell because I didn't look at her directly when I did it.

I only managed to pull the move off twice, and I had no idea if Thea noticed, but I felt good and sneaky. And a little like a chicken.

"Hubert," Valyn said when we were on opposite sides of the ballroom from Thea and Kazim. I looked at her. She had stopped staring at the other couple and was now studying me. "Why did you come to Seacrest?"

"Hm? Oh. Boredom, I guess." I winked.

"So you're not interested in the throne of Seacrest?"

"Absolutely not."

"And the queen?"

I shrugged. "Why should I be interested in the queen?" I chanced a quick glance at her and Kazim again.

By this time, we weren't the only two couples on the floor.

"You really do reek of onion," Valyn said again. "What do you do? Eat them raw?"

"They clear my head," I lied earnestly. "You should try one."

"I doubt the benefits would outweigh the unpleasantness."

"You might be surprised." *Might, but I doubt it.* "But since you brought it up, why do you ask? Isn't Kazim first in line to, um, to be king now?"

"Well, the counselors have made all the tests they care to make unless Theresa—"

"Who?"

"The queen."

"Oh. Oh, yes."

"Unless Theresa makes any more tests or at least makes a decision. She meets with the counselors tomorrow to discuss the most prominent possibilities."

"I bet the queen relies a lot on you for input about who to marry, huh?"

Valyn raised an eyebrow at me. Just one, which was fascinating. "A bit."

"So who do you favor?"

"Oh, *I've* been for Alain for a while, but Thea thought he was too vain. It's a shame he's not here tonight. No one has seen him since the tournament."

"Yeah. Alain's not a bad guy." Not that I had spoken with him much, but even if he was vain like everyone said, he wasn't too good to talk to an ugly noble, and that was something.

"If he doesn't show up soon, he won't get his dance."

"Hey, what? Alain gets a dance? With the queen? Why?"

"Well, because he was a second. Kazim gets the first dance and a kiss, which, if you ask me, Theresa needs some experience with, so I think she should give him a real one just to save face. But since Alain was second, he at least gets the second dance."

"And me? And me? I get a third dance because I was third place, right?"

"Ugh." Valyn held a hand up to my face. "No. You get the second dance because Alain isn't here. Reginald would have gotten the third dance, except he can't walk. And you should really do something about that onion breath."

"I have a better idea. Let Thea—ahem—let the queen

dance with whoever she wants, but I want the last one instead of the second or third or whatever because no one is sure how that's supposed to work anyway. Yes?"

"Um—sure. Our dance is over. And you should go drink some wine or something."

Sure enough, the minstrels stopped, and everyone clapped, and I released Valyn, who ran off holding her nose.

Then I looked around for Thea and Kazim.

They were gone.

Chapter 26

My heart began to pound. Where was she? Was she all right? What if she and Kazim were mouth-to-mouth somewhere? Not that I wanted to see that, but I had to find them just the same.

I scoured the ballroom, running past the tables of food and looking down all the chairs and weaving my way through nobles and suitors and maids and servers. I ran out into the hallway and looked up and down.

Where was she?

I ran back inside. Long curtains draped the far wall, evenly spaced. They must be hiding windows. I ran over and threw the curtain aside to find a great windowed door. Opening it led onto a long stone balcony that stretched across the outside wall of the castle. Thea and Kazim were there, standing on the edge about in the middle of the balcony, and I was far to one side. They were speaking and hadn't noticed me. I desperately wanted to know what they were saying. I tried to inch forward along the back wall, staying in the shadows. The curtains kept out most of the light from the ballroom except for the occasional long stripe. The noise from the ballgoers made it more difficult to hear the low voices of Kazim and Thea, so while I came closer, I had to read body language.

They were standing far too close for my liking. Kazim had his arm around Thea's shoulders, and they were facing. Kazim put a hand under Thea's chin and lifted her face to his. My breath got stuck halfway out of my nostrils.

No!

Thea stopped it, lifting her chin just out of his hands, and saying something gentle, holding on to his hand with both of hers and pressing it to his chest as if she were giving it back to him. Kazim said something gentle in reply, kissed her hands, and brought his other arm from around her, letting her go.

"I should get back," I faintly heard Thea say, and she walked behind her to the nearest window and slipped back in, fluttering the curtain as she passed.

Yay, Thea!

Not that the exchange had looked completely harmless, but she had stopped the kiss. That was important to me even though I had tried to convince myself it was going to be all right if it happened.

Kazim looked out over the balcony, the whole of Seacrest before him. He took a deep breath and just watched, obviously thinking. I had to slip back inside without him seeing me, but I was halfway between two doors. Without Thea distracting him, I had a feeling he would hear me if I made the slightest sound.

Kazim turned. He must have heard something I hadn't, but he wasn't looking in my direction. A cloaked figure approached from the farthest end of the balcony. Seht? No. The frame wasn't right. And I hadn't seen Seht wearing a cloak earlier. Not a hooded one, anyway.

"Good evening, Kazim," the figure said. I didn't recognize the voice because I had never heard the voice speak so seriously. But he pulled the cloak off his face and I knew him, wound fresh and red from earlier that same day: starting at his left temple, skirting an eye, running just past one nostril, slicing his lips, and ending on the right side of his chin.

Alain.

Seeing him gave me a deeper understanding of what it meant to be broken. Alain's spirit had been crippled. There was something wrong with his eyes, like he had gone mad. He pulled his straight long sword from his cloak and held it with one hand, pointing it at Kazim as he strode forward.

"Peace, Alain. I am unarmed, and we were in official combat." Kazim held up a hand and took a step away from the advancing Alain.

"You have no idea what you've done to me," Alain said in a hollow voice, as if he'd done a lot of weeping since his wound, but the wrong kind of weeping. "I am a prince of the kingdom of Lafestia. I *cannot* be marred so."

"But you *are* marred so, prince of Lafestia," Kazim said evenly. "And no amount of revenge will give you your face back. Go home. Go home and start again. You can still be king of Lafestia someday, with or without a flawless face."

"Your blow was deliberate," Alain continued in a sort of hiss. "You knew such a blow would hurt me worse than death. How *dare* you deal out misery so easily and yet counsel me to move on! I swear I will not rest until you have tasted just as much pain as I, and if you are still alive when

I'm through with you, I will hear your speech then and not before."

Alain lunged, and Kazim dodged. Rather than running away, Kazim charged, trying to close the distance between them so that Alain could not use his sword. Kazim knew well how good Alain was with his blade and must have known he couldn't contend without a weapon of his own. Kazim took a slice to his forearm getting close enough, but managed to grab Alain by his fists. They wrestled against each other.

Alain was a little taller than Kazim, but normally I would have put them at even odds. But not this time. Alain fought with a crazed fury that I knew Kazim would not be able to fend off for long.

Tiring, straining, Kazim uttered a loud stream of unintelligible sounds that must have been his native tongue. I understood only one word.

Seht.

The window nearest me, between myself and the struggle, shattered. Glass flew into the night like freed birds. Seht emerged, holding in one hand a wide curved sword, much less delicate than Kazim's. Kazim had told me his sword was good for slicing. This sword was obviously good for only one thing.

Chopping.

Kazim had fallen to one knee and Alain was bearing down on him. With an awful cry, Seht sprang forward and swung his sword heavily with both hands. Just once. And the struggle was over. Alain's body crumpled still holding his sword.

Alain's head came to a stop at my feet, angry broken eyes staring up at me from a maimed face.

Never to be king of Lafestia.

The sounds of the struggle brought everyone out onto the balcony. Women screamed. Nobles and guards poured out and then fought to keep the womenfolk back. I ran to the edge and was sick over the balcony, purging myself of wine, clams, and the beastly onion.

Guards and soldiers surrounded Kazim and Seht. They both stood calmly as if nothing had happened. Finally, three counselors appeared in their long dark robes.

"What happened?" my old friend Big Nostrils demanded, striding up to Kazim and Seht.

"Alain attacked me. If Seht had not interfered, I would have been killed," Kazim explained quickly.

"This is a great offense. Were there any witnesses?"

Kazim turned his eyes on me, and everyone else's eyes followed. I was leaning weakly on the stone railing.

I had a sudden thought. *What if I lied?* Wouldn't Kazim or at least Seht be locked up? Sent away to Lafestia for trial? Either way, Kazim would surely never be king of Seacrest.

But in the next instant I was filled with shame. Alain was dead. This was no time to be thinking of revenge; that was what had killed the prince of Lafestia. If Kazim had dealt unfairly, I would have told the truth in an instant. I couldn't lie now.

"What Kazim said is true. Alain attacked Kazim unarmed. Alain would have killed him. Seht was protecting his master." Though I wished in my heart something besides beheading could have been done to stop Alain. There was something sickening in Seht's eye. He had enjoyed the thrill of murder.

Nostril-flare straightened his robes and stood up straight.

"I see. It is unfortunate. We'll send a message to Lafestia straightaway and then the prince's body will follow."

Just then, the crowd parted enough to let two women through. Thea and Valyn. Thea gave a sickly screech as she inhaled, covering her mouth with her hands and turning immediately away. Valyn held her but looked as if she was about to faint herself.

Nostril-flare called two guards over to him. "Escort the queen and her lady to her chamber! The ball is over."

Just as quickly as they had entered, the crowd left. I slumped against the railing, breathing slowly. Kazim came and knelt in front of me.

"Thank you," he said softly, and, gripping my hand with his bloodied arm, pulled me to my feet. Once he was sure I wouldn't fall over, he released me and left, Seht following behind him without a glance at me.

I somehow made my way back to my chamber and pulled Alain's tunic off. As soon as I did, I noticed my patched fool's tunic and leggings laid out on the covers of my bed. Oaf's handiwork, no doubt. I tore them off the bed and threw them underneath it, trying to imagine Oaf dying as Alain had, but feeling unable because I still felt sick. Not in my stomach. I felt sick in my brain. In my head. Perhaps all fools felt like this when their stupidity caught up with them. How close to death I could be at any moment. How close death always lurked. I collapsed on my bed without getting under the covers and without undressing further, completely exhausted. I was vaguely aware when Alyss came in and pulled and pushed me into the covers, and then I knew nothing.

I slept late into the next day, and what woke me would be worse than all of my dreams of wide chopping swords and Alain's angry, dead, broken eyes.

Chapter 27

I felt myself being watched as I slept. I felt light on me from the windows and knew I should get up. Who knew what the day might hold? I had to be alert.

As soon as I opened my eyes, they were filled with the sight of Oaf's awful face only inches from mine. I swung out at him without thinking. Oaf jumped easily back, cackling.

"Good morning, Sir Farrago! You slept in awfully late, so I felt it my duty to come and bring you the news. Beautiful day for an engagement, isn't it?"

I sat up, trying to wipe both sleep and hatred from my eyes. I almost lunged at Oaf again, but then the last thing he'd said caught up to me. "What are you talking about?"

"The counselors stayed up late last night with the queen. And with Kazim, of course. It was quite a meeting. You should have been there. The counselors were afraid that the death of poor Alain might give Lafestia a reason to seek revenge and come against Seacrest. They wanted to stop dragging this out and get the kingdom settled at last. So, seeing as how Alain is no longer an option, Kazim is now engaged to the queen."

The emptiness inside me from losing my dinner last night widened into a painful chasm. "You must be jesting, Oaf. They would not name Kazim king. Lafestia will blame him for the death of their prince."

Oaf shrugged. "But it was not Kazim's sword that did the deed. Lafestia could blame anyone they wanted, even the contest for the queen's hand. In any case, whoever they decide to blame, Seacrest will be able to meet with them much more easily with a firm monarch on the throne than a recently overthrown government and an amateur queen who only knows how to be a scullery maid."

"She couldn't have," I breathed. Surely not. It didn't make sense.

"Oh, I don't know how the dear queen feels about it, but she understands that this is not about her. She has a kingdom to worry about, and Kazim *is* a handsome prince, *and* the best fighter and strategist, all things that the counselors favor highly. Messengers rode out early this morning to carry the news to and invite all the neighboring kingdoms. Some of the suitors are heading for home, like Sir Reginald. But others are going to stay for the wedding. What about you? What shall I tell her highness your plans are?"

I felt numb and in pain at the same time, as if my body was numb but my soul was on fire. "My plans," I said in my most dangerous voice, "are to see you thrown from the *highest* tower on this castle, you venomous boar!" I threw a pillow with all my might at him. I missed, of course, but sent Oaf hobbling with great leaps for the door, cackling gleefully as he did.

I threw on the blue tunic and gold leggings I had arrived

in; the ones I had taken from Gridian. I was going to see Thea. She owed me a dance anyway. She couldn't make a decision like this without speaking to me first.

The hallways were full of maids cleaning rooms that had just been inhabited by other suitors. It looked like most of them had left. Sir Leon was gone, as was Lord Percival. Prince Meldon was still around, and he gave me a friendly wave as we passed in the halls. I put on a pleasant noble face and waved back. *Oh, I don't care that my true love is engaged to another*, I told my face to say, and made my way straight to Thea's chamber.

Her room had two guards outside the door.

"I need to speak to the queen," I said, trying to look important but not very threatening.

"The queen has said she will see no one today," a guard said firmly. "Perhaps tomorrow."

Oh really?

"As you say," I said with a small nod of my head, and I turned and walked away. I went into the empty bedroom next to hers, stepped out the window, and worked my way along the stone ledge and past my gargoyle friend before I came to Thea's window.

Thea was marching restlessly back and forth as she spoke with Valyn, who was seated on Thea's bed, listening with her chin in one hand.

". . . So I'm completely where I said I was about my ability to choose, aren't I? Which is fine, I mean, as you said, it's not about me. Though I'm still not sure how well Seacrest will fare with a queen on the verge of—Augh!"

The window was shut, but not latched, so I carefully opened the outward-swinging hinge and hopped inside.

"What are you doing?!" Valyn jumped to her feet. "Get

out of her lady's chamber at once! She has already said she will see no one!"

"Well, *you're* here," I pointed out as I strode forward. "And I needed to speak to her lady, and that meant I had to see her."

Valyn rose with indignation pouring out of her nostrils. "*I* am the queen's lady-in-waiting and *you*—"

"Peace, Valyn," Thea said, silencing her Lady. "As a matter of fact, I have some things I would like to say to Sir Hubert. Perhaps you could go see that the chambermaids are keeping up with the new changes and that they all have their assignments to prepare for the upcoming wedding." Thea looked pointedly at me as she said the last part.

Valyn breathed out but managed to calm herself a little. "No. I'll be in the closet. I won't be a bother," she assured Thea. "Excuse me." She curtsied and vanished into a large walk-in closet brimming with queen's gowns.

"She will not cause us any trouble." Thea sighed. "And I am glad you're here." She stormed up into my face and pointed a finger a little too close to my nose than I was comfortable with. "Now listen, Sir Hubert. I know what you have been trying to do. I haven't missed any of your little *cues*. The dandelions, the comment about my hair—"

"Now I am sorry about that," I interrupted. "That was rude. But I did cover it up nicely later, you may recall."

"And the onion and your stupid chicken impersonation from last night. There. Now I don't know how you know him or why he sent you. I'm sure he thinks he's terribly clever and funny. Well, he's not. Because I-I might have loved him once. And I know that was never returned. So when you see him again, you tell him that it doesn't matter. I'm moving on and I'm getting married and I have a kingdom to think about now. I couldn't have had him anyway. If he wasn't such a fool, he would have gotten a *blasted* hint before I left!"

"Oh, I'll tell him," I said, nodding. "He'll be heartbroken."

"No, he won't!" Thea stamped her foot, scaring a few tears from her eyes. "And I *knew* you knew him! You had better stay and see the wedding so that you can tell him that you saw me married with your own eyes. Tell him to leave me alone."

"I will. But I already know something of what he would say in return."

"Go on, then." Thea folded her arms.

"Well, I'm sure he would say that there are risks if you fall in love with a fool. He might not get the hint very quickly. And he would also say, Thea, that you also run the risk of having that fool come after you, without plan or hope, knowing perfectly well that he can't have you."

I saw Thea go stiff when I said her name. And when I reached up to my nose to work the honey-stuck appendage off my face, I heard her breathing stop. The nose came off fairly easily, stretching strands of honey after it. I rubbed my wonderful beak and got honey all over my fingers.

"My goodness, but that feels better," I said. "Now if you'll picture me with longer hair and patches all over my clothes, including a light patch over my heart that you yourself stitched, you'll recognize me as—" I stopped because Thea's hands were over her mouth, and her eyes were brimming. She was trembling so much that I was worried that she might collapse. She squeaked something so high that I couldn't understand it. She often did that when overly excited. Finally, she brought it down just enough that I could make out her words.

"Farrago!" She took a deep shuddering breath and made a step toward me as if to rush at me, but stopped herself. "What—what are you doing here?"

I nearly felt my tongue get stuck in my mouth. Very all of a sudden. I didn't know how to answer her. "Well," I began slowly. "I guess I came because—because I missed you."

"Missed me?" Her hands were still over her mouth and her eyes almost too wide for her head. She came up to me until she was staring straight up into my eyes.

Oh, dear. I knew what she wanted. She would have all my masks off me. I felt my face muscles twitch. I had never liked Sir Hubert, but his identity was what was safe in this world. He suddenly felt deeply rooted in me. But when I had pulled him from my face, I found that it was not Sir Hubert, but Farrago himself that liked to hide his face. Why did taking off my masks for Thea terrify me so?

Because it required trust. Farrago in many ways entertained others but always kept himself hidden. Particularly that small boy that Fendral had rescued from the streets all those years ago. Who knew me without my masks? Fendral had, certainly. Leofrick. And even King Giles, a bit. I could take my mask of for Thea. I had to. I even wanted to.

But I was afraid. I had never had to think so deliberately about removing my faces for someone I already knew I trusted. This was different than Fendral and Leofrick. This was Thea. Whatever I felt for her was the same power that had taken Fendral from my life. It had driven me to forsake my home and name. It was powerful, and it frightened me. But I had come too far to back off now.

So, slowly, forcing myself, I closed my eyes and breathed and relaxed all the muscles in my face until I was sure that nothing but the deepest, most honest part myself was showing. And when I opened my eyes again, I was all me.

I was also trembling and felt tears brimming as well, but those I had to hold back because they would do nothing for my image.

"I came because I realized, a moment too late, that I loved you too, Thea," I whispered. "And before you went off and married some crazy Arabian, I needed you to know that I had come after you."

Thea finally brought her hands down from her face. "I wanted so badly to believe you had come after me, but I was afraid to, because I knew you couldn't." Her looked changed to pleading. "I will believe you and have hope again if you can forgive my doubts."

I felt my eyes lit up. "Deal." Fools should be able to forgive much as we bumble so much.

Smiling, Thea embraced me, and I bent to wrap my arms around her. After a moment, she lifted her face to mine, and almost without thinking I jerked back.

"What? What is it?" she asked, horrified that she had done something wrong.

"I-I can't," I whispered.

"Because I'm engaged? I'll have to fix that."

"No. It's not that." Certainly not that. "It's just . . ." I looked around the room. "You don't happen to have an onion on you, do you?"

Thea gave a short bark of a laugh and put one hand to her mouth as if to hold it in. But that didn't work very well. I loved her laugh. It was girly, but quite pleasant and it made me feel really good inside. "I've never kissed you without onion breath before." I smiled, shrugging. Pox, but it was good to be me again!

"Farrago," Thea breathed. "What are we going to do? I cannot . . . I cannot marry Prince Kazim now."

"Well, I can hardly blame you," I agreed. "But I hate being Sir Hubert. And I cannot be king."

"Why not?"

"Why not? Why not what?"

"Why not be king?"

It was my turn to laugh. "Thea," I explained, pointing a finger at my head. "Fool. *Happy* fool. Good fool. Not king."

Thea sighed and rested her head on my chest. "Maid," she whispered. "*Happy* maid. Good maid. Not queen."

I put a hand on the back of her head, stroking her perfectly calmed and smoothed hair and missed her old dandelion style.

"I'm sorry," I whispered back. "I wish I had a plan. I really don't want you to marry Kazim either."

"Farrago?" she asked softly.

"Yes?"

"Do you think you could manage to kiss me even without onion breath?"

I sighed a false sigh. "I guess I'll just have to get used to it."

And so I kissed her. And I was pretty sure I could get used to it.

Thea spread her fingers in my hair, and that was wonderful until she pulled too hard on the hair by my left ear. The same place Fendral had grabbed when he'd caught me stealing his juggle balls on the street, and the same place Constance had struck when I'd been eavesdropping in a barrel back in Gridian's scullery the night I'd heard Thea was queen.

"Ow!" I pulled back. "Ow. Not there. That's tender."

"Oh! I'm sorry. Here?" She stroked it gently, and the touch sent thrills of pleasure down my neck.

Smiling, Thea pulled my head down again to meet hers.

And then a shrill scream stopped us.

CHAPTER 28

I knew the only person that could be screaming was Valyn, and I didn't think a kiss was any reason to scream. It wasn't until Thea screamed that I realized the problem, that I felt it: a hard metal blade just under my neck, forcing my head slowly higher.

Seht's blade.

I let Seht lead me a step back from Thea. I already knew what his sword could do to heads, and he was looking far too happy.

"Stop it!" Thea screamed frantically. "Stop it! Stop it! STOP IT!"

I heard the strange language again and saw Kazim come through the door with three black-robed counselors.

Seht's blade lowered, the wide curve resting before my chest. I saw that the blade had the barest stream of blood on the edge. It was so sharp that I hadn't felt the cut. I still couldn't feel it. I hoped that didn't mean the pain would be worse when it caught up to me.

"Oh, dear," I heard a sigh behind me, coming from

Thea's window. What I wouldn't have given to have Seht's sword and Oaf's head just under it.

"Guards! Take this man to the gallows. At once!"

Nostril-flare had just given the order for me to be hanged.

"NO!" Thea screamed.

"No!" Kazim echoed, and the counselors paused to look at him. I did as well. Kazim had no reason to keep me alive that I could think of. I was now officially between him and his goal.

"To the dungeons," Kazim said. "I must speak with the queen. Do not let word of who this man really is spread. Do not harm him. Be quick."

The two guards each grabbed an arm and hauled me roughly out the door. I heard Thea call after them, "Don't you dare harm a hair on his head or I will have the same done to you!"

Bless her. It was a shame she had so little power. No one had even stopped for her orders. The counselors had paused only for Kazim. It was as if he was already king.

I fought back little against the guards; there was no point. They practically jogged me to my cell as if they couldn't wait for me to see it. Unfortunately, on the way, they obviously didn't take the order of "do not harm him" to mean the same thing as "be gentle." They pulled my arms back farther than they were supposed to go and rid me of my outer blue tunic and shoes before throwing me in the small, damp, cold cell with a vicious shove. The large wooden door clanged behind me and I heard the locks snap into place. There was a small window with bars on the upper portion of the door that I could look through, but that was all. Once they left, the light left with them.

There was something about being in the small dark cell that brought back all of my memories of living on the streets as a child. This wasn't much different than finding a place to sleep in a dank alleyway or on a garbage heap.

I heard faint chittering and small footsteps. Ah. My friends, the rats. I remembered how I had learned that if I didn't cross them, they would not bite me. I had taught many of them to approach me and sniff my hand. I even knew how to measure the days by how bad my hunger pains became. Three days was usually about all I could stand. I silently reproached myself. I was used to having plenty, certainly lately, and I had eaten nothing since losing my dinner last night. I already felt as if I'd fasted for about a day. Fortunately I could hear and smell water. It didn't take me long to feel along the walls where it dripped down. I touched the wall with my tongue. The water was good, but so slight, and I had nothing to gather it in. Still, it would keep me alive if I tried to drink often.

After a quick scour of my cell, I settled into the corner, making myself as small as I could for warmth. If I slept, I could numb the passage of time.

Trying not to think of Thea and what Kazim might be saying to her, I stayed still and eventually slept.

Guards passed by every now and then. I don't know how often. One time my door was opened and three guards came in. Two of them held my arms while a third threw blows at my chest and stomach. They avoided my face. I realized it was probably because Kazim had said not to harm me, and chest wounds could be covered more easily than face wounds. I could now finally feel the short strip of red along the bottom of my neck. It stung instead of throbbed like the rest of me.

I had memories of beatings. Fist blows I feared a little less than whip strokes. I had never had a proper whipping except for the odd lashes here and there when I passed too closely to the kingdom soldiers. Whip strokes took the breath out of you with their sharpness, and since my stomach was empty, the stomach blows didn't make me quite so nauseated. They would have if I'd eaten, so I began to regret my empty stomach less.

I didn't pay attention to their jibes. They were just the usual abuse of, "Thought you'd pretend to be a noble, eh?" and "Think you're better than the rest of us?" and other nonsense that I simply didn't mind. They grew bored quickly, especially when I didn't react or fight back, and they left me before too long.

Some rancid bread was thrown under a door slot three times. From what little I knew of dungeons, I suspected that meant three days. Unless they fed the prisoners twice a day here. Did they? I doubted it. I was even given some water. Stale, but in a small tin cup. Once I drank it I used the cup to gather water from the walls, cold and sweet. It only took a few hours, I think, to fill it.

I had endured such treatment before. I could endure it again. But what of Thea? What was going to become of both of us? Was I going to be killed? How long would they keep me here? How would Kazim have me killed? What was going on up there?

I was close to going mad with my questions, alone in the dark. I felt along every inch of my cell and eventually found three small chips from the walls, about the size of pebbles, barely heavy enough for me to feel. I juggled in the dark to calm myself. Juggling brought a bushel of good memories to mind that gave me some light in the cold darkness. And I waited.

I heard footsteps pass outside my door, but they didn't stop. From the faint sound of drunken singing, I wagered it was the jailer. Some light passed by. I went up to the bars on my door and tapped on the wood.

"Hey. Hey."

The jailer was only wishing he was drunk. He held a mostly empty bottle of poor ale as he patrolled down the cold hallway. His baggy clothes made him look a little bigger than he actually was. He looked up as if the voice had come from heaven.

"No. Over here."

The jailer finally found me. He came over and hit the short bars on my door with his fist.

"'Ey, get back in there!" he barked. "Down wi' ye."

"Want to see something?" I asked earnestly.

"See wha?" he asked, curious. How he dealt with the boredom of being a jailer probably involved beating prisoners and guzzling reject ale.

Five minutes later he was in my cell and I had both his shoes and the now empty bottle of ale dancing in the air. Bottles were fairly easy to juggle, but shoes were different for me. Still, it felt *so good* to be juggling again. Really juggling. Those darn pebbles were a little too light to feel, and in the darkness sometimes I was pretty sure I was only moving my arms and not really juggling anything.

My jailer was an attentive audience and was about to go get me two more bottles to add to my objects when four guards flowed down into the dark hallway. I caught my objects and set them down.

"What are you doing?" the front guard demanded of the jailer. The jailer opened his mouth to explain and I would have loved to hear it, but the first guard continued before he could. "The prince wants to see the prisoner. We're moving him to a higher cell."

"About time," I interjected. "Make sure this new one has a window. But I don't want new rats. I just got acquainted with my current ones, and we have an understanding."

The guard started as if surprised I could talk. My jailer chortled hard enough to nearly pass out. "Rats!" he wheezed.

I shrugged apologetically at the guards. "I'm the most entertaining thing that's ever happened to him."

The guard finally came to himself and fixed me with a stern glare. "That's enough out of you, then." He parted my shirt with his hands, seeing my bruises. "Someone's been beating on him," he said to his comrades. "At least they had the sense to avoid his face. The prince wouldn't like it if he saw it. Be sure his shirt covers the marks." And then the two others grabbed my arms and pulled me out of my cell. I didn't struggle as they dragged me away, but they weren't gentle just the same.

My new cell *did* have a window. Instead of a small window in the door, there was a small half-moon window in the wall about five feet over my head, which meant I was just under ground level. It was a little warmer. But as soon as I saw it, I pulled back as hard as I could against the guards. I wanted to go back to my old cell.

There were two reasons for this. One, there was a web in the upper right-hand corner with a dark spot in the middle. It was too high for me to reach, which in some ways was good, but in most ways was terrifying. The sight of it sent tremors through my chest that bounced against my bruises.

The other reason was the back wall. It had shackles built into it. They were going to chain me to the wall, and I'd have no use of my arms. And there was a spider in the corner.

I fought back with a terror and a strength I'd thought I'd lost in the last few days, and I think I surprised the guards with it, not that it mattered. There were four of them and one of me, and despite my best effort, they forced my wrists into the metal cuffs and closed the links, turning keys into great locks to keep them there. Attached as I was, I had to stand with my elbows bent like a square at my sides. If I slouched, my arms stretched above me. The cuffs were only barely too small, gripping just tightly enough to convince me there was no point in struggling. I couldn't pull very far away from the wall, but at least they left my legs free. I could lift them, but it used the sore muscles from my beating. And the best part: with my arms raised my tunic covered the worst of the beating marks. Only the red strip on my neck must have been visible. Kazim would never know. And I wasn't going to tell him.

CHAPTER 29

I hadn't been there very long, and already my fingers were beginning to feel funny when I heard angry conversation and running steps. Someone pounded against the door.

"Farrago! Farrago!"

Thea!

I heard locks rustling and then Thea ran through the door and threw herself at me, sobbing and clinging. The pressure of her against me hurt in several ways, but I wouldn't have traded it for anything. It was a good kind of hurt. And torture at the same time. I wished to heaven I could have used my arms to reassure her. Tell her that I was all right, at least for the moment.

Then Kazim appeared in the doorway, holding a burning torch, and the torturous feeling of everything worsened. Curse Kazim and his innocent face. I didn't believe a glance of it.

"I love you," Thea chanted over and over again. "I love you, Farrago."

"I love you, Thea," I whispered back. It wasn't nearly

as difficult to say as it had been the first time, nor was it to show her my real face, though I tried to hide my real terror for her sake. Her presence made me feel a little better. If only she could get rid of the spider for me. Not being able to see it made it a little worse. Who knew what it was doing or where it was crawling?

I shuddered at the thought. Thea released me.

"If I was really queen," she whispered, "I would be able to free you. But I won't have all my powers until I am married. Yet I need my powers to free you in order to marry you. It's an awful catch, isn't it? I'm sure my father didn't mean for it to go like this. I'm so sorry."

"It has been my doing," I tried to sooth her. "I knew the risks when I came. It is the fool in me that got me here."

"Oh, but, Farrago, I'm *so* glad you came!"

I beamed at her. "Me too," I said, and it was true. "Me too."

Kazim came and put an arm on her shoulder.

"Come," he whispered. "Let me speak with him. Let me tell him."

Thea nodded and, meeting eyes with me, slipped away, heading for the door.

"Wait," Kazim commanded. He beckoned with his fingers slightly, not looking at me or her. Thea came to his side and let him put an arm on her shoulders. "Now."

Thea started. "Now? I thought you wouldn't ask for it until—" Her voice broke. ". . . until the wedding. You cannot ask it of me *now*."

Kazim's face was locked in that perfect guileless expression of his, the one that made him look like a dark-skinned angel that could do no wrong.

"I do ask it now. I need some assurance that you will do your part and go through with the rest of it after he is gone."

Gone?

Kazim put a hand under her chin and lifted her face, and I understood what they were talking about. Thea still owed Kazim the kiss he had won when he'd become victor of the Tournament of Princes. Thea had thought he would not use it until their wedding, which meant they were still getting married, obviously, but Kazim was asking for it now. Here. In front of me.

Why? What possible reason could he have for that except to hurt me? Well, of course. That was his specialty.

In her shock, Thea didn't fight back—until the last second. Then jerking her head away, she ran out of my cell, leaving Kazim and I together. I was afraid to be with Kazim, but I was proud of Thea all the same.

Kazim sighed and turned to me. It was just the two of us. Not even guards stood outside. Why would they need to? I couldn't move.

"I think I have found a way to let you live, Sir Hubert," he began as if the incident with Thea hadn't happened.

"Farrago," I corrected. "My name is Farrago." I didn't want to be Sir Hubert ever again.

"Yes, that's right." Kazim nodded immediately. "Farrago. The great fool of Gridian Court." Kazim paced in front of me. "You did well," he began. "Even now, I am quite impressed that I never suspected you as a true threat. You had none of the characteristics most of my enemies have. No enemy has ever made me laugh. You told the truth about Alain's death, and you must have thought of what might have happened to me had you lied. Yet you did not. I admire you, Farrago. I do not understand you, but I admire you. I always," he said, struggling for words. "I always enjoyed your company."

"I'm touched," I said. "But I *am* chained to a wall in a dungeon, and I do not believe you are not going to kill me."

"I've found a way. To keep you alive, that is. There is a ship that leaves port tomorrow morning. It is a merchant ship sailing for my homeland. You will board that ship and be sold as a slave when it docks. The counselors have reluctantly agreed to do this instead of end your life. It took a lot of persuasion, but Thea would not stand talk of your death."

"Shouldn't I be sent back to Gridian for trial? I mean, that's where I'm from. I think the king of Gridian should decide how best to punish one of his subjects." I knew King Giles wouldn't touch me.

"If you'd been discovered to be what you are sooner, the counselors would have had to do that. But since you were caught with the queen, trying to usurp the throne of Seacrest, they have the right to punish you here and skip Gridian."

Which must have been why Oaf hadn't betrayed me sooner.

"Well then, you've got it all worked out. Good-bye then."

Kazim shook his head. "I have an alternate proposal," he whispered. "One the counselors do not know about. I was hoping you would stay, Farrago. Stay and become part of the court of the new Seacrest of which I will be king."

"Stay? Stay how?"

"I would disguise another prisoner as you and have him board the ship so that the counselors will not suspect. You would remain in hiding until we found a new disguise and identity for you. You would live here as a member of the court. You pulled off your last disguise well enough. I feel we could make a new one work."

I snorted. "Ah, the things Thea and I would do behind your back. The great scandals."

"I'm aware of that. It wouldn't exactly be behind my back because I would know about them."

I caught my breath. "You're really serious."

"Indeed. All I want is the kingdom. All you want is the queen. I have to marry the queen in order to get my kingdom, but I do not need to keep her. Besides, the queen is not good at putting on a face. She shows in her eyes what she feels in her heart. It would be prudent to have you around. She'd be able to maintain face better."

"Ah. So there it is." I smiled a mirthless smile. "You need me around to control your queen. At the very least you need to keep me alive in order to keep her happy and cooperative."

Kazim just looked at me and said nothing.

I seriously considered his proposal. I liked the idea of staying alive. I spoke lightly of my death to Kazim, but I knew that if death were actually looking at me, I would not be so casual. With Kazim's plan, I would be with Thea, but . . . not really. Only as far as secrecy and subterfuge would take us. Still, Kazim's plan, if he was in earnest, and I believed he was, was in many ways quite considerate.

"What did Thea say?" I asked him. "Did Thea agree to this plan of yours?"

"I'm asking you. What do you say?"

He wouldn't tell me. That must mean she hadn't agreed. I didn't think I'd be able to live the rest of my life not as Farrago. That certainly hadn't worked last time.

So slowly, and then more quickly, I shook my head. "No. I can't—I couldn't live like that. I'm sure you think you're being gracious, but—" The dislike I'd always felt for Kazim suddenly spilled over. "No!" I pulled against my shackles. "You're worried only about what you appear to be, Kazim, and not what you are! Well, what you are is despicable. I've seen the evil you are capable of. You do not see people as people. They are objects to you. Objects to be controlled or ruled or used or broken. Even now as you look at me, I am only and have only ever been entertainment, never alive. Never real to you. All your moves are calculated to an end that serves you. The best you can do is to *seem* like a king, Kazim, but you will never *be* one!"

Kazim's eyes nearly glowed with heat in the dark. "Just because I was second born does not make me less than my brother! I was always born a prince. I am not lower and I will *prove* that I am just as good as he! Better! Once I have this kingdom, I will sweep out until I have all the kingdoms under me, starting with your Gridian, and then I will overthrow my brother's throne, and we will see who the true king is!"

"A true king does not need a kingdom to prove it!" I shouted back. "He would simply *be* a king! Just as I am a fool even though I tried to be a noble. I hated it. It doesn't work. And you, you've almost convinced Thea that you care for her with your false niceties. She never would have seen them if you'd met her as a maid."

"Is that what she was? I don't care. I don't know why you're so worried about the queen. I will not be unkind to her."

"You can't afford to! You must convince everyone this marriage is real. You must convince them that you won her. Do you love her at all? Really?"

"I don't understand what you are talking about!" Kazim yelled back. "Where I'm from, a man rarely even *meets* his wife until they are married! I had no reason to believe it was any different in this country. This whole courtship thing seemed only to be a unique situation, even for here, because she was a queen and her father had made arrangements for her to be pleased."

"Then it's not that you don't love her, it's that you don't even believe such a thing exists." I stood up a little straighter. "Then I am in a better position than you are, Prince Kazim. Even chained to this wall as I am. I pity you, your ignorance. You have no concept of the love that I feel, and that is what makes you despicable. I have a lot of faults, but I see people as people. I see people and think of how to make them smile. So put me on that ship of yours. Sell me as a slave. I will be back. You have not seen the last of me. I am not merely an entertainment."

Kazim sucked in his breath slowly and then let it out. He was calming himself down.

"I suppose you are right about my proposal for you to stay. It would only have caused more problems later. And as you said to the counselors, there's no point in solving a problem if it only creates more issues farther along."

"Tell me, what did Thea say when you presented the plan to her?"

"Oh, she wanted to accept it, but she said nothing. She just wept. I felt certain that if I could have gotten you to agree to it, she would have followed. But I believe you are right, now. I thought it was worth the effort."

"Well then," I said calmly. "I guess our business is finished together."

But Kazim remained, an unsettling resolution on his face. "Not quite," he said softly. "As you said, as long as you're alive, you will find a way back to the queen. You would still cause problems for me down the road, and like you said, it is unwise to foster future problems. I told the queen I would let you live, but I didn't say in what condition. I'm very sorry, Farrago." Kazim pulled a rope that I hadn't noticed from his shoulder. It was attached to a clay jar I recognized. "I must break you."

All pretense at being casual or brave melted from me. "No, Kazim," I began to beg immediately. "I-I'll take your deal. I'll remain in Seacrest."

"No. It is your fear speaking now. You were right before. In the end, the other plan wouldn't have worked. You must be close to breaking already, but you were bolstered by the idea that you were going to live, and that must have given you hope. Still, the one you love is going to wed another. That must be difficult. I was hoping that the queen giving me the kiss she owed me in your presence would crack you further. But since that didn't work, I must rely on your unnatural fear of spiders."

Unnatural, he had said. Yes. That was the word I had never put to it. My fear of spiders was unnatural. If he let one loose on me now, the effect would be much worse on me than on a normal person. Kazim had no way of knowing how bad it would actually hurt me.

And I realized that that was a crucial ingredient when it came to breaking someone. It wouldn't be the spider alone. It hadn't just been the scar on Alain's face. It was the meanness of the act itself: the knowledge that someone was hitting you in your weakest place to cause you deliberate pain. If I was pinned under rocks in a rockslide and a spider crawled up to me, it would not be as bad as being chained to a wall in a dungeon while someone who knew I could not stand the sight or thought of spiders set one loose on me. It was simply inconceivable.

"Kazim," I continued to beg. "If—if you break me, I won't be *me* anymore. I won't be able to make people laugh. I won't juggle anymore. I—"

"I know," Kazim interrupted. "I know what broken people are like. Breaking is a delicate business. It is difficult to break them just enough so that they lose will without losing their life. Alain was cracked too far, and that is why he had to be killed." Kazim unwound the rope from the jar, holding it in front of him with one hand. "The camel spider is an aggressive creature, and he will charge as soon as I release him." He sighed. "I'll never be able to catch him again. Steel yourself."

"Please no," I could barely hear myself say.

"Farrago, I sincerely hope you survive."

"Kazim, I told you I had seen the evil you were capable of. Well, that's true. But you have also been kind. Like when you led my horse into Seacrest while I slept. When you got me out of the dining room when Oaf threw the spider at me. Kazim, you *don't—have—to do it.* Surely you can think of some reason to spare me. Surely you can think of something more important to you than your goal."

Kazim was silent for several terrible seconds. Thinking. Finally he shook his head. "No. Nothing." And he dropped the jug.

It broke into several large pieces. Almost before the jar

had finished breaking, a horrible creature perched on the edge of the topmost broken corner in the pile. It was the most horrible thing I'd ever seen. If the devil himself had suddenly appeared in my cell, I wouldn't have noticed him for the creature.

It was at least as large as my hand. Its bloated oval body was the color of pus and swollen like a boil. Its mouth had four lips, and on the tip of each one, I could see a small black tooth. It rubbed all four lips together. Its legs were large and hairy, and in addition to the eight legs coming off the horrid body, two small hairy arms were held up threateningly in front of it. It arched its back, turned its dark eyes directly on Kazim, and I swear on the name of the mother I never knew, it *hissed*. It was like a whispered scream. Quick as a dart it ran after Kazim, who leaped back and waved his torch at it. That stopped it, but it was not happy that it couldn't pursue its captor. After one more attempt, the camel spider backed up slowly, and then it turned and sprinted right at me.

The cell was suddenly full of the most horrid screams. I could hardly stand the sound of them and refused to believe I was capable of making such a terrible noise. I lost all control of my limbs and body. But still the spider managed to jump on my leg and crawl up my leggings. The weight of its legs coming slowly higher was more horrible than boiling oil. I pulled my legs up and flailed and pounded against the wall, but the spider continued to crawl right up me with that horrible power spiders have to walk on all surfaces regardless of their tilt.

I no longer had any concept of what Kazim was doing and I couldn't even find room in my mind for an image of Thea. I was cracking. The spider got to my waist and continued up quickly into my loose tunic, walking on my skin.

I went mad. The awful sounds increased. The whole kingdom must have heard me. This was the other ingredient needed to break someone: to push them a little farther than they ever thought they'd be able to endure. And still, I was pushed further. When the legs touched my neck, I escaped in the only way possible. I fainted. Never had darkness been so welcome.

I believe I never would have woken up except for the horrible pain in my arms. Without opening my eyes, I groaned. When I had fainted, my arms were forced to bear all my weight. What's more, they had been over my head for who knows how long. My arms felt as if they were ten times the size they were supposed to be and my hands were a deathly white and swollen. I wondered if I'd ever be able to use them again.

I was sagging in my shackles, held up by my wrists, but my arms weren't long enough to let me sit on the floor. Not yet, anyway. Maybe in a few more hours.

Once my mind got past the pain in my arms, I remembered where I was and why I was there. With a painful gulp of air, I opened my eyes. My heart was throbbing so hard that it bumped the bruises on my chest. There was a soft light in my cell from the crescent window over my head. A sliver of light with bars across it sat on the floor just a few feet in front of me. I was completely alone, and all I could hear was my labored breathing, as if instead of hanging there I'd been running all night. It was so quiet. I was so alone.

I made two attempts to stand up but didn't quite make it. My whole body shuddered as I tried to feel if the spider was on me anywhere. Had it bitten me? So much of me hurt, it would be too hard to tell. Were camel spiders poisonous?

Spiders. Legs. Crawling. Biting. Legs. *No*! Was this what it felt like to break? What if the spider came back? Was it on me? Where *was* it?

I thrashed in my shackles again. There was no point in it, but the thought of the legged demons still made me lose control of my body. I had nothing to do with it. It was the unnaturalness of my fear of them. A moment's pause, and my body did it again. Would it keep this up all night? I'd never be able to move properly again. Certainly never use my arms again. Oh! If there were only some way to ease the horrible pain in my arms. I tried to stand up again before the spasms came back.

Then I stopped.

I had seen nothing. No movement. But there was something new in the crescent of light on the floor. A shriveled black body. A spider, not the camel spider, was lying on its back with its legs curled in the air. Dead? It hadn't been there a moment ago when I'd woken.

In the next instant, with no sound whatsoever, the camel spider was there. It was five times as large as the still large dead one in front of it, standing just outside the beam of light where the black spider rested. No screams or horrible sounds came out of my mouth this time, though my body tried. It was one thing to scream or cry and not be able to help it or stop it, it was another thing to be so far gone that one couldn't even summon so much as a whimper from the throat. I went rigid as a dead man. If the spider came at me again, this time I doubted I would be able to move . . . or live.

The camel spider stared at me with its large black eyes.

Its front arms were still held in front of it, and slowly, it bent one, and then the other. Back and forth. It rubbed all four lips together. I couldn't move.

Then, with another bend of its front arms, the camel spider picked up the dead one in its mouth, stared at me a bit longer, turned, and darted away. Away from me. It had killed the other spider, and it was gone.

I don't know why, but despite the pain in my arms, and the pain in my whole body for that matter, I was filled with a sudden feeling of relief. I even laughed. Louder and louder. It occurred to me that I might still be breaking, but I felt so much better, not physically, but still somehow better.

Chortling, I managed to relax, at least a little. And leaning my head against the wall, I felt safe, and eventually drifted off again into something between a faint and sleep, welcome as ever.

When I came to again, it was morning, and I heard the locks on my door being fumbled with. I also felt sure that I'd never be able to use my arms again. The whole of them felt so swollen and bloated and cold. When the door swung open, it was Kazim. He looked like he might have had a rough night, though not nearly so rough as mine.

Kazim said something in that strange language of his, and while I didn't understand, I was pretty sure it was an Arabian curse.

"I hoped you'd be dead," he said.

And just the night before he'd said he hoped I'd survive. No wonder I didn't like him.

Kazim opened his mouth to speak again, perhaps to explain, but pushing him to one side, a counselor entered. It wasn't Nose-flare, though I saw several more robes standing behind him. The counselor standing before me was fairly short, and probably thin, though his robe hid that well. He looked happier than anyone visiting a dungeon should ever look. He came and put his face in front of mine.

He chuckled. "You don't know who I am, do you?"

I didn't answer because I didn't think a broken man would answer.

"Hee, hee! I suppose to a fool like you, we counselors all look the same. I lived in Gridian court for over twenty years, and as soon as you fools began to interfere, we became laughingstocks before the king. Well, no more. Gridian has been without its fool since you left. And the fool at Seacrest is much more accommodating than you *ever* were. You, always mocking us before the king, twisting our ideas, making yourself sound so clever. Well, today we counselors will have our revenge. Thought you'd escape on a ship, did you? Well, our dear Oaf told us of Prince Kazim's plan to send a double in your place and keep you around. Well, your double is ready."

I looked up. A broken man could still look confused, couldn't he?

"And I'm afraid we counselors don't take orders as well from a king-to-be as a king. Kazim does not decide what happens to your life today. We will have you broken *and* killed this day, dear Farrago!" And he laughed the most grating laugh my ears had ever endured. "Broken and killed! And the queen will never know. She'll think you've escaped on the ship. Well, let her think so. Guards!"

Two guards marched in. One of them began to undo the locks on my wrists while another began to fit a loose iron collar with a chain around my neck like a leash. As soon as my arms were free, they fell useless at my sides and I collapsed on the ground. I cried out at the pain moving my arms caused. One guard pulled me up by the chain on my neck, and though I was weak, I found my legs still worked. Seeing the way my arms flapped helplessly, the guards left them alone and just led me away by my collar.

They were leading me to my death. Between two guards I was marched, followed by a flock of happy black-robes and no doubt a slightly perturbed Kazim. Poor guy. I hoped my execution wouldn't ruin his day.

Pox him. Pox them all.

The ache in my arms was increasing. Or maybe the pain was just changing, but I managed to twitch my fingers. Twitch, but no more. My arms ached with every flap, but I couldn't use the muscles in them to stop them waving.

As soon as I was brought out of the dungeon, they led me outside. The air smelled wonderful, and I sucked it in as if it was the sweetest thing I had ever smelled. It was hard for me to believe that I was being led to my death. I had just survived the night with the most loathsome creature in the world only to be killed at sunrise? It couldn't be. Where was Thea? Would I really never see her again?

I was led to the front courtyard of the castle where a gallows was built. Normally, for a hanging there'd be a large crowd, but my death had to be done quickly and quietly with as few witnesses as possible so that Thea would never find out. Would she live the rest of her life waiting for me to come for her again?

As we marched, Oaf appeared and danced around me like an imp, cackling and singing.

"Going to have me thrown from the highest tower today, Your Majesty?" he mocked as he danced. Every now and then he jumped close enough to give one of my arms a good whap and send it flying. I managed to trip him once when he got too close, and the guards chuckled. It made me feel a little better, anyway.

Once we got closer to the gallows platform, instead of marching me up the stairs, the guards led me around it instead. And suddenly I realized that I wasn't going to be hanged. There was a chopping block resting on the ground all ready for me, and Seht stood smiling with his wide curved sword.

Oh. Decapitation. A nobleman's death. How considerate. Wait! No! Not Seht! Not a beheading! Though why a beheading should be any more fearful than a hanging I didn't know; dead was dead. But I didn't want to die at Seht's hands. Not that.

I pulled back uselessly on my collar. I must have looked pathetic being led as I was with my arms limp and bouncing. And my struggles didn't matter. The guard hardly noticed them. He just slipped the chain through an iron circle embedded in the ground and pulled it so my head was forced down over the chopping block, staring down into a bucket that would catch my head once it fell. The iron circlet on my neck was pushed up, leaving the bottom of my neck well exposed.

There now, it was just me and death. It was close enough for me to taste it. I could feel it coming with everything in me. Tears flowed slowly from my eyes, though my breathing was calm and no sobs came from my chest. Part of my fear had turned to resignation. What a way for a fool to go, though, wasn't it?

I saw Seht come to my side out of the corner of my eye. He raised his sword.

"I love you, Thea," I whispered, and closed my eyes.

Chapter 32

I tried to think only of Thea and not evaluate my life in the lengthened stretches before death. I tried not to think about what the sword would feel like, or if Seht would be kind enough to finish the deed with one stroke.

I heard a clunking metal sound and wondered if my head had hit the bucket. But I had felt nothing. Wow. Seht was good. I heard a collapse. Was it me? What was happening?

With trembling breath I managed to twist my head, which turned out to be still attached, just enough to see that Seht had dropped his sword and fallen to the ground. A knife hilt was sticking out of the left side of his chest.

What?

With a cry, Kazim ran to Seht's side, spouting urgent words in his native tongue that I, of course, didn't understand.

I heard the shouting and chaos of the counselors behind me as they ran off as fast as they could, shouting amongst themselves and fleeing for fear that they'd be next, but I heard no more bodies thump to the ground, and I assumed that Oaf must have followed them.

Trying to make sense of what looked like good fortune, I tried rather uselessly to look around as someone approached.

Then I felt a pressure on my shoulder, a hand. The hand squeezed in a warm, comforting way. It wasn't until this gesture that I realized I really wasn't going to die. Not right now. Not like this. Tears continued to flow. I did not yet understand what had happened.

Arms came down from behind me and began to undo the chain from its metal loop.

"It's all about the throws," I heard my rescuer say as he bent over me. "It's all about controlling the throws."

My eyes widened. He wasn't talking about juggling; he was talking about how he'd been able to kill Seht, and yet he was still talking about juggling. I began to tremble again. My goodness, but I was such a weakling. Or maybe every tender place in my body and soul had been pressed in the space of a few short hours.

With the slack in the chain I got to my feet, and slowly, too terrified to hope, I turned around.

He wasn't dressed in yellow, and he wasn't wearing bells. He looked like a common peasant. He was just a little taller than me, but I could look him in the eyes better than I ever had before. If there had been an angel standing there he could not have produced more joy in my soul than the man standing before me.

"F-Fen-*Fendral*," I choked through crippling gasps of breath. My eyes overflowed. My legs nearly gave way, but Fendral caught me so I wouldn't fall. My arms, completely dead an instant earlier, managed to lift themselves just enough to loosely return the embrace he wrapped me in.

"You perfect fool," he said in an admiring tone, or maybe he just thought I was stupid, but I could hear tears in his voice. "You perfect fool!" I hadn't felt so like a child since he'd left.

I had known that Fendral wasn't dead, but something in the way he had left had made me think I would never see him again. It was impossible that he was here.

"Ana has not been able to stop talking about you, *Juggle Man*," Fendral whispered to me.

"It's not possible," I heard Kazim say, aghast. "Sir Hubert had no manservant. No bodyguard. It was a jest. No man was ever there. He was never even a noble."

"Fendral," I repeated his name. "Fendral! What are you doing here? How?"

Fendral pushed me away still gripping me by my shoulders. "I will explain everything later, my Farrago, but first we must get to some high ground and make sure the queen is safe. Seacrest is under attack. By Gridian."

Fendral pulled another knife from his belt and held it by the blade, ready for throwing. "There is another for you, Prince, if you make a wrong move. I'm sorry about your servant. If I had gotten here sooner, I might not have had to kill him to save my charge. But Farrago did not deserve to be killed, and you knew that. He didn't even deserve to be broken."

I didn't mind reference to being broken, because I knew I wasn't. Actually, even despite my pain, I'd never felt more whole.

Kazim stroked the hilt of the small blade embedded in Seht's chest. I waited to see if he would pull it out and come at Fendral.

"If Seacrest is under attack," he said, "then I have other things to worry about." He got to his feet, leaving Seht on the ground. "Do we know why Gridian is attacking?"

"Yes," Fendral answered readily and put on the smile that was now mine as well. I was so pleased he still had one of his own. "They want their fool back."

Kazim glared as if Fendral was mocking him, and he very well probably was.

"No country goes to war over their fool," Kazim said.

"Well, it depends on the fool. And it sounds like you don't know Gridian very well." Fendral began to pull me toward the castle.

"Fendral," I said, leaning on him a little for support as I tried to keep up with his fast strides. "If Gridian was going to come after me, they would have done it a long time ago. And Giles hates war."

"No. Giles just needed the right person to convince him." Fendral winked at me. "Not that Leofrick hasn't been trying. Giles just needed to hear from me again. And just so nothing goes to your head, no, it wasn't just for you that Giles finally summoned his armies."

"I-I'm still not convinced I'm not dead yet." I winced as I tried to fold my arms on my chest so they didn't flap around so much. At least I was able to use them. Sort of.

Kazim was by our side when we entered the castle. Not too many people were screaming, but everyone was running around in a frenzy, maids and pages and nobles.

"Do you know where the queen's chamber is?" Fendral asked me.

"Yes. It's high up. Let's go." Kazim was already ahead of us. When we passed windows on the way up, I saw soldiers gathering in the front courtyard in rows. We came to the level just under Thea's, and generals and captains were speaking together about holding the castle and bringing the navy back in to attack from the rear.

"Wait." I stopped Fendral just as we passed a large conference room with counselors (none that I recognized from the chopping block) and captains. Thea was there. Kazim passed by us. I didn't know where he was going. I smiled as soon as I saw her, though she didn't see me. Thea's hair was back. The beautiful, glowing, dandelion head of hers, albeit with a small golden crown nestled at the top. Not that any of them seemed to care about her hair what with war preparations being made. Valyn stood next to the wall, just observing. She looked concerned, but she wasn't interfering as much I was sure she wanted to.

"Are all the troops gathered?" Thea asked. "Everyone?"

"Yes. And we've just sent a fast rig to bring in the navy, but they won't be here for several days at the least. Still, once they arrive, they could take Gridian by surprise from the rear if things have gone bad. The enemy is nearly at our gates. We need only the word from you, my queen, and we will stop them."

Thea was so different from the scullery maid she'd been not long ago. What, a month? Maybe? She'd gone from plucking chickens to giving the word for soldiers to go to war. How on earth had I won her? It didn't make sense, but I wasn't about to complain.

"That's right," Thea answered them, standing up straight and proud. "I'm sure I don't need to remind you that by word of mouth, and in writing in a long article given to the counselors, one of the few powers I was left with was the final command in the event we were attacked. Do you understand? I have final say on the movements of the army in all cases. If you deviate at all from what I say, it would be treason."

The captains nodded their heads quickly. *Of course*, they seemed to be saying. *Just give the word for us to attack, already!*

"Now, I have heard your recommendations and I happen to be very familiar with the kingdom coming upon us, so my final word is . . ."

All the captains leaned forward.

"Surrender."

At least one captain fell over. Two others only stumbled.

"What? My lady! We are under attack! You have stewardship over the whole of Seacrest! You *cannot* just surrender!" one captain insisted.

"I can!" Thea brought a fist down on a table spread with maps. "And don't you dare speak to me about the whole of Seacrest. The army is set to hold the castle and protect the nobles only! None of the villagers even have any protection, and *they* are the backbone of the kingdom! Gridian will be fair if we don't resist. We will save lives."

"But we'll lose the kingdom!"

Thea leaned forward until she and the captain were nearly nose to nose. "Yes, but don't you see? We'll lose it *to a good king*. You probably don't remember what those are like. But I do. I spent my whole life as a scullery maid in Gridian, and since Giles took the throne, things improved dramatically. He knows how to put people, not titles, first. You served well under my father, King Bennion, and he entrusted me with the future happiness of Seacrest, even though he didn't rule long."

"You'll be dethroned," another captain said.

Thea's face lit up. "Oh, I very much hope so."

"Gridian will not hurt the villagers." Fendral entered the room with me by his side. "I know their orders. In fact, they're entering with carts of food to placate the villagers before they come to the castle, and if you surrender, no one will be harmed."

"Fendral!" Thea looked almost as happy to see him as I'd been. Almost, but not quite, I was sure. "Farrago!" She ran to me and hugged me despite my folded arms. I was going to bear it like a man, but I couldn't keep just a small grunt of pain from escaping. Thea pulled back. "Farrago," she said, looking at me sternly, "are you all right?"

"Would you believe that in spite of being in a lot of pain and weak with hunger, I feel wonderful?" I gave her my best Fendral smile. *I've got everything under control.*

Thea laughed and kissed me lightly. That didn't hurt.

One of the captains was watching the troops in the front courtyard.

"They're at our gates," he said.

"Then we better let them in," Thea said calmly. "And you better go down and tell the troops to all surrender gracefully. I will hold you personally responsible if a fight breaks out."

Hesitantly, but obediently, the captains left and ran down to the courtyard. Welcome Gridian soldiers poured into the courtyard while the Seacrest army stayed on their knees, holding their swords up in surrender. Riding on the lead horse, looking much more dashing than he'd ever managed before, was Giles. He was helped a lot by his cape, of course. It made him look far bigger and more confident. He also had a really big sword. But, boy, did he looked relieved to see the army ready to surrender when he entered. Dismounting, he ran inside.

"King Giles is on his way," I said, watching his small form enter the doors with his sword drawn.

"I want to meet him in the throne room," Thea said.

Thea made the perfect image of a queen on the throne, even with her foofy hair. Valyn stood to her right, trying to keep her mouth shut, though it was clear she was having serious misgivings about the behavior of her queen.

Giles came through the doors not a second after she had sat down. He was followed by about twelve soldiers—no, thirteen—who lined the walls on either side of the throne room. Giles was a little out of breath, but still looked quite good for being him. I saw Valyn raise her eyebrows.

Giles looked cautiously around the room as if still expecting some kind of resistance. He kept his sword in hand. Fendral and I waved to him from behind the row of soldiers standing in front of us. They obviously knew we were on their side.

Deciding it was safe, Giles strode forward to Thea.

"Your Highness Queen Theresa Mary Angeline," he said as he approached her.

Thea stood.

"I am King Giles from the kingdom of Gridian. I'm

here to dethrone you. And," he said, looking a bit sheepish, "take over your kingdom."

Thea took her crown off and tossed it at his feet.

"Oh good. How about living the rest of your life as a scullery maid?" Giles asked.

Thea hugged him, which really surprised poor Giles. "You'll be a great king of Seacrest," she said as she stepped back.

"He might have been," a new voice said. The thirteenth soldier broke out of line and ran at Giles with a drawn scimitar. Valyn screamed and Thea tried to pull Giles forward as Kazim swung. Most of Giles's cape fell to the ground.

Kazim pulled off his knight's helmet and stood ready with his sword. Giles spun around and pulled out a sword of his own. The soldiers all pulled out weapons and began to charge.

"No, wait!" Giles lifted his hands to stop them. "Wait! Stay in ranks."

"That was a warning blow, King Giles of Gridian," Kazim said. "If you surrender now and take your army and leave, I will not dispatch you."

"Prince Kazim of Arabia," Giles said, holding his sword at the ready. "I have heard more of you than you think. I am merely striking first before you come against my own country."

"I am the king of Seacrest, and you will not take it from me," Kazim spoke as if swearing a deadly oath.

"No, he's not!" I shouted. "He only tries to *seem* like a king! Giles! You *are* one. You are a king already! You can beat him!"

"Kazim!" Thea shouted. "You will have to kill me too, for I will never marry you! You will never have Seacrest!"

Kazim did not look at her. "We will see," he promised. "King Giles, perhaps we can make this simpler. Let's keep this between the kings, shall we? If I win, your army retreats and you leave Seacrest to me. If you win, you may kill me and do what you will with Seacrest. What do you say?"

Giles did not answer right away. He was seriously considering Kazim's proposal.

"No!" I shouted at Giles when no one else did. "No, Giles! You don't have to make a deal! You have him! He's outnumbered!"

But Giles looked more pensive than I had ever seen him. "I have never felt like a king," he confessed. "If I really am one, as you say, Farrago, then let this battle prove it. Otherwise, I was never fit to rule. I accept, Prince Kazim. En garde."

Kazim's face became sinister, and he struck the first blow.

Giles, certainly to my surprise, blocked the blow, and many others that rained afterward. But I was terrified. There was no way Giles could win. I'd never even seen him fight.

"Fendral." I looked to him.

"I know." He held up his last knife and threw it.

It would have struck true, but Kazim, the fighter that he was, hit it out of the air before it made its mark and still managed to block Giles in the next second. They'd only been fighting for a short while, and Giles had lasted a short while longer than I had thought he would, but my money was still on Kazim. Not only because I believed Kazim to be the more skilled fighter, but because I was now fully convinced that Kazim was ruled by the streaks of evil I had seen in him, and was therefore the more deadly. Giles was mild. Always had been.

But he *was* a king. It wasn't a matter of seeming. He *was*.

"Do not help me!" Giles ordered, shouting at his restless soldiers as well as Fendral. "Let no hand help me but God's! I must be able to do *something*."

"It's a pity I do not know more about you," Kazim said as they fought, sweat dripping down both their faces. "I could have found a way to break you instead of kill you. As it is, I have only one option for defeating you."

Giles's face, eyebrows ever together with worry and concentration, suddenly relaxed just a little.

"Is breaking your style? My father was broken. So angry when no order could extend his life or ease his pain or make others love him. So angry when nothing made him happy anymore. He broke himself, and died. As for me"—their blades slid so the hilts clanged together—"the meek cannot be broken."

Kazim shoved Giles back. "But you *can* be killed." And with a quick thrust and a twist, Giles's sword flew out of his hands and landed on the floor with a clang.

I wished I had my flail. But even if I had, I could hardly use my arms. Pox with their deal; Kazim couldn't win!

Fendral, obviously thinking the same thing I was, ran for Giles. Thea and Valyn were screaming and the soldiers were coming forward, but Kazim was going to thrust before anyone got there.

But just before Kazim's arm was fully extended, he cried out and his arm jerked back in obvious pain.

Giles didn't bother to ask what had happened. He sprinted to his sword and snatched it up in the second granted him.

"Leave off, Fendral!" he shouted, and the old fool stopped in his tracks, backing obediently away. The soldiers froze as well, backing up to give the combatants room.

Kazim looked as shocked as the rest of us. Angered by whatever had stayed his blow, he struck again. Giles would have blocked him, but Kazim jerked back again, this time as if his back had seized up.

I saw a quick dart, a flash, as if a large pus-filled boil had just shot across Kazim's back, appearing again on his shoulder.

"Augh!" Kazim screamed. "Get off!"

The camel spider opened its demonic mouth wide and sunk all four little teeth into Kazim's neck. Kazim took up a great yell, but before he could swat it away, the spider had disappeared into his tunic. It hissed its familiar whisper-scream.

Was this God's way of helping Giles? Could God work through a spider? Really?

Now everyone had seen it. Giles did not take pity on Kazim just because he was being attacked by a demon-bug.

Flailing, Kazim blocked two more blows from Giles but could not keep face while the horrible thing ran around on his skin, biting him several more times. Giles disarmed him, catching the scimitar as it flew out of Kazim's hand. Kazim, trying to kill the spider, threw himself on his back, undoubtedly hoping to crush it. Giles held the tip of his sword at Kazim's throat, the point nearly puncturing the skin.

"Do you yield?" he asked.

The camel spider appeared on Kazim's chest, back arched and mouth open, holding its hairy little arms up. Kazim jumped back as much as a man on the ground with a sword at his throat could, but he managed to ignore the spider enough to address Giles as his most pressing threat of the moment.

"If I said yes," Kazim panted, "it would be a lie. I do not yield."

Giles, who for the past several moments had looked confident for the first time since I had known him, resumed his usual heavy demeanor. "I do not want to kill you. But if you insist that I must, I will."

"No."

Everyone looked at me like I was crazy. Which was incorrect.

"Killing was never Kazim's style. I say we break him."

Kazim laughed. "How? Even I do not know how I can be broken. Death would not break me, nor did the spider, angry as it is at me for locking it up for so long. Were I to yield, that might crack me, but I do not, and you cannot force me. What is your plan, Sir Hubert?"

"Fendral," I said, looking at him. "Find something to bind him with before I tell him."

With a last hiss, the camel spider darted off his chest so quickly I didn't see where it went. I was already standing well back, but several soldiers jumped out of its way. That made me feel a lot better. With the spider gone, I stepped more boldly toward him.

Quickly, Fendral and the soldiers tore off the ropes used to hold back the long curtains in the throne room and we bound Kazim's hands securely behind him, leading a rope down to his ankles, which we also bound, not worried about making the knots too tight.

"I am secure," Kazim assured us, kneeling with his hands behind his back attached to his ankles.

"Kazim," I said. "There is a ship leaving for your homeland today."

"It has already sailed."

"All castoffs were frozen to conserve manpower when Seacrest realized we were being attacked," Thea said. "That ship remains."

"And even if it had gone, there would be others, and you would be on one." I pointed at him for a moment before I had to lower my weak arm. "Once there, you will be sold as a slave—"

Kazim scoffed. "I am a prince. I cannot be sold as a—"

"—to your brother."

Kazim fell silent quite quickly. He looked at me as if I'd suddenly turned into a devil.

"With a long note explaining how you were beaten here," I continued. "By a meek king. By your own spider. And by a fool."

Kazim began to writhe against the bonds he had honestly assured us were secure. He had been telling the truth. "You cannot do that! You cannot do that to me! I am a prince of Arabia!"

"The second-born, second-best prince who will never be a king."

Kazim lunged at me. If he had caught me, the worst he could have done was bite me, but I still had strength enough to step out of range. Before Fendral or Giles could subdue him, Thea sent a knee into his stomach, stemming his cries of outrage.

I loved her.

Kazim doubled over, crumpling on the floor. At last he looked pathetic. Thea looked a little surprised and satisfied at the same time. I reminded myself to put this event in the note to his brother.

"Guards," Giles panted, sheathing his sword. "Take him to the dungeons and chain him there. Do not be gentle."

I had a feeling that Gridian guards were still going to be better than Seacrest guards, but I admired Giles for trying. Grabbing his wrists, three soldiers dragged a fuming Kazim away.

With a cheer, Thea hugged me, weeping. “Farrago,” she whispered. “We’re free!”

I hugged her back as well as I could. We *were*. Except for one thing.

Where was Oaf?

Thea clung to my side until I finally convinced her to let me put some proper clothes on and get cleaned up before dinner. Dinner would be just me, Thea, Valyn, Giles, and Fendral in the war council room, while the other nobles and the suitors that had stayed would be in the dining room. It would be heaven as long as I didn't smell like my cell or look like a waif.

My room felt foreign to me, as if it wasn't quite sure I belonged there now that I was Farrago to everybody again. The strength in my arms was coming back little by little, but they still quivered when I did the slightest things. Still, the strength would come back, so I didn't mind being patient. I poured water from my pitcher into my basin and washed my face, running the cold water up and down my arms and touching the bruises on my chest and the cut on my neck with cold fingers.

I dried myself and put on my fool's clothes that I had kept with me. It felt absolutely wonderful to feel all the familiar patches and to be able to glance across them and see the court of Gridian again. I was feeling much, much better.

Stepping out of my room, I hit something with my foot. It was an empty bottle of wine, very high quality. Suddenly my chest felt like lead. Oaf. And now that I thought of it . . .

Where was Alyss?

Picking up the bottle, I went into my room and filled it with the rest of the water from my pitcher. Then, as fast as I could, I ran down the hall, sticking my head in each room.

"Alyss!" I called, not too loud, into each one. She should be here. Somewhere.

Every now and then I passed another empty bottle of ale and ran a little more quickly despite how tired I still was. The halls were so empty. Maybe everyone was in the dining room. Maybe even Alyss was there. Maybe *Oaf* was there, for all I knew.

Another bottle, and then I realized that Oaf was most definitely not in the dining room. The bottles had started at my chamber and continued down the hall. Oaf was leading me.

This new knowledge made me more worried than ever.

The bottles led me up to another level, down another hall, and then a final bottle rested in front of the queen's chamber. I was afraid of what I would find when I opened it. I put my ear to the crack and listened.

A muffled whimper.

I wished I hadn't felt so worn thin. I wished I had a plan. But I didn't have time to run back for help if Alyss was in there. I still couldn't use my flail even if I'd had it. I wasn't even strong enough to go through the window for a sneak approach, not without being sure of my arms yet. So, used as I was to barreling in to situations without thinking, I gently cracked the door open.

Almost immediately, a knife sunk into the wood of the

door and I swung the door closed again. I heard a scream from inside.

"Oaf!" I shouted. "I really don't think you led me up here just to kill me so quickly. Stay your knives for a moment if you've anything to settle with me!" And I pushed the door open again.

Oaf was sitting on the window seat, yet another reason why coming in through the window wouldn't have worked. Several more empty bottles were scattered at his feet, and I could tell from across the room that his eyes were very bloodshot. Alyss had her arms tied behind her and was sitting on his lap, hunched over and trying hard not to look at me, but snatching glances anyway. With a flick of his wrist, Oaf suddenly had a new knife in hand, and I had no idea how many he had hidden. Still holding the knife, he took a swallow from a half-gone bottle of ale.

"I could have killed you just then," he said with a crooked smile.

"Hello, Oaf. Brought you something," I said, managing to heft the bottle just a little. I tried to make my voice sound casual and merry as if he had been Leofrick instead. I took a few steps closer.

"Not too close," Oaf said, holding up a hand to stop me and tightening his hold around Alyss's waist. "Is that king of yours dead yet?"

"Who? King Giles of Gridian? No. In fact, he's the new king of Seacrest. Gridian has taken over."

"Ah, so then that prince is dead."

"No. Kazim is due to be sold back home. The prince's servant is dead, if you wanted news of death."

Oaf showed his teeth in something he must have thought was a smile. "That will do. You must have your queen then."

"She's been dethroned, thank heaven. So, yes, I have my scullery maid ba—" Oaf sitting there with Alyss suddenly made me see something I never had before—something a little unsettling to me.

"What is it?" Oaf asked.

"Oh, nothing," I said, shaking my head. "Alyss, are you well?"

Alyss, if it was possible, buckled over a little more when I spoke to her and turned her face away.

"She won't speak to you," Oaf explained. "I've promised I'll send a knife straight to your heart if she does."

"Will you?"

"I might regardless." Oaf shrugged. "She takes me very seriously."

"She's afraid of you."

"Remarkable, isn't it? It took me so long to make anyone afraid of me. Years. It's not easy being born a cripple in such a cruel world. One's got to fight all his life for some sense of security. No one else is going to look out for you."

I saw something else that was even more chilling.

"Good thing you became a fool," I said. "And you fit it so well. Your foot. My nose. Those certainly help in our kind of profession. Best job there is if you ask me."

"Better still if you can please those in power to get what you want," Oaf continued. "Ale. Wine. Other little niceties poor cripples never find. Speaking of which, what's that you've brought with you?"

I checked my bottle. "Finest king's wine," I said. "Well aged. How about a trade?"

"Hmmm." Oaf groaned, swaying a little with drunkenness. "I can't think what to trade."

"Just give me Alyss," I said, taking another cautious

step forward. Oaf snatched up a knife very quickly, and I stopped. "Come on, you can't want her," I continued. "You're a man of the drink."

"Don't think that just because I am I can't still throw straight." Oaf jerked his wrist and the knife stuck in the floor at my feet. I had to hop back to avoid it. Alyss jumped and gave the smallest of shrieks. "And *you* can't want her either," he continued. "Like you said, you have your maid already." Oaf took another gulp from his bottle. "In fact, maybe you should tell her that. She was so thrilled when she heard you were not really a noble. Got her hopes all up. Tell her why you came to Seacrest and dressed up so."

Oh, he was like Kazim! Except that Kazim only seemed to hurt people for specific purposes and could be kind otherwise. Oaf was just trying to hurt her for no reason at all; just to make me squirm, I guess. But I had to play as long as Alyss was in danger.

"I-I'm in love with Thea. The queen," I said as gently as I could. "She was a maid and then she turned out to be a queen and I came for her."

"Ah. Now that's romantic," Oaf said with another slight baring of his teeth.

Alyss still wasn't looking at me, and I didn't blame her. I ached for her. Her shoulders were shuddering and some small splashes of tears landed on Oaf's leg.

There it was *again*. More hideous things. Similarities. Similarities everywhere. We were so alike it was making me ill. We were both fools. He had his foot and I had my nose. He had Alyss and I had Thea, one a chamber and one a scullery maid. Him with his sleight-of-hand and me with my juggling. And Alyss, who was obviously weeping because she liked the idea of someone coming after her, someone better than Oaf. It was so like when I'd heard Thea weeping to Valyn about wanting the same thing. Wanting something romantic like someone coming after her. But no. Oaf liked to torment her instead. He liked her to fear him. He liked to please the counselors instead of object to everything they said. Why weren't we more alike if we had so much in common?

Well, he must not have ever had a Fendral. Who knew where I'd be or what I'd be like without one. And Alyss, she certainly didn't have a Constance to bat away unwanted advances. Maybe otherwise they could have been like me and Thea.

And now what? I didn't know why Thea and I had been so lucky. It certainly wasn't fair. But that couldn't be changed. So now what?

"Oaf," I said with a drop of genuine concern in my voice. "I'll play your game. I'm *playing* your game! Just tell me what you want. There's a new king. Everything's changing in Seacrest. Just *tell* me what you *want*."

Pure confusion crossed Oaf's face, and I thought he might pass out from drink.

"I don't want to be executed," he said.

"I figured that."

"I don't want to end up in the dungeons or be sold with the prince."

"I figured that too. But I didn't ask you what you didn't want. I'm bargaining here for what you *do* want."

Oaf looked a little glazed over. In one hand, he gripped his bottle. With the other, he pulled Alyss a little closer. Oaf had become what he was because of fear. He was doing what he thought he had to do to take care of himself. As soon as things had gone awry, he had holed himself up in the grandest room in the castle with a lot of drink and even some company. He already had what he thought he wanted. What could he possibly ask for? And what could any of it have to do with me?

After a few moments of silence, which I gave him because he indeed seemed to be thinking, he made the knife vanish from sight and met eyes with me. His eyes were terrible, but he managed to hold up a steady hand to point at me.

"You and I are very much alike," he said seriously. What little piece of soberness left in him spoke. "I don't know if that has occurred to you. Oh, yes, we have our little differences, but overall, we are the same. But . . . ," he trailed off.

"Go on," I encouraged.

"You are . . . *happy*. I-I do not know why. I do not know why I never have been. But whatever is in you that soothes you"—Oaf took a quick swallow from his bottle—"I would have that."

Being at a loss for words had never been a problem of mine. In fact, having a quick tongue was one of my few strengths. But I didn't know what to make of Oaf's demand. Being happy had just been what I thought a fool's job was, but here was a fool lacking. And yet, my life, certainly lately, had been less than wonderful. Happiness, or maybe at least contentment, had been my usual state, but I had also just recently felt joy, as well as a lot of terror and sadness too. Perhaps Fendral had taught me to be happy. Perhaps it was just another talent of mine.

No. I didn't quite believe that. Oaf was doing it wrong, but I didn't know how or what to tell him. Certainly he could start by freeing poor Alyss.

"You're in luck," I said after a longer-than-usual-for-me pause. "I've put my own personal secret to happiness in this bottle." I held it up again.

Confusion returned to Oaf's already glazed-over expression. But I had all his attention, and after keeping it just a moment, I said, "Take it." And I tossed the bottle out the window.

Oaf jumped with the same reaction Alyss would have had if I'd thrown a baby. With a cry that was a mixture of drunken stupidity and crazed longing, he made a mad grab for it and began to tip too far.

Rushing forward, I knocked with my body more than pushed with my hands Alyss off the window-seat to one side where she landed with a thud. Oaf realized he was falling and seeing that I was the closest thing handy, grabbed my left wrist as he tumbled.

I screamed.

Oaf's full weight felt like it was tearing my arm from me. Doubled over as I was, I held on over the windowsill with my lower body, and that was the only thing keeping me from following him.

"Oaf, you fool," I managed to groan once my first scream was gone. "It was only water."

Oaf gave a strange dead smile and a faint chuckle. "Of course it was," he laughed. "Of course it was." And he fell.

His face changed to a mixture of soberness and realization in the instant he was close enough for me to see his face. Then his small image skidded along the tower wall, made weak grabs at other windows, and then I lost him in darkness. A second later I heard his faint thud below me.

I did not know if he let go or if he lost his grip. I certainly had not been holding on to him, and I wasn't sure I would have even if I'd had the ability. If he'd had any sense in him at all, he might have been able to cling to the stone gargoyle. Well, we fools often didn't do the sensible thing. Hence the name.

"Hubert." Alyss wept behind me, struggling against the ties on her wrists. "Hubert!"

I fell back from the window, my left arm as dead as it had ever been. "Farrago," I corrected. "Peace, Alyss. My name is Farrago, and I'm all right. Now turn around and I'll see if I can untie you."

With her cooperation and my right hand, I worked her bonds off.

"Hubert—Farrago," she continued to weep once she was free. "I'm so sorry. I didn't mean to—I-I know you love the queen—now. I'm just silly and stupid and you nearly died coming after me. I'm just a maid and I talk too much and I think too fast and—"

"Peace, Alyss," I repeated, motioning for her silence. "I'm sorry I cannot give you what you want. But I'm not done with you yet. Now, if you'll please be good enough to escort me back to the war council room, I would appreciate it."

Alyss would have done whatever I'd asked of her even if I'd told her to jump out the window herself. Holding my left arm gently so that it didn't flap around, she helped me back to the room.

"You're joining us," I told her as I pushed the door open.

Alyss jumped. "Oh no, sir! I could nev—!"

"It was not a request," I informed her, and pushed her inside with my good arm.

"Jug-oh man!"

With a smack that nearly knocked me over, Ana barreled into my knees, wrapping them both into a hug that put me even more off balance. Looking up at me, she suddenly stepped back.

"Oh, my nose." I went down on my knees. "It's all right, Ana. It's me. I-I wish I could juggle for you to prove it." Never had not being able to juggle felt so awful.

Alyss took off her apron and pulled my bad arm up into a makeshift sling. Ana stepped forward again and touched the tip of my real nose a few times. "Nose funny," she said. And then she patted my left arm too lightly for it to hurt. "Hurt arm."

A peasant woman with long brown hair picked Ana up.

"Mrs. Fendral," I said as I rose to my feet.

"Catherine," she said with a small curtsy to me, of all people. "We never really met. I hope you have not hated me all these years." She was genuinely worried.

"It did cross my mind, but I couldn't quite manage it," I said honestly. "I couldn't hate someone Fendral loved. It is good to officially meet you." And I bowed in return. I could still do that much at least. "Fendral!" I turned to him. "You have a daughter!"

"And you have a goddaughter!" he returned. "You should never have juggled for her. She loves that. She'll adore you forever."

"Like she adores her father," Catherine put in.

"She'll ask you for performances whenever she sees you for the rest of your life." Fendral winked.

"A goddaughter," I said, looking at Ana more closely. She was getting used to me, but she wouldn't be fully convinced I was her juggle man until I could juggle for her again.

And I would. In time. I just had to be patient.

"Who's your friend?" Fendral asked.

I turned to see Alyss ducking out the door.

"Alyss, get back here!" I ordered.

Alyss obeyed, but she looked like she was being tortured.

"Alyss, you remember the queen? Remember that she was a scullery maid back in Gridian. If she can sit and eat without feeling guilty, then you can too."

Alyss finally lifted her eyes.

I shuffled everyone so that she sat between Catherine and Thea. Thea and Alyss could talk maid stuff, and Catherine seemed to have a calming presence. Other servants began to bring in food, which made Alyss even more uncomfortable, but I let Thea talk her into believing it was all right that she was being waited on just this once.

I dove into the food as if I'd never eaten before. I was plenty hungry. Days and days on prison food after having been sick hours before and having eaten like a noble for most of my life before that had certainly helped my appetite.

"Um, Farrago?"

I glanced up with half a chicken in my mouth.

"When you get a moment to breathe, I was hoping to explain those questions you had earlier," Fendral said with some happy blue fire in his eyes.

I swallowed. *Ow.* I told myself to never swallow that much in one gulp again. "Questions?"

"About how I made you not dead."

I pounded the table. "That's right! I was curious about that, wasn't I? Fendral, *no one* managed to recognize me with my false nose. How did you even know I was here?"

"Well, first you managed to frighten poor Catherine nearly to death when she saw her daughter playing with some mysterious noble. The fact that Ana called you 'Jug-oh man' made it all the more confusing. I didn't manage to piece it together until the tournament."

"Ana was there!"

"Ana had come to see the tournament with us, but she slipped away while you were fighting Kazim. She was trying to come see you, and she was horrified when you were hurt. As I ran to get her back, I was close enough to hear the strange crack your false nose made as Kazim shattered it, but even then, I wasn't sure about you. But the tournament got me involved. I had heard that the true queen of Seacrest had been found in some distant kingdom, but the details were kept very quiet. But I recognized her at the tournament and decided to pay a visit to Gridian again to check up on things."

"You picked a fine time to visit! You could have come *anytime*. You took years to come back!"

Fendral laughed. "Well, I was always afraid that if I ever came back, Giles would never let me leave again." Fendral glanced over to Giles, who pulled his attention away from Valyn when he heard his name.

"Probably not." He shrugged, grinned, and turned back to Valyn.

"I only went back when I did because I knew there'd been some kind of upheaval, and I figured that *somebody* from Gridian Court should have been present. So I spoke with Constance, Leofrick, and Giles, and they told me everything about you and Thea, and then I knew who you were for sure. I mean, Ana knows what juggling is, and she wouldn't call just anyone a juggle man because, well, not many people know how to do it!"

"But—then you would have been in Gridian when I was in prison. You couldn't have known when to come or what was going on here."

Fendral shook his head. "Counselors," he said with a sneaky face, "are rather easy to eavesdrop on. Two of Gridian's former counselors joined Seacrest's court years ago because, well, because they hated you and me." He looked proud about that. "They had been plotting your death for quite a while and sending messages back and forth. Castle Gridian and Castle Seacrest are only two hard days ride away. I learned how Kazim's plans for expanding Seacrest and going to war against the neighboring kingdoms pleased the counselors. They were even going to poison Giles before Kazim got here so that the kingdom would be easy to take." Fendral stopped and turned to Giles again. "Which is another good reason why you should marry and have an heir."

Giles blushed. "We'll see," he said.

Fendral leaned over to me and put a hand on the side of his face, blocking Giles on one side. "Hey, what about Thea's lady-in-waiting for Giles? She's a noble, and she's familiar with Seacrest and its people. Do you think they would get on well?"

I leaned over to him. "She's a little bossy and opinionated, but she's the daughter of Sir Rupert, and we like him. Giles could use some of what she has, though. And if Giles could temper her a bit, then she'd be fine. I think it's a good match."

"Hey!"

Valyn had heard us.

Fendral leaned back in his chair with that same sneaky smile and continued as if we hadn't gone off topic for a moment. "So with the added information from the counselors, I managed to convince Giles that he had to go to war—to take back his fool and scullery maid, if nothing else. Still, the only reason we made it in time was because of the counselors. They kept you in prison as long as they did so that the counselors in Seacrest could tell the counselors in Gridian that you were going to be executed. Several Gridian counselors went to attend. The added time they took also allowed Giles to put his troops in order. The counselors left early one morning, earlier than we had expected. I rode ahead to try to get to you, and Giles and his armies came after."

"You cut it a little close."

"Not too close, though. You still have your head."

"Oh, I'm not sure I ever really had that, but I'm still grateful." I tapped the long thin scab on my neck lightly as I remembered Seht's blade. "I would never have thought you could kill," I whispered.

"Oh, I do have a few things that I would kill for," Fendral said solemnly. He stared hard at me and then at Catherine and Ana, merrily in conversation with Alyss and Thea.

In all my memory, I had no image of who my father might have been, but even if I had one, I can't imagine him lodging more securely in my heart than Fendral. "You have no idea what it was like for me to see you again," I told him quietly.

"Oh, I have some idea," Fendral returned. "I missed you too, you know. It was hard for me to leave."

"Why *did* you have to leave, Fendral?"

"Catherine and I—we—we wanted to be our own people. We just wanted to start afresh without the weight of Gridian's needs. We just needed to get away."

"And now? What happens now?"

"Well . . ." Fendral put a hand to his chin. "I don't know. I will have to speak to Catherine and see what she wants. Giles needs to go back to Gridian and set some things in order, but he's leaving Sir Rupert as steward here. I think perhaps that Valyn should accompany Giles back to Gridian so she can tell him more about what will be needed to run Seacrest and merge the kingdoms."

I saw Valyn glance up again at the mention of her name, but if she heard Fendral's proposal, she didn't oppose it.

"And us!" Thea came suddenly into our conversation. "We shall go back to Gridian as well, won't we, Farrago? I'll help in any way I can with the merging of the kingdoms. I'll tell the people what has happened and make them glad of it, but I must go back to Gridian, if even for a short while. I must tell Constance."

"Well, that's fine with me," Fendral said with a wink. "Maybe just long enough to marry the two of you at least. Let's all go back to Gridian."

CHAPTER 36

It was very odd how one could be generally achy all over and yet still so happy and at peace. I wondered if that was what Oaf had been talking about. Was there really something different about me? Something I couldn't see?

"Ready?" A beaming Thea in her full dandelion glory pressed against my side, looking more herself than she had since she'd left.

I forced myself to not lean away from her as she pressed all my bruises. I'd rather have her touch me and feel pain then to not have her touch me and feel less pain. And what would be the point anyway? I still hurt nearly everywhere all the time anyway, and I just didn't care.

"So ready." I put my good arm around her. My left arm was in a loose sling.

An assortment of carriages stood ready to carry us back to Gridian, and Sir Rupert was speaking with his daughter, ready to begin the reorganization of Seacrest.

A page boy ran up to the two of us.

"Um, Sir . . . Farrago?"

"Just Farrago," I said as I gave him my attention. "Something for me?"

"There's a man who wants to see you. He's been asking for you all night, but the physician wasn't done with him and he wasn't always awake."

"Awake? Physician?" I gasped. No. It couldn't be.

"It's Oaf, sir," the page boy said. "The servants found him last night. Both his legs are broken. And one arm. He likes to climb through windows sometimes even though he's a cripple. The servants think he must have fallen. The physician wasn't sure he'd make it through the night, but he's still alive and he's been asking about you. Will you come?"

Pox that Oaf. And pox my curiosity, but I had to see. "I'll come," I told him. I turned to Thea. "I won't be long," I promised. "But I must go alone. I'll be right back."

Thea, looking worried, released me. And I realized she wasn't worried about *me*, she was worried about Oaf. She was soft and she didn't know any better, even when it was Oaf. She didn't know half the things he'd done, and I probably wasn't going to tell her. Nodding to the page, I followed him into the castle.

He took me to one of the lower-level corridors to the servant's quarters. Oaf was lying on the stone floor on a thin mattress of straw, covered in thin blankets. He looked to be asleep for the moment, but I didn't trust him. Several empty bottles were around him still, and there was even an upright half-filled one near his hand.

"He usually calls for ale when he's awake," the page boy said. "And we give it to him for the pain."

Of course they did.

"Thank you. You may go," I said. He glanced at Oaf and then me before dashing off.

I sat by Oaf's bed, listening to him breathing. He was really asleep. I pulled the thin blanket off him. Both legs were covered in bandages and bound to sticks to keep them still and straight. His left arm was also bound from the elbow down. I noticed that his club foot had been straightened. Wrapped as it was, it looked like any other foot. Interesting. I replaced the blanket.

Oaf stirred and groaned. If I was still achy from my wounds, I could only imagine how he felt. "Ale," he rasped. "Wine." He reached for the bottle with his one good arm. I caught it before he did and moved it out of his reach. Oaf, feeling the bottle slip away from his fingertips, blinked several times and opened his eyes. I made sure to sit where he could see me. His face spread into a strange sort of smile.

"This isn't even the worst thing that's happened to me," he said with a chuckle that obviously caused him pain. "I can never seem to die when I want to."

"That's not my fault," I said.

Oaf's grin widened and then faded. "I'm surprised you're still here. I thought you'd be gone with your maid and never look back."

"Apparently you and I are not quite settled yet."

"Not quite." Oaf sighed. He closed his eyes and rested his head back on his mattress.

"So what do you want with me, Oaf?" I asked. I didn't have all day. Thea and I and everyone I loved were leaving to return to Gridian within the hour, and I had hoped to never see Oaf again. Not that it was awful for me to see him in this condition, but still, I felt finished with him. My curiosity was now satisfied.

"The worst thing that ever happened to me," Oaf suddenly started up as if he hadn't stopped, though he still looked like he was asleep on his mattress, "was being sold by my mother to the kingdom fool of Seacrest so that she could better pursue another affair. You see, my father was some Lord Edric of Somewhere-or-other, and my mother, well, there's no nice way of saying what my mother was." Oaf pushed himself to one elbow again. "I think I was about seven, and the only reason I know the name of my father is because she used to call me Edric II. She hadn't been awful before that, and even while I begged her to let me go with her, she smiled and assured me she would be back and that I would be fine and that she loved me. But the fool was an old waste who was never sober enough to teach me anything. So after a troupe of gypsies came to entertain the king one day because the fool was only funny because he was drunk, I became enraptured by a knife-thrower and practiced all day every day until I was a dead shot, sober or otherwise. It was a skill that used the part of me that wasn't crippled. But—"

"Oaf. Oaf. Oaf," I interrupted, feeling my patience all but vanish. "Why—why are you telling me this? Do you want me to feel sorry for you? Because I really hoped that that instant of—of *awakeness* I saw on your face as you fell and nearly ripped my arm off would be the last I ever saw of you. *What do you want of me now?*"

Oaf gave me a lopsided smile. "I want you to feel whatever it takes to do me a last favor," he said. "You're so soft I thought it might take a drop of pity for me for you to finish what should have happened yesterday."

I said nothing. He was going to explain anyway, but I had a feeling in my stomach I didn't like as he spoke.

Oaf reached toward the far corner of the room, and I turned to see where a small lump of clothes sat.

"Those are the things the physicians removed from me

as they bound my broken legs and arm," Oaf said, wincing with the effort of pointing. "Please. My left shoe. The one that fit on my uncrippled foot. I can't get it."

I fished around in the limp pile and pulled out Oaf's left shoe.

"In the heel," Oaf directed, lying down again and clenching his teeth. "There's a vial."

It took me a moment, but I eventually worked a small vial out of the wooden heel of his shoe.

"What is it?" I asked.

"Poison," Oaf said. "I got it a long time ago. I thought it might come in handy one day."

"What do you expect me to do with it?"

"Farrago, that vial was never supposed to be for me, but since last night I've changed my mind about execution."

My surprise was too great for me to hide it from my face.

"I know there have been many who haven't liked me," Oaf said, pointing out the obvious. "But no one has ever pursued the most obvious way to kill me." Oaf pointed a weak and shaking finger at the bottle I had moved just out of his reach. "Poison in my drink," he said. "I thought"—Oaf shifted and winced—"I thought you might oblige me, seeing as we're such good friends. That is, if pity is what you need. Everything I've told you is true. Or would it help if I gave you more reason to despise me? My mother did come back when her affair failed. I set the castle hunting dogs on her."

"Stop talking, Oaf," I commanded abruptly as I picked up his bottle and stood with the vial of poison in one hand and his drink in the other. Well, wasn't this quite the reversal? Only the night before he had sat with a helpless Alyss on his lap, flinging knives and drinking to his heart's content as I tiptoed around him.

But . . . I did pity him. Lying helpless as he was, how could I do anything else? There was something wrong with Oaf. I didn't know exactly what it was. Maybe whatever was in me that drew people to me was broken in him. Maybe he needed to be broken again to fix it.

"Oaf, never have I come across anyone that I've disliked so thoroughly and so strongly as you. I think it's because we're so alike, as you said last night, and yet so different.

"Now, I've made many threats to you, Oaf. I told you I would throw you from the highest tower, and I seem to have done that. I also told you I would dry you out. Since you're alive, I intend to do that too, which means that I cannot oblige your request for poison. I'm sure I've made many other threats, but I can't remember them right now, and if I can't remember them, I'm quite certain that you and your ale-filled head can't either. So we'll both forget them. And since you called for me, I'll be the one to decide what is done with you. I'll arrange for you to come with us to Gridian." I turned to go.

"Farrago." I heard Oaf shift some more and groan in pain. "Farrago!"

I stopped and looked at him. He was sitting up just a little, and he beckoned me back with his good arm. I sighed and returned as he lay back down. He beckoned me closer as if he wanted me to lean in so he could whisper something. Suddenly I was overcome with a surge of anger. In that moment I knew his thoughts as well as if they had been my own. I grabbed his arm as roughly as I could and felt the knife concealed in the sleeve. Since my left arm was still dead from Oaf's weight tearing it off the night before, I wrestled the knife out with just my right hand and stormed angrily away.

"Farrago!" Oaf shouted after me, angry now too. "What do you intend to do with me? Just kill me outright or don't play! Farrago!"

I heard the shattering sound of glass and made no attempt to stifle a broad smile. Oh, I had a pretty good idea of what I would do with him. Oaf needed to be broken. His insides were crippled and he needed to be broken if they were ever going to straighten. And it just so happened I was more than happy to do that for him, old friends as we were.

Thea was asleep against my shoulder. It was my left shoulder, so of course it still hurt, but I'd eventually convinced her it didn't. And I didn't feel any remorse for that lie, either. None. Alyss was next to Thea, asleep against the side of the carriage.

We'd been traveling for just over three days. Oaf had finally quieted down on the floor between us and Fendral, Catherine, and Ana sitting just across from us. Giles and Valyn were in another smaller carriage alone. Oaf's bottom half was strapped to a plank to keep his legs still and to keep him out of trouble. Catherine and Thea and even Ana had been quite worried about him for a while. For the first day, Oaf had just yelled at me and then the second day he had screamed for ale, which made me feel very good to deny him. Fendral was even going to give him some at first until I'd had a quick talk with him. But finally it was quiet, and everyone but me was asleep.

Thea stirred and glanced up at me. I kissed her forehead.

"You know, things are a little unfair in my favor," I whispered to her.

She sat up and stretched. "How do you mean?"

"I mean that every day I get to see your face, but you're stuck with seeing mine."

Thea rolled her eyes and gave my ear a light flick with her finger. I yelped and clapped a hand to my ear, making everyone in the coach jump in their sleep except for Oaf.

Thea was mortified. "Farrago! I'm so sorry! Did I hurt you?"

"No," I immediately confessed, winking.

Thea jabbed me in the side and I squealed in an unmanly way, not bothering to try to keep from laughing as she tried to jab me again. I grabbed her fists and managed to get a peck on her cheek as she squirmed. At least we were both laughing.

And then suddenly I realized where we were.

"Wait! STOP!" I rapped on the top of the carriage and yelled as loud as I could. "Hold up!"

The carriage came to a sudden stop, and I heard the horses whine in protest. Oaf cried out as he was jostled and everyone jumped awake.

"What is it?" Thea rubbed her eyes as she sat up.

"I just have to pick someone up. I'll be right back," I said as I jumped out the door.

Tom glowered at me from the driver's seat. "I am not a coachman," he told me sternly.

I gave him an apologetic smile. "You happen to be a great coachman. I should know. You're doing great. Sorry for the sudden stop. I'll just be a moment."

Tom grunted, which I took to mean I was forgiven, and I hurried on.

We had just entered Gridian, and we'd just passed a small cottage at the outskirts of the kingdom. A small stream flowed in the back and clay pots littered the front porch.

I ran up to the door and knocked urgently. "Spinster! Spinster! I mean, Lady—something or other!"

The door opened and my spinster stood in the doorway. "Farrago!" She cupped my face in her hands. "You're back! You're alive! How did it go? Your arm! What happened?"

"Everything happened! But I think it went well. Look!" I pointed behind me. The spinster's eyes widened at the sight of the crowd of carriages, or the fact that Giles was poking his head out of his door window.

I tucked the spinster's hand in my arm. "We're just getting back now. I wanted you to come with us and meet the girl I chased after. Will you come? You could even stay. You could be Lady Whatever again. Giles wouldn't mind. Please."

Her mouth was open, and she was still surprised, so I took that as a yes and pulled her to my carriage.

"It's a little crowded, but we're almost to the castle anyway. Pay no attention to the cripple on the floor."

"Kind lady!" Oaf began to implore as soon as I opened the door.

"Oaf! I'm suddenly remembering that I once told you I'd cut your tongue out. Do you want me to keep that promise?"

Oaf glared at me again but kept his mouth shut.

"Lady Spinster, this is Thea." I helped her to her seat. "And you might recognize the old fool of Gridian, Fendral. And that's his wife, Catherine, and their daughter, Ana. The one on the floor is Oaf and we don't talk to him. Everyone, this is . . . um . . . I'm not really sure what to call her, actually. So I'll let her introduce herself and I'm going to sit up top with Tom because it's crowded in here."

The last thing I heard was some happy high-pitched sound as the spinster clasped hands with Thea and they began to talk girl talk. I hoped Fendral wouldn't mind. I bet he wouldn't. And I hoped Oaf hated it.

"Hello, Tom," I said as I jumped up next to him in the driver's seat.

"I still can't believe I spent all that time coaching a fool," he said.

"Oh, but you don't regret it. Besides, I'm a really good fool."

"Oh, I don't doubt that."

"I mean juggling. Once my arm gets better, I'll show you."

Tom grunted. I liked Tom.

Gridians came out of their homes to see us and we waved heartily to each other. It was so good to almost be home!

We finally passed through the gates of Gridian Castle. Various servants came out ready to take luggage inside, but one person stood out more than the others.

"Constance!" I stood and waved in my seat. "Constance!"

I dismounted from the carriage in one leap, which again, wasn't a good idea, but I didn't hurt myself much. I ran to Thea's door and threw it open. If I'd had full use of both my arms I would have carried her. All I could really do was grab her hand and pull her after me.

"Constance!" I shouted again. "Look!"

Constance's face lit up faster than a torch, and if I live to be a hundred I won't forget her expression. Somehow she wasn't nearly as ugly or fearsome as I'd once thought her.

"Farrago!" she shouted. "You did it!"

She met us halfway and completely covered Thea in a bear hug.

"Well, I don't know if *I* did it but . . . it's done!"

Constance scooped me up next.

"Augh! No, Constance! Gentle! I'm broken!"

She released me suddenly.

"You perfect fool! What have you done to yourself?" she said as she madly dabbed at her eyes with her apron with one arm still around Thea.

"Oh, everything. It was great. Spiders and princes and fights and—and I have something for you!"

"Something?" Constance asked.

"Yup. And someone." The carriages had met us and people began pouring out. I opened the door, helped Catherine and the spinster out as Fendral carried Ana and helped Alyss out while I beckoned Constance over.

"This is the something." I said, nodding my head at Oaf.

"What are you doing, Farrago?" Oaf asked in a highly suspicious tone as he sat up just enough to look at me.

"He was the fool of Seacrest, but he's a bit broken as well. I mean in the head, and he needs a heavy hand. And you're the only one I could think of who could handle him. He's devilishly tricky. I figured you could do with someone to watch now that Thea is—well—mine."

Constance narrowed her eyes at me.

"And by mine, I of course mean that Thea and I will be around. You just won't have to guard her as much, you know? We might be back and forth a bit. But it's all right! Because I also have a some*one*!"

There was a thump as Tom alighted from his place at the driver's seat and began to speak to the horses.

"Constance, this is Tom." Tom looked over at me. "He was a blacksmith at Seacrest. A good one. He's going to make a nice pair of leg braces for Oaf and some shackles. And—"

Hey, Tom was actually a little taller than Constance, and he had that same *I-might-squash-you-if-you-cross-me* look that Constance sometimes used. "*Aaaand* he might stick around to help you with Oaf. Just in case you need a break. Tom's a great coach. He could handle Oaf too. Hey, Tom? Could you carry Oaf inside for her? If we don't get him out of the way, he'll start to scream again. Oh, and no matter what he says, don't give him any ale or wine."

"Farrago!" Oaf yelled at me.

Tom opened the carriage door on the opposite side where Oaf's head was and jerked Oaf and his plank out in one motion, carrying Oaf under one arm. Tom and Constance walked side-by-side. Twisting his top half, Oaf looked back at me as Tom carried him away. Oaf was a good actor, but I'm quite certain that the worry on his face was genuine. I gave him an eager smile that Ana would have been proud of and waved at him. He spat at me. Tom jostled his plank. I was happy.

"FARRAGO!"

Sprinting toward me was someone I'd never seen sprint.

"LEOFR—!"

I would have finished his name if Leofrick didn't knock the wind out of me. Picking me up, he squashed me in a man-hug and then shook me by the shoulders.

"Farrago! I'm so glad you're back. This whole time I've been trying to explain without really explaining where you went and I'm really no good with the counselors and I was thinking that maybe you wouldn't come back because you'd be dead and *then* where would we all be? Hello, Thea! Glad you're back. (Hello, Leofrick! Glad to be back.) I mean it's not like I could keep up pretending to do your job because I don't even juggle not even a little bit and—"

"Ow, ow, OW! Leofrick! Do you see the arm? I am in pain. No more shaking. Bad. But I am glad to see you. I've no doubt that you did exactly what I hoped you'd do while I was gone."

"Farrago, I couldn't convince Giles of a blasted thing! The counselors did most of the talking and I couldn't pull off the war thing at all! If Fendral hadn't shown up and if we hadn't learned about the counselors, then—!"

"Leofrick! I don't care! Anymore. It turned out fine. And anyway I have someone for you. Do you have your mandolin?"

Leofrick pointed to the strap that held the mandolin on his back.

"Fine. Leofrick, this," I said, pulling Alyss away from the carriage where she'd been trying to stand unseen, "is Alyss. I want you to play her something until she smiles. And then play some more. Trust me, this is payback. I owe you one."

Leofrick raised his eyebrows and looked at me. He tried to say several things, but nothing came out. Alyss's cheeks went very pink. Red, even.

"All right, fine. We'll get inside the castle and get something to eat first." I linked arms with Thea. "Like this, Frick."

Slowly, attentively, Leofrick linked arms with Alyss and we walked inside. Giles was already escorting Valyn inside and were talking with Fendral and Catherine and Ana.

"Jug-oh man! Jug-oh!" Ana demanded from behind me. "Jug-OH!"

"Soon, Ana." I sighed hopefully. "Soon."

I stood anxiously in the church before the priest. I wore patches of gold silk. This whole process seemed a bit formal for me, but since Thea wanted it, I wasn't about to complain. My left arm was doing much better, though it was still weaker than my right. I flexed it a few times as the organ-player continued to organ. Finally I heard the doors open behind me and turned to look.

Escorted by Fendral, my almost-wife came in at last. I hadn't been allowed to see her for nearly a whole day, which had been horribly unfair. But it was worth it now.

Thea's hair had been tamed a little, which I guess I didn't mind. She did look beautiful. I just worried that we made an uneven pair if she insisted on mellowing her one great flaw. But she made up for it wearing a beautiful gown covered in patches of white and gold. You'd be surprised how stunning that looks. Why other women hadn't figured this out was beyond me. It was like we matched.

I suppose a better man would have been able to remember something of what the priest said. I can't remember a thing. I suppose I must have said whatever I was supposed to say at the right time, because without taking my eyes from Thea's face for a second, Thea was suddenly kissing me, and I had time for a quick thought of *Aw! I was going to eat an onion first!* and then that was my last thought until Thea broke the kiss off. I knew it hadn't been me.

Constance and Valyn and the spinster were crying. Fendral was laughing from that wonderful rich well of mirth of his. Catherine and Alyss and Leofrick and Ana were applauding. Giles was smiling, something he rarely managed, though he'd been doing it lots more since Valyn had come. Tom even looked pleased. Wow. If I could have lived the rest of my life in that moment, I would have died from bliss. It was a strange instant of powerful happiness that nearly knocked me over. I had never experienced it before.

The intensity lasted only a moment though, because I suppose a moment was as long as I could handle it. A firm happiness filled me in its wake. Smiling naturally, I picked Thea up and ran, yes ran, all the way back down the isle. I clicked my heels as I passed the doors and helped Thea into a waiting carriage. We waved to all of them as Tom caught up to us and clicked the reins for the horses to drive us to Seacrest where we'd be honeymooning. Our carriage pulled a small cart filled with my weight in pastries, compliments of Constance. Thea laughed and cried at the same time. Well, maybe that was me. Maybe it was both of us.

And then we kissed again and didn't have to stop for a long time.

I wasn't involved in all the details of merging the two kingdoms. Giles and Valyn were the most heavily involved in that, though Thea had responsibilities too. We traveled often between the two kingdoms. Castle Seacrest was eventually remodeled to be more of a school/ hospital, and Giles decided to rule from Gridian. Actually, Seacrest lost its name to Gridian, I think. All I really knew was that I was to perform in the old Seacrest castle in a week's time for some kind of celebration about the merging.

I had been practicing for days. Becoming frustrated, I threw one of my balls as hard as I could against a wall in the Gridian hallway as Thea came down.

"What's wrong?" she asked gently, stroking the place by my ear that was so tender.

"It's like I have to learn to juggle all over again," I said. "My arm keeps giving out." Oh, her fingers in my hair felt good. I calmed down.

"It will come," she promised. "And if it doesn't, I'll perform in your place." She took the two remaining balls from my hand and tossed them both in one hand.

I smiled. "You're getting better."

She grinned back with a face that said she had more than one secret. "Giles received a message today from Arabia."

I perked to attention. "Really?"

"Kazim made it. His brother wanted to thank you and Giles, and he'll be coming to visit."

"That's *wonderful*."

"There's more."

"I guessed as much."

"Giles is thinking of announcing his engagement at the celebration next week."

"ENGA—!" Thea clapped a hand over my mouth. I started again, but in a whisper. "I didn't know he was engaged! Does Valyn know?"

Thea laughed and gave my face a light slap. "It's not official yet, but Valyn has been telling me all about it. It's only a matter of time. I've never seen Giles so happy."

"I know. It's about time."

"Valyn is beside herself. She's so much calmer when she's around Giles. They're so good for each other."

"I take some of the credit for that. It was my idea."

Thea nudged me. "It was Fendral's idea. You get credit for Alyss and Leofrick. I haven't heard anything about an engagement for them yet, but I've never seen them apart."

"Good." I closed my eyes. "Very good."

The hallway filled with the familiar step-thunk of someone approaching. Oaf stopped when he saw us, gripping his crutches. "Fancy running into you here. I hope I didn't interrupt you kissing or anything."

"Hello, Oaf!" I said brightly. "You know, it's still strange seeing you with your foot straight. How much longer does Tom intend to keep you in those braces?"

Oaf grunted. "Until I die, I think."

"Does Constance know you're up here?"

"OAF!" Constance's voice thundered from down the hall. Oaf jumped so badly that he fell over. I helped him up and hid him in the window curtains as Constance came huffing down the hall.

"Hello you two," she gasped. "Have you seen that Oaf? He's so lazy. If I'm not on him every minute he runs off, and I need water brought in from the well."

"I thought I heard him in the gardens," I said. "How's he been lately?"

"Irritable. Especially since I dragged him away from the wine storage two weeks ago."

"You've sure been running him around a lot."

"It keeps his mind off the drink. And the physician says he should be made to use his legs so they don't go all stiff. It's good for him."

"And you enjoy it."

Constance grinned at me. "There's something about the cries of those being made to do something good for them that they hate that just does me good."

"Well, if you have trouble, I'm sure Tom would be happy to help you."

Constance forgot to take a breath. "Now don't you start to teasing. Tom's a fine fellow and I won't have you pestering him."

"Oh, I wouldn't dare. I was just noticing that he seems to be hanging around you lately."

Constance flushed. "Well," she said. "Maybe he does appreciate my style with Oaf. He's a good man." She cleared her throat. "You let me know if you see that Oaf." And she went back the way she came.

I waited until she was gone before I let Oaf out.

"That woman," he sighed and rested against the wall.

"Want to give her the shock of her life? Show up in the kitchens with the water. And if she gives you a hard time, you can always mention Tom."

"She's going to be the death of me," Oaf said.

"No, Oaf. She's the life of you. *You* would have been the death of you."

Oaf snorted, then sighed again. "You dropped this," he said. And with a flick of his wrist, he held the juggle ball I'd thrown. "Lady." He nodded his head to Thea. My goodness, but he was tired. He was much slower when he wasn't on the drink, and his eyes weren't nearly as red. He was almost decent-looking. Almost.

Oaf shouldered his crutches and began to hobble slowly away.

"OAF!" This time it was Tom yelling. Oaf vanished down the hallway as if he didn't know what tired was.

Chuckling after him, I took Thea's hand. "Come on. I want to go find Ana and practice with her. I always do better when she's watching."

Thea nodded, but her expression changed as we walked.

"What is it?" I asked her. "What are you thinking of?"

Thea hesitated. "I was just thinking of . . . Ana."

"Ana?"

Thea nodded. "I was just wondering what she would look like if she was a little younger. With wavy hair that sticks out like a dandelion and"—she glanced up at me—"and maybe a nose that looks like a beak."

I stopped dead in my tracks, easily picturing such a character. "Poor thing," I whispered. I leaned over and put my forehead to hers. "But I would dearly like to see such a child."

Thea beamed at me. Catching her hand, we jogged down the hall together to meet Fendral and Catherine and Ana.

Leofrick had said it right. It was going to be a lot of fun being me.

1. This work is told in first person through Farrago's eyes. Do you think he is a reliable narrator? Why or why not?
2. Farrago's identity comes largely from his trade and his connection to a few specific people in his life. What are other ways people define themselves? What elements in your life contribute most to your own identity?
3. Of all the villains, Oaf hits particularly close to home for Farrago, being a fool himself. What did you think of Oaf's "redemption"? Why did Farrago help him out in the end? Do you think there's any hope for true change in Oaf?
4. After hearing more of Oaf's background, is any of his behavior justifiable or more understandable? Do you think you'd have become someone similar to Oaf if you had the same background?
5. Do you think Kazim would have made a good ruler? Why or why not? What do you think ultimately made him a villain?

6. Was Thea right to give up her position as queen? Was she shirking her birthright responsibility and being selfish, or was she doing what was best for her and her kingdom?
7. Do you think that Kazim's punishment was fair? Why or why not?
8. Fendral gave up a job that he thrived in and other responsibilities for love. Farrago was unwilling to pretend to be someone else to be with his love behind the scenes. Were they right to make the decisions they made regarding the ones they loved? What would you be willing to give up for someone you loved? What would not be worth it for you?

About the Author

Bethany Zohner Herbert was born in Salt Lake City, and aside from a short amount of time living in England and the South, she is back in her native Idaho where she grew up. She has been a fan of books since before she could write. She earned her bachelor's in creative writing from BYU-Idaho and her master's in literature and writing from Utah State University. When not coming up with weird stories, she likes participating in and teaching Zumba, making crafts (silly ones like puppets), reading, and dating her husband.